## THE WELCOME WAGON

Three of the men from out front of the abandoned saloon walked toward them down the middle of the sagebrush-littered street.

"Stop right there, you're close enough," the ranger said when the men got within ten yards of them.

"Close enough?" The three stopped, but the one in the middle said, "This ain't close enough to carry on a civil conversation."

"It's close enough for our purposes," said the ranger. "We've got nothing to talk about anyway."

"Well, I'm afraid we do, Ranger," said the young gunman, tightening his jaw. "See, that's our well you and your horses are using."

"Turn around and go," said Burrack, not even offering a reply.

The men stood firm. "Maybe you don't understand about the well, Ranger," the young man said. "Now that the town has pulled up stakes, we've taken over. Hueso Seco is our town now. So the fact is, you're going to have to—"

"Tackett," said the ranger, cutting the man off.

Sheriff Tackett swung the sawed-off double-barrel up from under his coat, cocking both hammers with his thumb. The three men stiffened on the spot.

"See what I meant by 'close enough'?" said the ranger.

# HELL'S RIDERS

## Ralph Cotton

A SIGNET BOOK

SIGNET
Published by New American Library, a division of
Penguin Group (USA) Inc., 375 Hudson Street,
New York, New York 10014, U.S.A.
Penguin Books Ltd, 80 Strand,
London WC2R 0RL, England
Penguin Books Australia Ltd, 250 Camberwell Road,
Camberwell, Victoria 3124, Australia
Penguin Books Canada Ltd, 10 Alcorn Avenue,
Toronto, Ontario, Canada M4V 3B2
Penguin Books (N.Z.) Ltd, Cnr Rosedale and Airborne Roads,
Albany, Auckland 1310, New Zealand

Penguin Books Ltd, Registered Offices:
80 Strand, London WC2R 0RL, England

First published by Signet, an imprint of New American Library,
a division of Penguin Group (USA) Inc.

First Printing, May 2004
10  9  8  7  6  5  4  3

 REGISTERED TRADEMARK—MARCA REGISTRADA

Printed in the United States of America

PUBLISHER'S NOTE
This is a work of fiction. Names, characters, places, and incidents either are
the product of the author's imagination or are used fictitiously, and any resem-
blance to actual persons, living or dead, business establishments, events, or
locales is entirely coincidental.

For Mary Lynn . . . *of course.*

# Prologue

————

An empty whiskey bottle fell to the ground in the stirrup-high wild grass. Cinco Diablos grabbed Morton Toller's forearm as Toller raised his big Starr revolver and started to take aim at the bottle. "What do you think you're doing, you *cerdo hediondo*?" said Diablos. "That shot will be heard from here to *infierno*!"

"Lift your hand off my arm, half-breed," said Toller, "else you won't have enough fingers left to pick lice off your ass come morning." His left hand came up quickly, grasping the wooden handle of a long Brazilian machete he carried in a sheath hanging from his saddle horn. Sunlight glinted along the machete blade.

But Cinco Diablos held firm. His right hand had not been idle. In it he held a snub-barreled eight-gauge Spanish shotgun, its buttstock cut down to a pistol grip, its original long, ornate barrel replaced with one three inches long and flared on the end. "Tell your fat belly *adios*!" Diablos said, his teeth clenched squarely beneath his black mustache. At the slightest move from Toller, Cinco would drop the hammer and send a blast of nail heads through the man's barrellike stomach.

"Damnit, boys!" said Jessup Earles, bumping his horse into theirs, but careful not to get between them.

"No wonder I'm always short on good fighting men!"
His dark eyes shined into Toller's. "You can cleave
his fingers off tonight if you have to! Right before
supper, if you really want to bake his beans!" His eyes
streaked from Toller to the half-breed. "Cinco! You
shoot that bomber this close up, you'll be wearing
Toller's gullet in your beard for the next month! We
all will! Now let down, the both of yas."

"He will *cut* me," said Cinco Diablos, not backing
off an inch.

"He's right, I *will*," said Toller, himself unyielding.
"I allow no *white* man to touch my personage in any
manner, let alone a *half-breed*."

"Boys, let your bark down," said Haddon Marr, his
voice low and calm but carrying both a threat and an
authority that needed no further statement. Both
men's eyes turned from themselves and to Haddon
Marr. He sat relaxed in his Spanish-style Hope saddle,
his hands crossed on the wide, flat saddle horn. In his
left socket he wore a yellow glass cat's eye, and its
vertical pupil seemed alive and watching every move.
He'd taken off his right glove and held it loosely in
his left hand. From his saddle horn a bundle of long
black scalps hung intertwined as one against the shin
of his knee-high Mexican boots. Amid the scalps hung
a dried and blackened foot with two toes missing. He
wore a black leather necklace strung with accumulated
human teeth, ears, and spindly finger bones.

Both Morton Toller and Cinco Diablos relented
their position at the same time, slowly and grudgingly.
"I should have brought more whiskey." Toller grumbled, watching Cinco's horse sidestep a safer distance
back from him. "I'll kill you another time, half-breed,"
he said in afterthought.

"I will kill you first," said Cinco, giving a slight shrug. "There are five devils in me, only one in you. We will see who dies and who lives." He let the hammer of the snub-nosed shotgun down, still stepping his horse away from Toller.

"If everybody is finished killing everybody else," said Jessup Earles, looking around at each man's face as he pulled a wad of chewing tobacco from a pouch made from a bull buffalo's scrotum, "let's get chawed up and ride out there." He passed the tobacco pouch to Haddon Marr on his right. Marr took the pouch but didn't dip into it. Instead he passed it along to the nearest man, a thin, elderly man known as Uncle Andy Fill. A wide saber scar ran cheek to cheek across the bridge of Uncle Andy's nose, leaving an ugly slice of it missing, the remains lying flat against his face. Uncle Andy took a wad of tobacco and passed the pouch on to Taos Charlie, a gunman turned scalp hunter who wore a brace of short-barreled Colt Thunderers on his left hip and his favored gun, a big, long-barreled Remington, on his right. In his saddle boot stood a long half-stocked Sheets Plains rifle with a silver eagle inlaid in its walnut stock. Taos took a small wad of tobacco and pitched the pouch to Crosseyed Burton Stowl. "I never killed me a white woman before . . . except a whore once in Nebraska," said Taos. He worked the tobacco into his jaw as he spoke. Stowl fumbled with the pouch until his eyes managed to focus on it. He pulled out a thick pinch of tobacco and passed the pouch on to Morton Toller.

"What's wrong with killing a white woman, whore or otherwise?" Jessup Earles asked Taos in a firm tone. "If the Hun says he'll pay double for yellow hair, we'll give him all the yellow hair he wants." He looked from one grim face to the next for support. "We'll give him enough yellow hair to stuff his mattress, far as I care."

"I never said anything was wrong with it," said Taos. "I just said I never done it. . . . except that whore that time." He looked at the others, spit a stream of tobacco juice and grumbled something profane under his breath.

"Remember," said Jessup Earles, adjusting the ragged stocking cap down on his head, "once we hit the flat stretch where they can see us from the supply store, ride like hell, kill anything that moves, burn down what's left standing." He also spit a stream, then wiped a hand across his mouth. "Any questions?"

"Let's get 'er done," said Haddon Marr, jerking his big spotted horse around toward the stretch of flatland, then staring expectantly at Jessup Earles, awaiting his lead.

"That's what I say," Earles called out, "let's get 'er done!" He booted his big bay hard, sending the horse into a run. Haddon Marr rode only a foot behind Earles. Following the two, the rest of the men rode bunched up until their horses hit the wide flatland. Then they spread out and rode abreast, the horses' hooves raising low thunder from the earth beneath them.

Fifteen miles from Wakely, in the settlement of Clifton Wells, no one saw the riders coming across the plains until it was too late to offer any armed resistance. An old buffalo hunter named Dagas Bright rolled out of a hammock as the sound of splashing hooves crossed the small creek at the settlement's perimeter. But just as he reached for his rifle leaning against a tree, the firing began. One of the first shots hit Bright in the chest and knocked him backwards.

Dark arterial blood spewed from his buckskin shirt. Other men and women made a desperate effort at defending themselves as the riders pounded through the settlement. Yet, within moments their bodies lay strewn in the dirt alongside those who had only tried to flee.

When the screams of the wounded and dying had dissipated, and the sound of gunfire had fallen silent, Jessup Earles and Haddon Marr stepped their horses calmly among the carnage while the rest of the riders leapt down from their saddles, their knives in hand and made quick work of anyone unfortunate enough to still be alive. "No sign of any yellow hair so far, Jessup!" Morton Toller called out, standing over the body of a young Mexican teamster, a bloody dark scalp hanging from his left hand, his knife in his right.

"Keep looking then, *damn it!*" shouted Earles. He gave a searching glance back and forth and said to Marr, "I saw two womenfolk with hair as yellow as sweet corn when I scouted through here yesterday. One was full grown, the other one was young, her cub most likely. The grown one gave me a dipper of water. I know they're still here somewhere."

"If they're not, we've sure come a long way out of our way for nothing," said Marr, reloading his big Walker Colts as he spoke. The barrels of the guns were still warm as he shoved them back into the double holster rig mounted down over the pommel of his saddle. For a raid such as this, the big Walkers had served him well over the years. On his hip he also carried a newer single-action Frontier Model Colt for what he called "personal protection." "We've been this side of the border near a month now. I'm ready to head back to Mexico before we pick up a posse on our tails."

Giving a low, dark chuckle, Earles nodded toward the bodies lying about them and said, "Do you really think there's a posse this side of hell wants to lock horns with us?"

"What I think is, we're off our prowl over here. If I wanted to be in this country I never would have left."

Jessup Earles started to reply, but before he could he heard Morton Toller call out, "Hey! Over here! I believe I've struck that yellow hair we's looking for!"

Earles and Marr heeled their horse to a spot where Morton Toller stood over the body of a young man wearing an out-of-place pinstripe business suit, his string tie undone and stuck to his chest by a thick puddle of blood. A rifle lay only inches from the young man's hand. "Down in that dugout!" said Toller to Earles and Marr, and the others as they gathered closer. He pointed with his bloody knife toward a plank door standing closed at the bottom of a short tunnel just below ground level. "I caught a glimpse of yellow hair slamming the door!"

"Get down there and get her!" Earles barked.

"Huh-uh!" Toller shook his head. "I can't go underground! You knew that when we took up, Jessup!"

"Damn it!" Earles looked down at the dugout door, knowing that whoever had taken shelter there had no way out. He took his time, stepping down from his saddle, Haddon Marr doing the same beside him. With their guns drawn, the two walked down to the plank door. "Hello, the dugout!" said Earles. He took the thick leather strap that served as a door handle and shook it hard. The door only rattled slightly. "Open up, else we'll burn you right out of there. You and your nit! I saw you both yesterday. I'm the one you gave a drink of cool water." He grinned at Haddon

Marr standing beside him. "Guess she'll think twice next time, helping a wayfaring stranger."

Inside a dim circle of lantern light in the dugout, the young widow, Greta Gusstabt, clutched her twelve-year-old daughter to her bosom and whispered a prayer in her broken English. All the while she worked frantically with a sharp skinning knife, cutting long handfuls of hair from her daughter's head and letting it fall to the earthen floor. In the same hand that clutched the knife she held a crushed letter she had carried with her all the way from Philadelphia.

"Mama, what must we do?" the child sobbed hysterically, her face buried against her mother's bosom, feeling her hair leave her head in long wisps. When the men had arrived, Greta and her daughter had been in the wagon near the stream, readying themselves for the last fifteen miles of their journey to Wakely. Seeing the gruesome work begin, she had grabbed the child and run to the dugout. She knew that cutting her daughter's hair would not save her life, only that it might spare the child unbearable torture should she still be alive when the scalpers got their hands on her.

"Pray, Hilda! Only pray!" said the woman. "Pray to a merciful God!" As she spoke in a trembling whisper, the woman gathered most of the child's remaining hair and hurriedly sliced it off close to her head. "Pray that we are forgiven the sins of this life, and that—"

Her words were cut short as the sound of heavy boots began to pound on the plank roof of the dugout. "Come open this confounded door, woman!" shouted Jessup Earles. "Your string is run out on you!"

"Please spare my child!" Greta called out through the sound of the heavy boots and the falling dirt from the planks covering the dugout.

"Sparing ain't what we're good at!" Earles laughed.

Marr backed up a few steps and looked up at the men atop the planks and sod covering the wide hole in the ground. "Come on down here . . . knock this door in! Let's quit all the fooling around!"

The men hurried, Morton Toller calling out without venturing down toward the door, "Can we all get some of that woman before we kill her?"

Inside in the dim light, Greta watched the door burst open, spilling a shaft of harsh sunlight on her and the child. She closed her eyes tightly and prayed, seeing the silhouettes of the men crowd into the dugout.

"Ain't this a sight," said Jessup Earles, stopping everybody for a second with his arm outstretched, holding them back. In the swirl of dust and sunlight they saw the woman facing them on her knees, cradling her daughter, her arms wrapped around the child, her hands steepled, the letter still crushed tightly in them. Greta had loosened her hair and spread it forward as if in an offering. Earles smiled with satisfaction. But then his smile faded as he saw the child's close-cropped head and the pile of long, silken hair lying on the dirt. "Well, I'll be a son of a bitch!" he growled. "Woman, you expect mercy after pulling a stunt like that?"

"Let *us* have her!" said Uncle Andy Fill. "We won't hurt her hair none."

"What's going on down there?" Toller called out from ground level. "Are we going to pass that woman around? Me and Cinco want some too!"

"No, not me," said Cinco Diablos. He stood holding the horses, looking down toward the open door, his blood-stained knife in his left hand, along with a scalp he'd just taken from one of the dead.

Ignoring Toller, Earles wrenched the child from the

pleading woman's arms. "Why the hell not?" he said to Andy Fill. He raised a boot and kicked the woman backwards onto the dirt floor. Then he passed the terrified girl to Haddon Marr as the three men rushed past them to get to the woman. "Here, you can have this bald-headed little nit!"

Haddon Marr looked the child up and down, holding her out at arm's length. "Mine to keep from now on?" he said. "Do you mean it?" The child trembled violently, in deep shock, unable to even scream, let alone fight for her life.

"Hell, yes; far as I'm concerned, do what you want with it. It ain't worth nothing to us." Earles growled. "Not until its hair grows back."

Uncle Andy Fill, the first to reach the woman, reached down, grasped the woman's dress, undergarment and all, and ripped them from her. "Whooieee! Look at these things!" he shouted, seeing the large, pale white breasts spill from her torn cotton undergarment. She tried to crawl away on her back, but Cross-eyed Burton Stowl grabbed her by her ankles and pulled her back to them, jerking her feet wide apart, exposing her soft white flesh.

Atop the ground Toller watched Haddon Marr walk up out of the ground carrying the child.

From the dugout Toller heard catcalls and laughter and called out, "What's going on down there? Don't forget me! I want her too!" His eyes went hungrily to the child in Marr's arms.

"Don't let it cross your mind, Toller," Marr warned. "This one belongs to me, nobody else." He held the girl in his left arm, his right hand poised near his holstered Colt.

Toller turned back toward the dugout below. "Hey, damn it! Bring her up here! This ain't right!"

Suddenly the hooting and laughing stopped. After a second of silence, Uncle Andy Fill cried aloud, "Damn it to hell! She's stabbed herself!"

"Pull it out of her! She's all right!" said Taos Charlie. "A little blood never hurt nothing."

"She's dead, damn it!" said Uncle Andy Fill. "Pull it out of her yourself, it ain't my knife."

"Where'd it come from?" Burton Stowl asked, sounding disappointed.

"I reckon she had it hidden," said Fill. "Says a lot for you jacklegs, a woman rather die than accommodate yous." He laughed darkly.

"Hell's fire!" said Uncle Andy Fill, the three of them arising out of the dugout, dragging the woman's naked corpse by her ankles, her scalp already having been taken by Jessup Earles.

At ground level, they dropped their hold on the woman and stopped and looked at the child cradled in Marr's left arm, her bare feet and legs dangling limply. Marr covered the child's eyes with one hand. "Why did you have to drag her up here?"

The three looked at one another with no answer. Then they looked at the little girl.

"Maybe we get to do ourselves some good after all," said Taos Charlie.

"Walk wide of her, boys," Haddon Marr warned them, his right hand raising his Colt and cocking it. "She's mine and mine alone. Earles gave her to me." He stood in a way that both sheltered the child from the men and kept her from seeing her dead mother on the ground with the knife handle protruding from her chest.

"Like hell!" said Uncle Andy Fill. "She belongs to all of us. I'm taking my bite of the biscuit right now!" He took a step forward, saying to Taos Charlie and

Burton Stowl, "Come on, he's talking out of his head."

Haddon Marr raised the cocked Colt. "So long, boys!"

"Haddon, *no!*" shouted Jessup Earles, walking up from the dugout, the woman's long blond hair hanging in a bloody tangle in his left hand. Blood dripped steadily to the ground. "Let's try to act like civilized men here!" As he spoke he slung the scalp as if he were popping a whip toward the ground, getting rid of excess blood and matter. "These boys did their share just like you did."

"Didn't you just give her to me?" Marr asked firmly, although it really wasn't a question.

"Well, yes, I did, but damn, Had. . . ." said Earles. "Just look at yourself. You're acting strange."

"You said 'mine from now on,' to do what I wanted with her." He kept the Colt cocked, stepping back away from the men, toward Cinco and the horses. "I'm not giving her over to nobody unless I damn well feel like it." He sat the stunned child up onto his saddle, then said, "Look at her. Hell, she's just a strip of a kid yet."

"She's twelve if she's a day," said Earles. "My ma was that age when she had me!"

"That's you," said Marr. "I'm keeping her away from all of you until I figure what I want to do with her." He swung up onto his saddle.

"I said she's yours until her hair grows out, Had," said Earles, pointing a long, bloody finger at him.

"No, you didn't." Marr snapped back at him. "You never said a damn thing about her hair growing back."

"Then I'm saying it now!" Earles growled. "We're in the hair-lifting business. It goes without saying! Soon as this nit's got anything worth selling, I'll skin

her quicker 'n a cat'll skin a fish! Do we both understand that?''

Haddon Marr glared at him without answering.

"Do we agree?" Jessup Earles repeated, reluctant
to push anything much farther with Haddon Marr.
Earles and the others stood watching as Haddon Marr
backed his horse a few feet and sat staring at them.

"Well . . .?" Marr said.

"Well what?" said Earles, not understanding
Marr's attitude.

"Well, let's ride," said Marr. He offered a tight unyielding smile, still holding the cocked pistol pointed
loosely in Earles' direction. He lowered his chin over
the girl's close-cropped head and nestled it in against
his chest.

"You didn't answer me," said Earles.

"I didn't intend to," said Marr.

Earles stared for a moment, puzzled. Then he shook
his head and began to chuckle under his breath.
"Had . . . I swear to God, you beat all I ever seen."

# PART 1

# Chapter 1

The ranger, Sam Burrack, followed the long rise of black smoke until it led him to Clifton Wells. When he saw the burnt hull of the supply store and the line of bodies on the ground with blankets thrown over them, he stopped for a second, then winced and rode forward slowly. Two men lifted the bodies and laid them into a buckboard. Grim faces turned toward him as he led his prisoner past the charred remnants of three wagons, the smell of burnt flesh, of both man and animal, filling the air. He carefully pulled the lapel of his riding duster open to reveal the badge on his chest, lest anyone here mistakenly question either his intent or purpose. Faces changed at the sight of his badge—while their expressions remained grim, they appeared far less suspicious. A few yards ahead of him the ranger saw a man in a black linen suit standing over a body with his hat off and his head bowed.

"What's happened here?" the ranger asked another man standing with a rifle in one hand and a shovel in his other.

"Scalp hunters, the way we make it out," the man responded, eyeing the prisoner closely.

"Who's in charge?" Burrack asked bluntly, going straight for the top man.

"Sheriff Boyd Tackett," the man responded, still

staring at the prisoner. He jerked a thumb toward the
man in the black linen suit standing ten yards away
in front of a dugout. Then he asked in a tight voice,
"What's this man done?" his hand growing even
tighter around his rifle stock.

"Obliged," said the ranger, ignoring his question,
touching a finger to the brim of his wide gray sombrero. He recognized the name Boyd Tackett, and he
gave a soft tap to the sides of his big Appaloosa stallion and moved forward, the prisoner close beside
him.

"Do you see the way they're all looking at me?"
the prisoner asked in a whisper. "You'd think I had
something to do with all this."

The ranger said without turning to him, "A terrible
thing has happened here, Riley. Seeing you in tow
represents the criminal element to these men right
now. Ride along real quiet like, keep your head
down."

"Rest assured, I will," whispered Ted Riley, in a
deep Southern accent. He lowered his head quickly.

A hot wind lifted a corner of one of the blankets
covering the dead as the ranger and his prisoner rode
on slowly. The ranger saw the grizzly handiwork of
scalp hunters and swallowed the dry, bitter taste that
their kind of savagery always brought to him.

"Lord God almighty," Riley whispered, riding
closer beside him, the length of lead rope hanging
slack between them. "I wish I'd never seen that."

Another man, this one carrying a shotgun and
dressed in drover clothes, reached down and flipped
the blanket corner back over, covering the dead face
with its tortured expression and a streak of its bare
skull shining through a mass of bloody gore. He gave

both Riley and the ranger a hostile look as they passed him.

Stopping a few feet back from the man in the black linen suit, Sam dropped the lead rope and his reins and stepped down from his saddle. Riley looked around nervously without raising his head. A few of the men began to gather in closer around him, looking him up and down.

"Sheriff Boyd Tackett?" the ranger asked quietly, stepping up closer and stopping, noting the sheriff still held his hat in his hand, looking down at the body lying out front of the dugout.

The broad-shouldered young sheriff turned to face him, his hair and his string tie fluttering on the hot wind. His eyes and expression were sad and distant, made even more so by the long, drooping black mustache mantling his lip. Cocking his head slightly, he looked past Burrack at the prisoner, then looked back at him and said, noting the badge on his chest, "Yes, I'm Sheriff Tackett. What can I do for you?"

"I'm Ranger Sam Burrack, and it's not what you can do for me. I spotted the smoke a long ways back and followed it here. Is there any way I can help?"

Sheriff Tackett took his time answering, first looking at the big Appaloosa stallion, then at the prisoner again, then back at Burrack, shaking his head. "Not that I can think of." He stood slumped, staring back down at the blanket-covered body on the ground for a silent moment before sighing and saying, "Sam Burrack, huh? I've heard of you."

"I've heard of you too," said the ranger. He waited.

Sheriff Tackett turned his eyes from the body long enough to give a nod toward the Appaloosa stallion. "You're the ranger who killed Junior Lake and his bunch . . . avenged Outrider Sazes after one of them shot him."

"Yes," said the ranger. "You're the sheriff who shot Cordell Dickson and cleaned up Cottonwood."

Tackett nodded, turning his eyes back to the body on the ground. "Dickson wasn't nothing, neither was cleaning up Cottonwood."

"Neither was Junior Lake and his bunch," said Burrack. Tackett raised his eyes again and the two men stared at each other in silence, each sizing up the other as if for future reference.

A townsman wearing a bright red Scotch plaid riding duster and a brown bowler hat stepped in and said to Tackett, "Pardon me, Sheriff. We've looked everywhere. There's no sign of any little girl."

"Keep looking, Kirby," Sheriff Tackett said firmly.

Pushing up his brown bowler hat, he said, "Sheriff, we're running out of places to look!" He gave the ranger a glance, as if asking for their help.

Burrack looked at Sheriff Tackett curiously.

Tackett took a deep breath as townsman Kirby Romans turned and walked away. He reached inside his black linen coat, pulled out a wrinkled letter and handed it to the ranger without commenting. Burrack read the letter to himself, then looked at Tackett, seeing the sheriff stare down at the body as if he and the blanket-covered corpse were the only ones there. After a long moment of silence, the ranger said, "Sheriff . . . I'm sorry."

Tackett only nodded without raising his bowed head.

The ranger looked all around the settlement, then out across the endless barren land. The only sound to be heard came from the whir of hot wind and the crackling of embers in the smoldering fire where once the supply store had stood. "This child she mentioned, that's the child you're still looking for?"

"Yes," Sheriff Tackett said in a lowered voice. "She came all this way, her and her little girl. I told her it would be safe . . . no trouble with Indians for years now." He paused, then said, "I told her I would be a good, faithful husband to her, and that I'd be a good father to little Hilda." He dropped his gaze and said, "You see, Ranger, little Hilda is what you call 'slow.' She's twelve years old, but her mind hasn't grown as quick as she has. I just wanted to make life right for her ma and her."

The ranger only nodded, knowing there were no consoling words to offer. He folded the letter carefully and handed it back to the sheriff. As they stood there, the ranger raised a hand and motioned for Ted Riley to step down and bring the horses forward. When Riley stood next to him, he asked the ranger in a lowered voice, "What is it, Ranger?"

"Stick close to me, Riley, we're going to be looking for a little girl here," the ranger said, just between the two of them.

"Certainly, Ranger," said Ted Riley. "You can trust me. I am a man of honor who would never take advantage of this kind of situation. I'll do whatever I'm told."

The ranger looked into his eyes. "Keep that attitude and you'll be back out of prison before you know it."

"I have no choice but to keep that attitude," Riley replied. "I come from a long line of honorable men."

"Good for you," said the ranger, passing his words off.

Before they had taken three steps away from Sheriff Tackett, a voice called out from down in the rubble of the collapsed dugout roof. "I've found something!"

The ranger and Ted Riley stopped in their tracks and joined the others who hurriedly surrounded the dugout. "What is it, Jake?" asked Kirby Romans, stepping down along a fallen roof timber. A hot breeze lifted the tails of his Scotch plaid duster.

"This!" said the dusty, black-smudged face of the man down in the rubble. He stood up from beneath a timber he'd crawled under and held a thick wad of hair in one dirty hand and a lit lantern in his other.

"Oh, Jesus!" said Kirby Romans. "It's the child's scalp!"

"No, it's not," said Jake Winslow, scooting up onto the timber, holding the hair out for him to see it better. "I thought the same thing myself. But it's not a scalp. It's just loose hair, see?" He shook the handful of hair back and forth, showing no sign of any blood or scalp matter. "Her hair was all cut off! No sign of her! Just her hair, laying in a pile on the floor!"

The ranger looked at Sheriff Tackett, seeing the grim, tortured look on his face as he stared into the collapsed dugout at the silken blond hair.

"What do you want us to do, Sheriff?" Kirby Romans called out, taking the handful of hair and holding it up for Tackett to see.

Seeing that the sheriff wasn't able to reply right then with a clear voice, the ranger called down, "Bring it on up here."

Tackett stood in silence as the two men climbed up from the collapsed dugout and Kirby Romans held the long blond hair out for one of the lawmen to take. Seeing that Sheriff Tackett wasn't going to take the hair, the ranger reached out with his gloved hand, took it and looked it over. He said quietly to Romans and Winslow, "I'll hold it for now. The sheriff can

have it when he's ready." He noticed one long strand
held together by a red ribbon, and the sight of it
caused him to wince slightly and have to look off
along a distant hill line as if searching for something
there. In a moment he folded the hair gently, tucked
it into his shirt pocket and buttoned his pocket flap.
Two men stepped in quietly, picked up Greta's body
without removing the blanket and carried her away to
the buckboard.

Seeing the two men carrying Greta away, Kirby Romans shook his head. "I reckon we best get the dead
on in to Wakely, huh?" he asked the ranger, seeing
that Tackett had stepped over to the dugout and stood
staring blankly into it. "I expect the sheriff will want
to get some supplies together so we can get right on
these killers' trail? That would be my guess. What do
you think, Ranger?"

Before he could answer, Sheriff Tackett cut in without facing them, saying, "No! I'm not going back to
town. I'm getting on these men's trail right now, while
it's still fresh."

The ranger only watched without speaking.

"But Sheriff Tackett, we'll need supplies, enough to
last all of us a week or more," said Romans. "Besides,
most of us have jobs or businesses to run! We need
to get back there and make arrangements before we
go riding off in a posse!"

"Then go on back to town," said Tackett. "I'm
sticking on their trail." He continued to stare down
grimly into the collapsed dugout.

The other men began to gather closer, listening to
the conversation. "Ranger, maybe you can talk some
sense into him," said Romans. "We rode out here
with him because a party of wagons didn't show up

when they were supposed to! It's terrible what's happened here. But all we can do is take these poor pilgrims to town and get them buried!"

"Then go on home," the sheriff cut in. "I'm not stopping you."

"But you're *our* sheriff," said Romans, the wind still licking at his plaid duster tails. "We need you in town, not out here traipsing after these scalp hunters. We need to notify the army outpost. Let them handle this bunch. Besides," he continued, pointing a finger along the ground, "these killers' tracks are headed due west, probably on their way back across the border right now. That's where most of them drop their spurs anyway."

The ranger listened and watched, knowing that what this townsman said was true. The sheriff wasn't even dressed for a long ride, wearing his linen suit, his white shirt and string tie. He imagined the sheriff had dressed that way to impress his soon-to-be bride. He wondered if the sheriff had even carried any extra ammunition other than what he had in his holster belt. But judging by the look on the sheriff's face, Burrack realized nothing the townsman said was going to make any difference.

"All of you listen up," Sheriff Tackett called out to the gathering men, craning slightly, making sure he could be heard. "I'm riding after the men who did this. I know you have obligations in town. So, any of you who want to ride along with me, get on back to town, get supplied, do what you have to do, then get on my trail and catch up to me. I'll leave a clear sign for you any way I can."

The men looked at one another, nodding and murmuring among themselves. "What about the ranger?" asked Otto Baugh, the town barber.

"What about him?" said Sheriff Tackett, before the ranger had time to respond for himself.

"Is he riding with us on this?" asked Baugh. "He has more legal jurisdiction to go after them than we do. This is more his job than yours, Sheriff."

Sheriff Tackett turned, facing the ranger. Burrack knew he had to make a quick decision. He glanced at his prisoner, then at the sheriff and the rest of the men. "I'm going to ride as far as I can with you. I've got a prisoner here I've got to deliver. But that will have to keep for the time being." He paused, then added, "Just so nobody gets any wrong idea and decides to do this man harm. Let me make it clear that he is no murderer or outlaw." He looked Ted Riley up and down as he spoke. "His name is Ted Riley and he was convicted of forging an express agent's name on a delivery receipt. Two years from now he will be walking the streets among you, a free man, having paid for what he did. Does everybody understand that?"

"A forger?" said Otto Baugh. "I'll be surprised some convict doesn't kill him before he gets his time in! I'd be ashamed to tell anybody if that was all I done!"

A short laugh rose then fell among the men. "If you drag this prisoner along," said Jake Winslow, still slapping dust and bits of debris from his forearms and clothing from his crawl beneath the fallen wood beams, "is he going to slow us down? Can he keep up? This could turn into an awfully hard ride for a pencil-pushing *forger.*"

The ranger looked at Ted Riley and asked, "What about it, Riley? Are you eager to get on to prison, or do you think you can keep up with them, live on the trail awhile?"

Riley said to the ranger, "I'm in no hurry to get to prison." He lowered his eyes and said to the men, "I'll do the best I can not to slow you down or get in your way."

The ranger looked Riley over appraisingly, listening to him speak. He would never have gone on the trail with a prisoner without first sizing him up. He'd cautioned himself not to underestimate Ted Riley. He had the look of a man who'd been around and seen his share of the frontier life. Granted this man had a gentlemanly mild manner to him, but the ranger knew better than to judge a man simply by his manner. "I'm not going to have to put cuffs and chains on you, am I?" the ranger asked, watching Riley's eyes closely as he made his reply, looking for whatever sign of deception might be revealed there.

Yet the ranger read nothing but sincerity . . . and that in itself put him on alert.

Ted Riley said in an even tone, "No, Ranger, cuffs won't be necessary. You have my word I won't try to escape. In Alabama the word of a Montgomery Riley is held in the utmost esteem."

"All right, enough talk," Sheriff Tackett cut in. "You men get to town, get supplied and get back out here. One of you go by my office and bring me a change of clothes and the new bag of coffee beans I left on the corner of my desk."

The ranger looked at the sheriff and felt a little better hearing him snap out of his anger and grief enough to concentrate on what he needed. Sheriff Tackett's eyes met the ranger's as he spoke. "Bring as much ammunition as you can afford to carry. Any rifles you need, take them from the gun rack." He lifted a small key from his vest pocket and pitched it to Kirby Romans. "Be sure and sign for them." He looked away from the ranger, toward the buckboard loaded heavily with the dead. "See to it she gets a proper burial. I'll pay for it out of my own pocket when I return." He stepped back, put his hat on and squared his shoulders.

The ranger nodded slightly, assuring himself that the sheriff would be all right once they got on the trail. As Sheriff Tackett and the rest of the men turned to their horses, the ranger and Ted Riley did the same. In moments a silence fell across the deserted settlement as the buckboard and the riders moved away toward town, Kirby Romans in the lead, his bright plaid duster tails flapping behind him. The ranger, the sheriff and the prisoner rode west, following the tracks of what appeared to be seven running horses. For the next twenty minutes the three rode at a steady, moderate pace. On the ground, the hoofprints they followed remained long, the seven horses still running hard.

"It would sure be something if they blow their horses out and you catch right up to them," said Ted Riley, as they rode abreast along the trail, the ranger and the sheriff keeping a close eye on the ground.

"Yes, it would," said the ranger, "but I don't look for that to happen. These men know what their horses are capable of doing." As he spoke he slowed his Appaloosa to a slow walk and leaned down the horse's side, studying the hoofprints. "They're used to being on the run. The business they're in, they move away fast because they always figure there's likely to be somebody on their trail."

"As bad as their horses are shod, at least they'll be easy to follow," said Riley. He had noted as they'd started out that the hooves of the seven horses were either shoeless or poorly shod. Only one horse appeared to be wearing a full set of shoes, and at that the shoes were worn thin.

"They won't be too easy to follow," Tackett commented. He'd slowed down alongside the ranger, and also leaned down, studying the tracks.

"How's that?" asked Riley.

The ranger answered for Tackett, saying to Riley, "You can expect men like these to pull off the trail onto rock or harder ground the first chance they get." He straightened in his saddle and looked back over his shoulder, judging they had gone over three miles. "I'm surprised they didn't leave this trail before now."

But another mile passed beneath their hooves before the tracks they followed veered off the wide trail toward a stretch of low rounded hills over a thousand yards away. "There's where the tracking gets harder," said Sheriff Tackett, slowing his horse for only a moment, then heeling it out across the hard rocky ground. The ranger and Ted Riley did the same, keeping their three horses abreast until they reached a narrow path leading up over a surrounding wall of sunken boulders. Sheriff Tackett stepped his horse carefully up among the boulder caps, the ranger lagged back and motioned Riley ahead of himself, keeping the prisoner in plain sight as they began winding their way through the rock.

"I expect they'll drag us over every sharp rock and through each bottomless gully they can find," said Tackett. "That's one thing you can count on from a bunch of vermin like this. They figure if anybody's on their trail, they'll make it as tough as they can to follow." Looking all around, he added, "They know that it's terrain like this that turns any ordinary posse around and sends them home with their tails tucked—"

"Hold it, listen!" the ranger said, cutting him short and jerking his Appaloosa to a halt.

Tackett and Riley stopped also, their eyes searching the surrounding rises of blackish doomed rock, ears straining. For a second the only sound was that of the hot wind rolling and snaking its way among the stone. Then, from a stand of taller rock a few yards to their left, the sound came again and the ranger honed in on it. "Over there," he said in a whisper, "a horse nickered."

The three stepped down from their horses as one, silently, and crouched on the ground. Taking Sheriff Tackett's reins, the ranger handed both of their horses to Ted Riley and motioned for Riley to stay back with the animals while he and the sheriff checked things out. Riley looked down in surprise at the reins in his hands. But his expression changed when he saw the handcuff click around his wrist. He watched the ranger pull his arm over and click the other cuff around the stirrup to the big Appaloosa stallion. The ranger whispered in the Appaloosa's ear. The big stallion appeared to plant his hooves more firmly in place.

"I gave you my word, Ranger Burrack," Riley whispered.

"I know that, Riley," he whispered in reply. "This is just to keep you reminded of it." He gave Riley a trace of a flat smile, then stepped away quietly.

Tackett had crouched down and leaned against a boulder. When the ranger joined him, he whispered, "I hope you didn't just give our horses away to that forger."

"That stallion won't take him anywhere. He'll stand

there through a twister unless I tell him otherwise," said the ranger.

"So will my bay," said Tackett. Looking back at where Riley stood crouched with his wrist cuffed to the stirrup, he grinned and added, "For your prisoner's sake I hope so anyway." He nodded toward the taller rocks where they'd heard the sound of the horse nicker. "I'll move to the right, take up a flank position above the rocks, in case this is an ambush."

The ranger nodded. "I'll give you time to get in position before I close in." He raised his Colt from his holster and checked it as he continued. "But I don't think this is an ambush, unless they left somebody behind waiting on a posse. And that ain't likely unless they knew *for sure* that somebody was tracking them."

"Then what do you suspect?" Tackett asked, still in a whisper.

"A lame horse, more than likely," said the ranger, not cocking his Colt, but keeping the barrel pointed up, a gloved thumb over the hammer. "But we better treat it serious, just in case."

The two moved out silently, snaking their way, moving farther and farther apart, the ranger allowing the sheriff to get ahead of him. Judging how long it would take before he could count on Tackett getting into position above the taller stand of rock, the ranger stopped and waited, close to the spot, listening for any further sound, hearing none. When he decided the sheriff had had plenty of time to get in place, he eased forward on his belly until he reached a spot where he could peep around the stand of rock into a small clearing. Doing so he let out a tight breath and lowered his thumb off his Colt, seeing a horse standing with a front hoof raised in pain, just as he'd suspected. Still searching the clearing, the ranger stood up cautiously and walked forward toward the animal. "Sheriff Tackett," he called out, keeping his voice at a level tone. "Come on down . . . it's what we thought it was."

The ranger waited until he heard the sheriff began to struggle down the side of the rock.

Tackett leaped down the last few feet and walked into sight, slapping dust from his linen coat and looking the lame horse up and down. "What *you* thought it was, you mean," said the sheriff, uncocking his Colt and letting it hang at his side. "I flat out missed it. Never even thought it might be a stone-bruised horse."

"You would've thought of it, if I hadn't," said the ranger. He walked to the suffering horse and raised its muzzle in the palm of his gloved hand. Looking down at the horse's front leg he saw a streak of blood running along the break in its shin where the leg twisted sideways at an odd angle. "But it's no stone bruise. Its leg is badly broken."

"I reckon they didn't shoot it because they didn't want to risk somebody hearing the shot," said Tackett."

"Yep," said the ranger, rubbing the poor horse's muzzle as he gazed off in the direction of the hoof scrapings on the hard ground, "and neither do we."

"Dang it," said Tackett, shaking his head. "I hate what tracking men like this can force a person to do." He took a deep breath and looked levelly at the ranger. "Do you want me to do it?" he asked.

Burrack shook his head, still rubbing the horse's muzzle. "Why don't you walk on down, let Riley know everything's all right," he suggested quietly. "I'll be along in a minute."

When Sheriff Tackett walked out of sight, the

ranger reached down and drew the long bone-handled knife from his boot well. "We'll be lucky if this is the worst thing we have to do," he said to himself.

At the horses, as Tackett walked down, Ted Riley stood up slowly and asked in a lowered voice, "Where's Ranger Burrack?"

"He's coming," said the sheriff. "You don't have to talk so careful now. It was a lame horse, like the ranger said."

"I'm still talking careful because I don't want to say anything that might spook this animal," said Riley. He held the cuff up enough for Tackett to see. "I've got an arm invested in this animal!"

"Yeah, I suppose that would be a problem if he took off real sudden like," said Tackett with a straight face as he took the reins to the other two horses' reins from him.

Riley stared at him and stood close to the big stallion, rubbing the animal soothingly now with his free hand.

They waited in silence another ten minutes before the ranger finally came meandering down between the boulder caps. When he grew closer, Sheriff Tackett asked above a whir of wind, "Is everything all right?"

Burrack shook his head. "I've got bad news." He walked in closer as he spoke. "I followed their tracks a little ways on foot. They didn't cross these hills. They headed back down this way."

"What?" Tackett looked surprised. "Why?" His eyes went along the trail at the bottom edge of the hills.

"I figure whoever lost their horse must've been somebody big enough in the ranks that they're going to replace it as soon as possible. These boys don't want to ride double no longer than they have to." He nodded along the trail. "Unless I miss my mark on this, we'll find their tracks coming down somewhere along there."

"Dang it!" said Sheriff Tackett. "If they head that way, there's a relay station at Stone Pass. If they get horses there, there ain't a thing to keep them from riding right on into my town!"

"Then we best get moving," said the ranger, "that *is* where they're headed." Reaching down with a key he unlocked Ted Riley's handcuff from the stallion's stirrup.

# Chapter 2

Relay station attendant Al Doone first heard rifle and pistol fire resounding from a long way off and thought it might be some cowhands letting off steam on their way to town. But when the intensity of the firing continued, he told himself these were no cowboys; and soon he saw the boiling rise of dust on the horizon, coming up from a good two hundred yards west of the stage trail. He scratched his head, pulled up his drooping gallows, hooked them over his shoulders and stepped out of the shade of a flapping canvas overhang into the scorching sunlight. He knew there were no stagecoaches coming through until the next morning. *But wait . . .* He questioned himself for a moment, making certain. Then nodded to himself. Hell, no there weren't.

"Mecila," he called out over his shoulder above a rush of hot wind, "fetch me out that coach gun by the door."

The short, stout Indian woman came running in her bare feet, carrying the twenty-inch double-barrel, holding her long gingham skirt hiked up with her free hand. She handed Al Doone the gun without question and stared out through the swirling heat at the dust, seeing it move sidelong on the wind. "I know," Doone said, as if replying to something she had said, although she had not murmured a word, "I was wondering that myself."

The Indian woman only nodded, visoring a hand above her eyes, staring intently at the riders rising into view.

"I hope you've got that big shooter up twixt your legs, just in case," said Doone, breaking the shotgun open, checking it as he talked.

She lifted the front of her belled skirt and revealed the National Arms revolver standing in its holster, strapped to the front of her thigh.

"Good," said Doone, "now get back inside and keep watch through the window. Anything that don't look jake all of a sudden, you commence spitting fire at 'em through the fire hole."

She nodded, looked once again at the riders drawing closer, then hurried inside and watched through a gun slot in a closed wooden shutter. Soon the distant firing stopped and the dust settled for a moment before rising even thicker than it had been. Another twenty minutes passed before the riders came thundering into the station. In the midst of the riders the buckboard loaded with bodies slid sideways to a halt, almost tipping over in the billowing dust before stopping completely. "Hold on now!" shouted Al Doone, stepping forward with the shotgun raised, seeing the brown bowler hat and plaid riding duster through a swirling haze of dust. "What the hell do you think you're doing here?"

The rider's horse reared and spun slightly in the dirt. "You've got to help us, mister! We're from Wakely. We've got scalp hunters trying to kill us for our horses!" He clamped a hand down on the bowler hat to keep it from flying off as the frightened horse came down hard on its front hoofs.

"Scalp hunter?" Al Doone shot a glance at the bodies stacked onto the buckboard.

"That's right," said another rider, pointing a finger at the bodies. "There's some of their handiwork! We found them massacred at Clifton Wells! They never had a chance!" As he spoke a gloved hand reached down and flipped a blanket off one of the bodies.

"Lord God," said Al Doone, turning his eyes away from the grizzly sight.

"How many gun hands do you have inside?" he asked Doone, nodding at the closed window shutter.

"There's just me and my Ute squaw here," said Doone, "but we'll take as many down as we can. I hate a scalp hunter worse than anything!"

"Then get ready, they're right behind us!" the leader shouted. "We've got to take cover before they get here!"

"All right, hurry up!" shouted Al Doone, shooting a frightened glance out across the dust-streaked land. "Everybody inside!" He watched the riders drop down from their horses and hurry toward the building. "Mecila! Open the door! Don't shoot!" he shouted.

But the Indian woman fired the big revolver through the gun slot, sending one of the men tumbling backwards with a bullet through his chest.

"Damn it, woman!" shouted Al Doone. "I said don't shoot! These are townsmen from Wakely!"

But the big revolver barrel only roared again through the gun slot in the wooden shutter. This time the men managed to duck away from her line of fire. Mecila shouted something in her native tongue, but before Al Doone could make it out one of the men turned to him laughing and said, "Damn if that squaw ain't got a good eye on her!"

"Huh?" Al Doone gave the man a puzzled look,

seeing the gun pointed at his stomach. Then he noticed the bloody bullet hole in the man's plaid riding duster and the string of bones and teeth strung around his neck as the duster fell open in front. Realization struck him, too late. "You sonsabitch!" Doone managed to shout before the man's gun belched a blast of fire into his stomach.

"Fooled you!" Jessup Earles laughed as he stepped away, watching Al Doone fly backwards, dead on the ground. Keeping out of the line of gunfire coming from the window, he walked around the side of the building where the rest of the men had gathered. Cinco Diablos stood with his back flat against the wall, keeping count of the number of pistol shots. Squatting in front of him, Taos Charlie wrapped a rag around the end of a stick, making a torch.

"You've got about five minutes to smoke her out of there," said Earles, "else we'll shoot her to pieces, take what horses are here and get going."

"Damn it, hurry up then, Taos!" said Morton Toller, giving Taos a nudge with the toe of his boot to speed him along. "I'm getting damned tired of being denied every woman we come across!"

"If you're going to do something with her, you best do it pretty quick. I'm taking her scalp. Ute looks the same as an Apache. Besides, we owe her something anyway for shooting poor Uncle Andy!"

Uncle Andy Fill had crawled around the building from out front where the Indian woman's shot had dropped him in the dirt. He sat bowed, blood running from a gaping chest wound, both hands trying to hold back the dark heavy flow spreading down into his lap. "Somebody stick a rag in this for me!" he shouted, his voice wheezy and full of blood. The others only stared at him for a moment. "Damn, Uncle Andy," said Taos Charlie. "I believe that Indian has kilt you sure as hell."

"Will somebody do me some good here?" Andy rasped in a blood-filled voice.

Morton Toller untied a ragged bandanna from around his neck and pitched it into Uncle Andy's lap. "There, stick it in yourself and shut up about it!"

Two more pistol shots exploded from the gun slot. "There, that's it!" said Cinco Diablos. "She has to reload!"

Morton Toller and Taos Charlie ran to the door and slammed their shoulders into it repeatedly until the thick plank door gave way and busted in onto the floor. But as Jessup Earles and Cinco Diablos joined them to rush inside, the Ute woman brought the reloaded revolver back into play. "Uh-oh!" said Toller, ducking back out onto the porch as splinters from the door frame exploded near his head. "Everybody back! She's loaded and game as a bulldog!" He jumped back off the porch as another shot resounded.

"To hell with this!" said Earles. "Taos, get in there and get her alive if you boys want her! Else I'm killing her right now!"

"I'll get her!" said Taos Charlie. He rushed inside as another shot slammed into the door frame. The sound of a brawl came through the open doorway. Taos let out a scream of pain. Cinco Diablos and Morton Toller rushed in to help him. Jessup Earles stood on the porch and shook his head impatiently. As the sound of unarmed battle continued, he looked back along the trail and saw Haddon Marr ride in through the raised dust with the girl on his lap, cradled in his left arm, her face hidden against his chest.

"Glad you could join us, Haddon," Earles said with

a snap of sarcasm, eyeing the girl up and down. He
stepped off the porch while the sound of shouting and
scuffling resounded from inside the relay shack. The
young girl kept her face hidden, her hands over her
ears. Haddon Marr had wrapped a thin blanket
around her. Still, every few minutes he could feel her
shiver against his chest.

"What's going on in there?" Marr asked, circling
his horse wide of the porch, craning his neck for a
glimpse inside the shack.

"They've got themselves a Ute squaw treed," said
Jessup Earles. He grinned as he heard Toller let out
a curse and something or someone slam against the
inside wall, jarring the shack on its foundation.
"Maybe she'll take the edge off them for awhile."

"Now that we've got your horse replaced," said
Marr, gazing over at the four horses in the small corral, "we could have rode around this place. We picked
three other spare horses from the dead posse men
back there."

"We've never got *enough* horses, Haddon," said
Earles. He flinched at the sound of a chair crashing
inside the shack. A silence followed as he stepped up
onto a horse and flipped the tails of the red plaid
riding duster out and let them hang down the horse's
sides. The two heeled their horses toward the corral
at a slow walk as Morton Toller and Taos Charlie
dragged the dazed Indian woman out by her heels and
dropped her in the dust. A large knot glistened with
blood on the side of her forehead.

"As soon as we finish up here, we best get back
across the border," said Marr, tucking the blanket up
around the child's shoulders.

Watching him with a curious look, Jessup Earles

said, "I've been studying things over, and I ain't so sure we need to be in any hurry getting back across the border."

They stopped their horses at the corral gate. Marr looked at him. "We best get back across. It don't take much studying to figure that."

"I can understand you feeling that way. You're in a hurry because you got something to occupy your time for awhile," said Earles, glancing at the youngster on his lap. "Me and the boys ain't been near as lucky this trip. What'd be the harm in raiding a town or two before we call it quits?"

"Whatever it is you think I want to do to this kid, you're wrong, Earles," said Marr. "I ain't letting none of you get your hands on her, is all."

"Whatever you say, Haddon." Earles spit, then by-passed the subject. "The thing is, we've been living leaner than we have to in Old Mex. Scalping is what you might call a dying occupation these days. I believe there's money to be made in raiding towns. . . . Hell, there has to be." As he spoke his eyes moved off across the wavering flatlands in the direction of Wakely, twelve miles away.

"There's money in lots of things, Earles," said Haddon Marr, "but that doesn't mean we've got to try it. If scalp hunting has run its string, maybe we need to think about settling in somewhere."

"Yeah? And what?" Earles spit again. "Plant a garden?" He reached down, lifted the latch on the corral gate and rode in. "It's a shame I'm all dressed up in this fancy hat and duster and got no place to go. We've got a wagonload of bodies that'll get us right into that town before we have to fire a shot."

Thinking about things for a second, Marr stepped his horse inside the corral and kicked the gate closed behind himself. "All right. If them clothes and the bodies will get us into Wakely, let's hit it and just see how it goes."

"I knew I could count on you, once you thought about it." Earles grinned, turned his horse around and headed back for the gate, having looked the four horses over. He turned his gaze to the men and the downed Indian woman in the dirt out front of the relay shack. "Looks like everybody's had their fun. Let's go shoot that squaw and lift her hair, else we never will get these boys to leave."

In the dirt, Uncle Andy Fill sat with the bandanna pressed against his chest, staying the flow of blood. A long string of red saliva hung from his bloody lips. He stared glazed-faced at the naked, dust-coated Indian woman as she tried to struggle to her feet. "Somebody better knock her in the head again," he rasped, seeing the stout woman regain her faculties and look down at herself. She raised a hand, pushed back her long black hair from her face and felt the bloody knot on her forehead. Realizing what had been done to her, she snarled in rage and staggered toward the man standing closest to her, her teeth bared, her arms spread like a warring grizzly. She caught Morton Toller off guard and off balance, strapping his gun belt around his waist.

"Whooa now!" Toller shouted, seeing her come at him swinging, her first roundhouse blow knocking his hat from his head. He reached for his pistol, but in doing so lost his hold on his loose gun belt and dropped it, gun and all, in the dirt. "Get her off me!" he shouted to the others.

The Indian woman grabbed him by his long hair and slung him back and forth while he screamed and cursed. The others tried to help him, but as they came

at her she used Toller like a club, swinging him back
and forth at the men.

"Lord God!" said Uncle Andy Fill, watching in disbelief. "She'll kill the lot of us!" But then he flinched
when a shot from Jessup Earles' pistol hit the woman
and sent her slumping back down into the dirt, Morton
Toller, still in her grip, landing atop her.

Cinco Diablos cursed under his breath, stepping in
and helping Toller free himself from the woman's
death grip. "Come on, hombre. Get up and shake
yourself off. Lucky for you Earles shot her."

"That dirty bitch!" Morton Toller shouted, kicking
the body, holding one hand to the top of his head.

Crossed-eyed Burton Stowl laughed. "Damn,
Toller! We're the ones supposed to be lifting scalps,
not getting *ours* lifted!"

The others laughed with Stowl. But Toller would
have none of it. He snarled and jerked his big knife
from his belt. Stowl looked stunned, but then he saw
that he was not the target of Toller's rage. Toller
jumped astraddle of the Indian woman, reached down
and gathered her long black hair in his left hand.

"Before you go any farther," said Jessup Earles,
"you best understand, that's *my* scalp you're about to
take. I killed her."

"I don't care about her damned scalp!" shouted
Toller. "After her doing me that way, I just want to
be the one cuts her!" He gave a quick, violent slash
of the blade and pulled the scalp free with a tearing
sucking sound. He stepped back and slung the blood
and fluid from it. "There, Earles," he said, pitching
the grizzly trophy to him. "It's yours, with my
compliments!"

Jessup Earles caught the scalp, held it up at arm's
length appraising it, then wrapped the long hair

around his saddle horn and let it hang down his horse's side. He looked around at the men's horses, each animal with a modest string of scalps hanging from their saddle horns. "You men listen to me," said Earles. "Marr and me have been talking things over. This trip ain't been as good as ones in the past. It seems we make less and less every time we take scalps back to the Hun. I decided maybe it's time we ride into a town and take what we want from it." He looked from one dusty face to the next.

The men looked back and forth among themselves, then glanced at Haddon Marr to judge his opinion on the matter. "You're talking about robbing banks and such?" Morton Toller asked.

"Yeah, banks," said Earles, "and stores, and saloons, and whorehouses, and what the hell ever else we feel like robbing at the time." He grinned and shrugged. "We are limited only by our imagination."

Crossed-eyed Burton Stowl stepped forward, scratching his head up under his floppy hat brim, and said, "Earles, I ain't so sure that's a good idea. I ain't earning what I'd like to earn, scalp hunting, but at least it's something we know. We get enough law on our tails as it is this side of the border. We go to taking folks' money, they're going to get real upset with us."

Earles gave him a flat look. "More upset than us taking their scalps? Is that what you're saying?"

"All right, I see what you mean." Burton Stowl backed off. "I was just thinking out loud, I reckon."

"You wasn't thinking *at all,* Stowl," said Earles. He didn't like the idea that the men had all given a look to Haddon Marr when he'd told them his plan. "The fact is, this ain't something I was asking your approval on," he said, giving everybody a harsh stare. "What I said is, *I decided* that's what we're going to do. I'm the one running this bunch. Anybody doesn't like it, can get their knees in the wind right now and don't look back." His gloved hand pushed back the bright plaid duster, went to his pistol butt and rested there as he spoke. "Is that clear enough for everybody?"

The men stared, not about to say anything.

"All right then," said Earles. "Drag Uncle Andy up onto his saddle and let's get going."

Uncle Andy Fill said in weak, wheezing voice, "Maybe I better sit here awhile, see if I get to feeling some better."

Earles stared coldly at him. "Either get up and ride, or take a bullet and be done with it. I ain't leaving you behind alive to tell anybody our business."

"That's awful damn hard of you, Earles," Uncle Andy grumbled, "as long as we've been together . . . as much as we've been through." He wiped blood from his chin and struggled to his feet with the help of Cinco Diablos and Morton Toller, who stepped in and steadied him until he stood upright on his own. Then the two backed away and left him on unsteady legs.

"Bring me my damn horse, somebody!" Uncle Andy demanded.

Taos Charlie led the animal over to him quickly. Uncle Andy grabbed onto the saddle to keep from falling on his face. Cinco Diablos gave him a shove upwards and Andy tumbled into his saddle, cursing in his blood-filled voice. "You're the most awful sonsabitches I ever fell in with! Damn ever last one of yas!"

Earles grinned; the rest of the men laughed out loud. The bullet hole in the back of Uncle Andy's shirt billowed in and out, spraying a fine red mist with each word he spoke.

"Look at this fool!" said Taos Charlie, pointing at Uncle Andy's bloody back. "He's too damn mean to die!" He gave the horse a sound slap on the rump and sent it forward, Andy weaving side to side before steadying himself in the saddle.

"Taos," said Earles, "you get over there and drive the buckboard. We're going to haul those bodies into Wakely with us."

"They're getting awfully ripe," Taos Charlie warned.

"Keep the wagon moving forward." Earles grinned. "We'll stay in front of you till we get close to town." Seeing Andy Fill ride away, Earles nodded his head, saying, "Yep, Uncle Andy'll be all right till we get him to Wakely." He turned his horse and slapped his brown bowler hat on the animal's rump. "Let's ride!" he shouted over his shoulder.

# Chapter 3

Sheriff Tackett, the ranger and the prisoner had been riding abreast at a fast steady clip when they came upon the site of the slaughter. To make better time the ranger had taken the lead rope from Ted Riley's horse and let him ride on his own. Upon seeing the dead sprent randomly across the rocky soil, Riley murmured, "My God!" and let his horse canter quarterwise as it slowed to a halt. Kirby Romans wandered aimlessly among the bodies, his hat and duster gone, his shirt bloody front and back and hanging from him in shreds. He turned at the sound of the three horses approaching and stood in his sock feet, a pistol hanging from his hand. A mass of black, glistening blood matted his hair where his left ear had been sliced away. He struggled to raise the pistol toward the three riders, not recognizing them in the wavering heat and sun glare.

"Hold your fire, Romans!" Sheriff Tackett shouted. "It's me, Tackett . . . and the ranger and his prisoner."

"Sheriff Tackett . . . ?" Romans said, his voice sounding foggy and uncertain. "Where have you been? Can you believe this? They cut off my ear!"

"I see they did, Kirby," said Sheriff Tackett, stepping down, swinging his canteen from his saddle horn.

"But we're here to help you . . . now take it easy."
He hurried to the injured man, sat him down on the
dirt and lifted the pistol from his hand gently. He held
the canteen to the man's parched lips and poured a
trickle of tepid water into his mouth.

But in Romans' stunned condition he only took a
short sip, then began talking as water ran down his
chin. "I never seen anything like it," he said, his eyes
shiny and dilated. "They just come up out of the earth
like something from hell, they rode straight through
us, shot everybody down then swung back through for
the kill." He pointed with the canteen toward the bodies in the dirt. "Winslow dead, Otto Baugh dead,
Macy dead, Redding dead, Tindall, dead . . . all of
them dead."

"Take it easy, Romans," said Tackett. "Don't talk
right now, save your strength."

"I've been saving it," said Romans, flatly, his face
pale, bloodless and streaked with dust. Bluish blood
vessels stood out on his chalk-white forehead. "They
took my new duster, my hat. Look at me! I'm a ruined
mess. Thank goodness I'm not hurt though . . . nothing
worth mentioning anyway."

The ranger and Riley had been looking Romans
over as he spoke. They looked at each other curiously,
seeing no sign of bullet wounds on him. Suddenly, as
if stricken by a dark realization, the ranger stepped in
closer and tipped Kirby Romans forward by his shoulder, revealing what was left of the back of his head.
"Oh, Jesus!" Ted Riley gasped, seeing the exposed,
gaping wound in the upper section of Romans' skull.
Down Romans' back lay a thick coating of drying
blood and gore.

Sheriff Tackett winced and looked away for a second. "Oh, that . . . ?" said Romans, dreamily, raising

a hand toward the back of his head. "That's just a graze I got when they rode through. It ain't all that bad is it? I can't feel nothing up there."

The ranger reached in quickly and took his dusty hand, keeping him from probing the terrible wound. "Let us take care of it, Romans," he said in a calm voice. To Riley he said, "Go to my saddlebags, get my clean shirt and tear it into strips."

"Lord have mercy, Ranger," Sheriff Tackett whispered in private to Burrack as Ted Riley hurried over to the horses. "This poor man ain't going nowhere. He'll be dead before we've gone a mile." Kirby Romans gazed about as if in wonder at having awakened in some strange new place.

"But he's alive right *now*," the ranger whispered in reply, giving the sheriff a determined look. "That's all you and I have to go on." He realized that the sheriff was thinking about the unsuspecting townsfolk in Wakely, and what the scalp hunters would do once they arrived there. But the fact was they weren't close enough to reach these monsters in time to stop them anyway, Burrack thought. "We can't leave him here alone this way, can we?" he said. It was not a question that needed answering.

"No, of course not," said Sheriff Tackett, the two of them speaking low as they watched Kirby Romans gaze all around the barren land as if in a trance. "But dang it, I don't even know what to do for a man with his brain hanging out. I've never seen anything like this, have you?"

"No, I haven't," said the ranger, "but we've got to cover his head, keep dirt out of it, try to get him to a doctor. That's all I know to do." Ted Riley came back from the horses tearing a blue cotton shirt into bandage strips.

"Much obliged, Riley," Burrack said, taking the strips of cloth from him. "Now go among those bodies and see if you can find me a hat . . . the bigger the better."

Without a word Riley walked off quickly among the dead.

"Maybe if I rode on out of here I might be able to catch up to these rats before they hit Wakely," Tackett said, realizing as soon as he said it how hopeless it would be.

"What would that get you, Sheriff?" said the ranger. "All you would do is ride your horse to death and end up stuck on foot out here while the scalp hunters go ahead and hit your town anyway."

"Dang it!" said Sheriff Tackett. He slumped and took his hat off and wiped his sleeve across his forehead. "I know you're right, Ranger, but I feel like I've got to do something! These people elected me sheriff to keep the town safe. I'm failing them, that's all there is to it."

"When you haven't done the best you can do to protect them, that's when you've failed them," said the ranger as he carefully wrapped the strips of cloth around Kirby Romans' shattered skull. "I can't think of anything more you can do right now than what we're doing. Don't forget, my job is also to protect innocent folks, your town and every other town in the badlands outpost. This bothers me as much as it does you."

Sheriff Tackett let out a breath. "I know that, Ranger. It's just that this thing is eating me up. I've let my town down, I've let that poor woman down, not to mention that poor child." He sounded crushed and looked all around as he spoke. "I don't even know if that child is dead or alive."

"Keep thinking she's alive then," said the ranger. "If she ain't laying here and we didn't come upon her body along the trail, odds are she's still alive. These men wouldn't go ten feet out of their way to drag a body out of the road."

"Are you always this sure of yourself, Ranger?" Sheriff Tackett asked. There was no resentment in his words. He asked, hoping the answer would offer him some advice, a way to hold up under the crushing hopelessness he felt.

The ranger eyed him as he continued wrapping Romans' head and tucking the end of the cloth under to keep it in place. "You haven't let anybody down, Sheriff, not yet. Not unless you've given up and quit. All anybody can ask of you is the best you've got. As long as you're giving that to your badge, you're staying square with the world. You do want to stay square with the world, don't you, Sheriff?"

"Dang right I do," Tackett said, sounding a bit irritated at the question, which was exactly the response the ranger wanted to hear. It showed him this lawman still had some bark on him, that this terrible situation might have staggered him, but it hadn't knocked him to his knees.

"That's good to hear," said Burrack. He held Tackett's stern gaze for a moment, then he looked at Ted Riley, who came walking back slapping a tall, dusty Stetson against his leg.

"Will this do?" Riley asked, handing him the large hat.

"It should," the ranger replied. He took the hat and snugged it down gently but firmly over Kirby Romans' bandaged head. Romans raised a weak hand and felt all around on the hat as if in a trance. "You keep this hat on, Romans," said Burrack, pushing his hand away gently. He turned to Ted Riley and Sheriff Tackett, gesturing a hand around the bodies on the ground. "I figure they got the horse they needed here along with some extras if they need them."

"But why did they take the wagon?" asked Ted Riley. "Especially with all those bodies still on it. Why didn't they at least empty it?"

The ranger and Sheriff Tackett both looked at him, surprised that he had taken such an interest in the matter.

"They took the wagon with the bodies still on it because it will get them into Wakely before anybody there has time to figure what they're up to," said Tackett, coming out of his dark despair. "That's why they took Kirby's plaid duster too, I figure."

"They seem to like the element of surprise," the ranger said quietly, almost to himself. "We'll have to keep that in mind." He turned to Ted Riley, saying, "I want you to ride double with Romans."

Ted Riley nodded in agreement and reached down to help Romans to his feet. The ranger turned to Sheriff Tackett. "I've got a feeling that relay station along the trail will be gone when we get there. But there'll be water there. Let's push for it and see how Romans does."

Sheriff Tackett nodded and turned quietly toward the horses.

They mounted and followed the hoofprints off the trail, heading in the same direction parallel to the trail but across sharp rock and through cutting brush. They rode along at a careful pace to keep from laming their horses. "They say you can tell the man you're hunting by the road he rides," Tackett observed.

The ranger nodded.

"If that's the case, these men must've rode straight

up from hell," said Tackett, looking at the harsh route the riders had led them onto. Two hundred yards to their left the trail lay flat and inviting, in spite of its ruts and rockiness.

Riding beside the ranger, Ted Riley sat behind his saddle with his arms around Kirby Romans, supporting him. "If we knew they were headed for the relay station, why didn't we stick to the trail until we got there?"

"We could have stuck to the trail," said the ranger. "But if we don't cover the same ground and they drop the child somewhere along the way, we'd never know what became of her. The longer we keep an unbroken trail between us and them, the better the chances of us finding the little girl . . . whatever her condition." He gave Sheriff Tackett a quick glance.

"He means 'dead or alive,' " Tackett said bluntly to Riley.

"That's right," said Burrack, "dead or alive."

Sheriff Tackett heeled his horse up ahead of them a few yards and remained there until they topped a rise and saw the drift of smoke moving low and side-long on the horizon.

"There's our answer about the relay station," the ranger said, letting out a breath. "Let's see if anybody is lucky enough to still be alive." He looked at Riley and said, "Take it easy with Romans. We'll ride on ahead and meet you at the station." Taking his canteen from his saddle horn, Sam handed it over to Riley. "If we've gone on once you get there, follow the trail on into Wakely."

"Right, I will," said Ted Riley.

Burrack looked at Tackett, who sat staring in disbelief. "Let's go, Sheriff," he said.

"Wait a minute!" said Tackett. "I can't leave Kirby

Romans with a man who might toss him off on the
ground and cut out!"

The ranger gave him a flat, level gaze, saying, "You
had thoughts about leaving Romans where we found
him so we could get on to Wakely."

"If I did, I kept them to myself," said Tackett. "But
I can't trust this man the way you seem to, Ranger."

"Riley," said the ranger, turning to him, "do you
realize what would happen if you left this man to die
out here?"

"I expect instead of two years in prison, they would
just go ahead and hang me, Ranger Burrack," Riley
replied.

Turning back to Sheriff Tackett, the ranger said,
"This is a day of big decisions, Sheriff. If you don't
like mine, tell me yours. I'll go with it."

Tackett looked back and forth between the two,
then said, "Dang it, let's ride." He jerked his horse's
reins sharply and heeled the animal forward at a
faster pace.

"See you soon," the ranger said to Riley, giving a
resolved look.

"That you will, Ranger Burrack," Riley replied
firmly, returning the same look.

The ranger sent the big Appaloosa forward at a
quick trot, catching up to Sheriff Tackett at the beginning of a flat stretch where the land became less rocky
and less covered with brush. "You have to realize
something, Ranger," said Sheriff Tackett. "On top of
everything else I've got on my mind here, I ain't used
to working with another lawman."

"I understand that," said Sam. "If that was my
woman they killed or daughter these men took, I
would feel the same way you do. I have nothing but
respect for you, Sheriff."

"Same here, Ranger," said Tackett, the two of them traveling along at a faster pace. "It dawned on me after I rode away that you'd rather take a chance on that forger escaping and on a dying man getting left behind than break a tight trail between us and the little girl."

"That's pretty much the whole of it," said the ranger. "Even if we get Romans to Wakely and save his life, I ain't sure it's something he'd be thankful for. If he could decide right now with a clear mind but knowing the shape he's in, I figure he'd tell us to forget him and go for the child. You know better than I do, what do you think?"

"Yes, that would be his decision," said Tackett. "If it wasn't, he wouldn't be worth saving anyway."

"There you have it," said the ranger. "Ted Riley will have to work out his end of this thing. We've got a child to save."

"I salute your decision," said Tackett.

"It's the same one you would make if this wasn't all so personal to you," Burrack replied.

"Yes, I expect it is," said Tackett.

They rode on.

When they reached the charred remains of the relay station and saw the bodies of Al Doone and Mecila lying in the dirt, Tackett and the ranger stepped down and led their horses the last few feet until they stood over the woman's naked body. "This is the worst bunch I've ever come up against," Sheriff Tackett said in a lowered voice. The woman's head had been scalped almost entirely, leaving only a thin line of hair on the back of her neck and the same along the side of her head above her ear. From the looks of her, it was clear what else had gone on before she'd died.

The ranger reached up and jerked a blanket down

from behind his saddle. He shook it out and stooped down and laid it over the woman, stirring a rise of blowflies from atop her head. Staring closely at her head for a moment, he said before flipping the blanket over her face and lifting her in his arms, "There are *rurales* in Mexican villages who still pay for Apache scalps. I don't like it, but there's nothing we can do about it."

"Neither do I," said Tackett. "But all they needed was enough scalp to prove they made a kill. They didn't need to go this far. This just says they enjoyed what they were doing here." He spit on the ground toward the puddle of blood they could tell did not come from Al Doone or the woman. "Whoever this blood belongs to, I hope it's taking him all day to die."

Behind the burnt relay station a plank toolshed had been pillaged by the scalp hunters but left standing. The ranger carried the woman's body there and laid her inside on the dirt floor. "This is the best we can do you right now," he murmured as if the woman could hear him. They walked back and carried Al Doone to the shed and laid him beside the woman. The ranger closed the plank door and, with the side of his boot, raked a rock over against the bottom edge to keep it shut.

"I've looked all around," said Sheriff Tackett, "there's no sign of the child."

"I know," said Burrack. Then, seeing the troubled look on Tackett's face, he added, "Keep thinking of her as being alive, Sheriff. It's the only choice we've got for now." Looking off in the direction of Wakely, seeing the wagon tracks and hoofs sticking to the trail this time, he said, "Let's get on into Wakely and hope we don't find the same thing awaiting us."

\* \* \*

The two army deserters came out of the hill line,
following the smoke like wolves on the scent of prey.
One rode a bone-rack of a mule, the other trudged
along, wearing one worn-out cavalry boot and a broken dress shoe held together by bits of fence wire.
They both wore ragged scraps of what had once been
their uniforms. The one on the mule carried a poorly
serviced Army Colt shoved down in his waist behind
a dirty rope he wore for a belt. The big revolver carried only one gray, corroded cartridge in its cylinder.
The man on foot carried a long bayonet affixed to the
end of a hickory shovel handle, serving as both a
weapon and a walking stick. Approaching the burnt
hull of the relay station, the man on foot cautiously
raised the hickory handle as if it were a rifle.

"Watch your step, Roland," said the one on the
skinny mule. "Just because you don't see anybody
don't mean there's nobody here."

"Just keep your eyes peeled, Dubbs," said the man
on foot, "I don't want any surprises." He stopped at
the charred framework of the station and looked past
it at the plank toolshed.

"I don't plan to tarry here long enough that we get
blamed for this," said Dubbs, stepping down from the
weary mule. The animal plodded immediately to a
water trough beside a well and stuck its muzzle into
the tepid water.

"You better hope whoever did this killed the old
man and his squaw," said Roland, sidestepping around
the burnt hull and moving to the shed, the long handle
with its bayonet point extended out before him. "I
don't want to tangle with either one."

"Nor do I," said Dubbs quietly, stepping over beside him in front of the shed door. He gave a stained
grin through his long, scraggly beard. "But I'll admit

I've dreamed many nights of killing them in their sleep and taking what we wanted out of here."

Roland rolled away the rock with his foot and jerked the door open, stepping back quickly and pointing his bayonet stick out in front of him. Blow-flies buzzed heavily and careened out the open door. "Good Brother *Joseph!*" he gasped, slapping at the flies with one hand, still holding the extended bayonet.

"It's them, ain't it?" said Dubbs, craning his neck forward for a better look.

"It looks like somebody has made your dreams come true for you," said Roland, stepping inside, looking down at the bodies, then around for anything of value the couple's killers might have left behind.

Fanning the flies out with his floppy hat, Dubbs rifled through a few tin cans of food left standing on a shelf. Other cans lay on the dirt floor. Among other scattered items left lying in the dirt, Roland found a battered harmonica, blew through it, then pitched it aside. He rummaged quickly through some spilled dried beans, a wooden comb, and a half-used quarter shank of jerked elk meat, which he raised to his nose and sniffed before shoving it down inside his shirt. "Wouldn't it be something if we found ourselves some tobacco?"

"You bet it would," Roland agreed, "but what kind of fool would leave tobacco behind?" As he spoke he stuffed fallen tins of food inside his shirt, all the while looking around the floor of the small shed for an empty bag they could use to carry their newly acquired supplies in. Suddenly his eyes went to Al Doone's body and widened in delight at the sight of a bulge in the dead man's shirt pocket. "Hold it!" he said, almost squealing in glee. Both of them scooted through the dirt to the corpse. Roland plunged his hand into the shirt pocket and came out clutching a small cloth bag of tobacco.

"Open it! Open it!" Dubbs shrieked, resisting the urge to yank it from Roland's hand.

Roland loosed the drawstring on the bag and stared into it, poking his finger into the brown loose tobacco. "Oh, my god! Oh, my god!" he said, pulling up a pinch of chopped tobacco and letting it fall from his fingertips back into the bag. "We have struck the mother load!"

"Thank you, Jesus! Thank you, Jesus!" shouted Dubbs, half rising to his feet, and jumping about in a crouch. His pistol spilled from his waist and thudded onto the dirt floor. As he reached to pick it up, a boot descended out of nowhere and clamped down on the pistol butt.

"Huh?" Dubbs tried to look up, but just as he did, the man standing over him shoved him hard into Roland, sending both of them scrambling on the dirt floor amid the tins of food and scattered debris.

Roland's instincts made him snatch the long hickory handle from the dirt. But before he could raise the bayonet, the sound of the big Army Colt being cocked filled the shed. "Leave it where it lays," said the voice.

Roland and Dubbs both looked up at the gun pointed at them.

"Hell, mister," said Roland. "That gun ain't got but one bullet in it. And it would probably blow up in your hand if you pull that trigger!" He lowered the hickory handle back to the dirt floor, but he kept his hand wrapped around it.

"We'll see what one bullet will do to your friend here if you don't take your hand away from that pig sticker," said Ted Riley, his feet shoulder-width apart, the Colt extended, the tip of the barrel no more than six inches from Dubbs' nose.

"Mister, I'm telling you the truth," said Roland, stalling, still wanting to make a move with the bayonet. "If you pull that trig—"

"Damn it to hell, Roland!" shouted Dubbs, cutting him short, looking up the long barrel of the Colt. "This ain't the time to argue! Look at the spot I'm in!"

"Are you a lawman?" asked Roland, his hand still on the long handle. "Are you with the military?"

"No," said Ted Riley, eyeing the ragged remnants of their uniforms, "I'm no lawman. I'm not with the army." As he spoke he sidestepped around to a wall full of shelves and rummaged up and down them with his free hand, searching for anything he might use. "Now get your hand away from the bayonet or you'll be wearing this man's brains in your beard."

Roland and Dubbs both backed away a step, half raising their hands. "We already searched them shelves, mister," said Dubbs. "There ain't nothing of any value here. Careful you don't jerk up a rattlesnake."

"Oh, really?" Ted Riley's hand had reached behind a flattened feed sack and came out holding a Remington revolver.

"I'll be damned," said Roland, "as much as this shed has been rummaged, this fellow walks in here and comes up with a pistol?" The two deserters gave one another a sour look.

Riley flipped the revolver open, saw that it was fully loaded, then flipped it closed and shoved the big Army Colt down in his waist, turning the Remington on the two men. "You were too busy searching a dead man for tobacco," he said.

"By rights, that's our pistol you found," said Roland. "We would have found it sooner or later had you not horned in on us."

"You might be right," said Riley. "But who has time to look at things that way?"

"I expect you'll be turning us in for the government reward?" Roland asked, trying to think of what they might do to distract this man and make a lunge for the revolver.

"What reward?" asked Riley, giving a shrug. "Do you mean the one hundred dollars a piece for turning in deserters? No, I'm not interested in it."

"Well, excuse us for not being notorious desperados!" said Dubbs.

"Quiet, Dubbs," said Roland. Then he said to Riley, "If you're neither a lawman nor a provost officer, why are you bothering with us?" He gestured a stiff nod toward the two bodies on the dirt floor. "We had nothing to do with any of this, so help us God we never."

"I know you didn't," said Riley. He waved the Remington revolver toward the open doorway, past the buzzing flies and the terrible smell of death. "Come on, we can talk outside."

"Talk?" said Roland. He and Dubbs gave each other a baffled look. "Talk about what?"

# Chapter 4

When Ted Riley had told the two deserters about his situation, the two deserters looked at one another curiously. "Well, hell!" said Roland. "You ain't but just a little bit different from me and Dubbs here. Only thing is we run off from the army instead of getting our scalps lifted by the Mescalero back when they were on their high horse."

"Yeah," said Dubbs. "Looks like all you'll have to do is give that idiot a shove and head for the hills." He grinned, giving Kirby Romans an appraising look. Romans sat slumped in the saddle while the horse watered itself at the trough. Blood and fluid spread beneath Romans' snug hat brim through the bandages. A string of saliva bobbed from his parted lips. "He ain't looking none too spry anyhow," Dubbs chuckled.

"We'll even take you in with us if you want us to. Won't we, Dubbs?" Roland cut in.

"It makes me no difference," said Dubbs. "One thing for sure, where we live, you'd never have to worry about any law dogs sniffing around for you. Only times we have to watch our step is when we come down here to see how the pickins are." He spread a hand, taking in the relay station. "Of course now I reckon this place will go back to the ground it sprung out of."

"And once your footprints soak into the sand," said Roland, "it'll be like you was never even here."

"I gave my word I'd take this man on to Wakely," said Ted Riley, still keeping a safe distance between himself and the two deserters. "That's what I intend to do."

"Oh, your *word*!" said Roland, giving a short laugh. He and Dubbs looked at one another, then both began laughing. *"Now* I understand! You gave your *word*!" The two laughed harder.

"Stop laughing!" Riley demanded, leveling the Colt at them.

Roland and Dubbs looked puzzled, but their laughter stopped abruptly. "Take it easy, fellow," said Roland, "we thought you was making a joke . . . about giving your word to a lawman."

"I don't joke about serious matters," said Riley.

"We see that you don't," said Dubbs, placating him. "But you have to admit, it sounds a little crazy, to hear a man say he's going to risk his life, take a chance running into them scalp hunters, just to deliver a dying man with no mind left to a lawman who's gonna take him on to prison as soon as he gets there."

"The whole thing makes you sound a little touched in the head yourself," said Roland, eyeing Ted Riley closely, as if trying to figure him out.

"It's a matter of personal honor," said Riley.

"Some honor," said Dubbs, shaking his head.

"You said *two years* is what you've got to pull in prison?" Roland asked.

"That's right, two years," Riley replied. He let the pistol droop a little as he spoke and gave himself a chance to ponder his situation.

"That's going to be the longest two years in your life," said Dubbs.

"You must've been tempted to make a run for it," said Roland. "Why else would you even be telling the likes of us about it?" He gestured a dirty hand up and down their ragged uniforms, their worn-out boots.

Riley stood silent for a moment as if thinking about it. "You're right, I expect I did feel tempted there for a moment, riding in."

"Aw! See?" Roland tapped a finger to his forehead. "You were tempted—so you're no better than we are, are you? If you was thinking about it you just as well go on and do it, eh? Your honor blew away on the wind the first minute you felt yourself tempted."

Riley seemed to think about it for a second, then he said firmly, "No! My honor just became stronger. How valuable is a man's honor or integrity if it's never put to the test?"

As if they had no idea what his words meant, Dubbs said, "My freedom is worth more than my honor any day."

Riley's horse raised its wet muzzle, both horse and mule having drank their fill. Backing away toward his horse, Riley said to Dubbs, "You gave up both your honor and your freedom a long time ago."

"Aw yeah?" said Dubbs. "What makes you so damn smart on the matter?"

"How long have you been hiding out up in the hills?" asked Riley. As he asked, he lifted the Army Colt from his waist, opened the cylinder with his free hand and dropped the single bullet to the dirt.

The two deserters looked at each other for an answer. Finally Dubbs said, "We've been here *quite a while*, that's how long."

"There's been no Apache around here for almost three years," said Riley. "They've stayed over in Mexico." He stepped up into the saddle and reached his arms around Kirby Romans, the Remington still in his hand.

"Three years? Damn, it don't seem that long," said Dubbs. He scratched his head wearily.

"You would have been out of here long ago," said Riley, "getting on with your lives somewhere."

"Still," said Roland, "we might have gotten ourselves kilt. Then how much better off would we have been?"

"You'll have to answer that for yourself," said Riley. "Death is the only risk in life." Giving a look at the two, then off toward the bleak, lonely hills, he said, "I'll drop this Army Colt alongside the trail a hundred yards from here. I wouldn't want to leave you unarmed out here."

The two didn't answer. Instead, Roland stepped forward and asked, "What does that mean? Death is the *only* risk in life? There's all kind of risks in life! That makes no sense!" He'd become angry all of a sudden. "Who the hell do you think you are, mister? We would have found that Remington ourselves before we finished here! We know who the hell we are, mister! At least we ain't in no prison but our own!"

"I'm not your judge," said Riley, backing the horse, keeping an eye on the two as he turned toward the trail.

"The hell you ain't!" shouted Roland. "You've been judging us ever since you rode in here. You and your *honor*! Well, how do we measure up?" He spread his arms. "Does this suit you, you son of a bitch!"

Ted Riley heeled the horse forward in a soft lope along the trail toward Wakely. When they had gone less than a mile he said into Kirby Romans' ear, "We happened into those two at about the right time.

Seeing them answered any doubts I might have been having."

Romans stared blankly down at the saddle horn, more dead than alive, yet Ted Riley answered aloud for him, saying to himself, "Teddy, boy, I raised you to do the right thing. I never doubted you for a minute."

"It's hard though," Riley said into Kirby Romans' ear. "I think of the next two years sweating it out in that stone quarry I've heard so much about . . . sleeping nights in a steel cage. It would be easy to turn tail and disappear. I could slip across the border, take a ship anywhere in the world and just lose myself. Nobody would ever know. Years from now I could come back a new man, with a new name, a new life." As he spoke he felt himself overcome with a deep yearning. For a moment his eyes welled. But he shook it off and rode on toward Wakely.

Nearly a mile farther down the road he said aloud, "Why can't I do it? Why can't I just do like any *other* man would and start anew?" He slowed the horse down almost to a stop, looking southwest in the direction of the border. "Why is it so important that I always do the right thing, no matter what the cost?" He sat in silence for a moment, hearing only the whir of hot wind. Then he sighed deeply, heeled the horse forward and rode on, staring almost in resentment for a moment at the battered hat and the spreading blood in front of him. "Well?" he asked, appearing to expect an answer. But no answer came to him.

The scalp hunters had cut the telegraph lines four miles back along the trail. Now they stopped again and took cover in a low dip in the land long enough to rest their horses, getting the animals prepared for a hard, fast run. In the distance, across a stretch of brush and flat rocky ground, the roofline of Wakely stood amid wavering heat. Jessup Earles stared at the town for a moment, then drew his horse back and joined the others. "Everybody make yourselves presentable," he said, smoothing down the front of the bright plaid riding duster. He ran a hand around the front brim of the brown bowler hat and added, "Bring that stinking mess of bodies up here beside me until we make sure the town gets a good look at what we're doing."

"Why don't we get shed of these stinking wretches and load the wagon with rocks?" asked Morton Toller. "All we want is for them to see how heavily the wagon is loaded anyway."

"Because it just looks different," said Earles.

"You're saying a wagonload of bodies rides different than a load of rocks?" Toller asked in a skeptical tone of voice.

Earles nodded at a dead arm hanging over the side of the wagon. "Rocks don't do that," he said. "Besides, what if somebody went to the trouble of raising a telescope on us and sees a load of rocks coming toward town. Wouldn't that give them an idea they might be about to have the hell shot out of them?"

"If they raised a telescope they'd see it wasn't the right man wearing that coat and hat any damn way," Toller persisted. "So I don't know that these bodies would make much difference."

"You want to throw off these bodies?" said Jessup Earles, getting a wild-eyed look to him. "Is that it? You want to throw them off and gather some rocks? Then let's stop everything right here, *right now* and you go do it!" His hand pulled back the plaid duster and poised near his pistol butt.

Still Toller pushed. "Alls I'm saying is, we don't have to smell these stinking sumbitches all the time!"

"Let go of it, Toller!" Haddon Marr snapped at him, seeing the argument could only end one way, with one of the two men killing the other. "We've brought that wagonload of bodies this far, let's go do what we come here to do!"

"Hell, yes then!" Toller shouted, "Let's get it done!" He spun his horse and reined it over beside Taos Charlie.

Charlie gave him a fierce look and said under his breath, "What the hell's wrong with you? You know better than to argue with Earles, drunk or sober."

"Yeah, don't I know it," said Toller. Then looking at the empty holster on Taos Charlie's right hip he said with a teasing grin, "Where's your big Remington, *amigo*? You might need it if we're gonna be shooting people."

"What the hell?" Taos Charlie slapped his empty holster, realizing for the first time that his big revolver was missing. He shot a wild glance around at the others. "If this is somebody's big idea of a joke, it ain't funny. I ain't laughing!" His eyes went back to Toller, fixed and angry.

"Whoa!" said Toller. "I just saw it missing and told you about it. Don't go accusing me of anything!"

"Oh, no!" said Taos Charlie, his expression suddenly changing from anger to regret. "I remember now. I laid my gun on a shelf back at that relay station. In all the commotion with the squaw, I plumb forgot all about it. Damn it, my best gun!"

"Left your best gun behind?" Jessup Earles said in disbelief, overhearing the conversation and reining his horse over closer to Charlie. "Tell me you ain't *fool* enough to let some squaw cause you to forget your damn gun!"

"I'll go back and get it when we finish here!" said Taos Charlie. "It could have happened to anybody!" He looked humiliated.

"I can't tell you how important it is that we don't lose our guns!" said Earles, in a taunting, rage-filled voice. "It just slows up everything we got to do!"

"Damn it! I've still got plenty of guns!" said Taos Charlie, cutting him off. He reached down and jerked the Colt Thunderer from his left holster. "And I've got a Sheets rifle too. Nobody has to slow down on my account!" He lowered his eyes to the pistol in his hand, checking it until Jessup Earles pulled his cold stare away from him and looked at the other riders.

"There's nothing new about how we're going to do here, men. We hit hard and fast, don't stop until the town is bellied up. We're not taking any scalps this time though." A wide grin of satisfaction came to his face. "This time it's all about taking *money*! No trophies, just cash!"

Holding the girl in his lap, her face hidden against his chest, Haddon Marr added, "So don't none of you forget yourself and lop off some fool's ears, or fingers, or topknot."

"What if we just can't help ourselves?" asked Toller.

The others laughed aloud.

"If you can't, you *can't,* I reckon," laughed Earles, tightening the bowler hat down onto his head. "But while you're counting bloody fingers and ears, the rest of us'll be rolling in piles of money." His laughter stopped abruptly; his grin fell away, replaced by a mask of harsh determination. "Let's ride, by God!" he shouted, booting his horse forward.

Handling the wagon, Cinco Diablos slapped the reins to the horses' backs and sent them forward up onto the flat land behind Earles. Beside Cinco on the rough wooden seat sat Uncle Andy Fill, his arms wrapped across his abdomen in pain, his horse tied to the rear of the wagon, running along in the stink of the dead.

Haddon Marr waited for a second, letting the others get ahead of him. Then he said to the frightened child, "You sit still and don't worry. I ain't letting nothing happen to you. You belong to me now."

The child offered no answer or response, but Marr felt her quake in fear against him. He grinned and stroked the back of her hastily shorn head. "Silly little thing, ain't you," he whispered. He booted his horse forward, riding hard and fast until he overtook the other riders and the wagon and had to slow his horse to keep from riding past Earles.

From the main street running the length of Wakely, only a few people took notice of the coming riders until they drew close enough for Jacob Evans the blacksmith to recognize the plaid riding duster and bowler hat at the head of the billowing cloud of dust. "Looks like our sheriff's posse is returning from Clifton Wells."

Otis Townsend, Wakely's telegraph clerk, craned his neck and stared out through his thick wire-rimmed spectacles. "Kirby's sort of hard to miss with that loud plaid duster on." The onlookers stared for a moment until they got a clearer view of the heavily loaded wagon. Noticing the naked arm hanging stiffly over the wagon's side rail, Otis said, "Uh-oh. Looks like the news from Clifton Wells isn't good. And here we are with our telegraph lines down."

"Our *lines* are down?" the blacksmith asked warily.

"They sure are," said the clerk. "I just tried sending a message through and couldn't do it. I was getting ready to ride out and look for the break."

The blacksmith considered things for a moment, but then seemed to dismiss his thoughts. Seeing how low the approaching wagon rode on its springs, he said to anyone listening, "We better get the doctor out here in case he's needed."

"Yes, indeed," said the telegraph clerk. "I'll go have Reverend Danforth ring the church bell. This looks like something the whole town will want to know about." He hurried toward a new brick church a block away.

"Wait!" the blacksmith said. But it was too late. Otis had already bounded off through the gathering crowd.

"Wait for what, Mister Evans?" asked Dick Tyson, the blacksmith's young helper, who stood beside him.

"Something ain't right, Dick," the blacksmith replied secretively.

"Oh? What's that?" asked Tyson, staring off at the approaching riders.

"Sheriff Tackett would never allow an arm to dangle over the side that way. Doesn't that strike you as being disrespectful to the deceased?"

"Well, yes, now that you mention it." Tyson scratched his head. "Do you suppose he just hasn't noticed it? Maybe it just happened?"

"I don't know," said Evans, studying the riders as they drew closer. "It just doesn't strike me the right way. Plus, our telegraph lines are down?" he said questioningly. He looked all around at the street filling up with people. "I don't want to be called foolish, always thinking the worst, but let's you and me go quietly to my shop and get ourselves armed."

"Armed?" Dick Tyson looked startled.

"It's probably nothing, Dick," said the blacksmith. "But let's be safe instead of sorry." They turned and moved through the gathering crowd toward the blacksmith shop.

At a distance of two hundred yards, Jessup Earles and the riders watched the wide street fill with people. Church bells resounded. He called back over his shoulder to Haddon Marr a few feet behind him, saying in a loud voice above the rumble of hooves, "I love this! They're swarming together like bees! We'll just dip in there and take *all their honey*!"

Haddon Marr only grinned and nodded, not hearing Earles' words but getting a good idea, seeing the number of people in the street grow as they drew closer. At fifty yards, he saw expressions on the townsfolk change, looking wary as they backed away slowly, uncertain now of what they were watching descend upon them. Seeing Earles lift his pistol from its holster, Haddon shouted back to the rest of the men, "Commence shooting!"

A woman screamed as the riders' shots began exploding. But her scream was quickly lost in a rich, curious mixture of gunfire and church bell. A man in the crowd managed to jerk a small pistol from inside his coat, but before he could return fire, he fell backwards with a spray of blood appearing above his head. "My God! They're *killing* us!" a man shrieked, his arms coming up instinctively, catching a woman when a bullet struck her dead center and flung her against him. He fell to the ground with her as the scalp hunters' horses trampled through the stunned crowd. Cinco Diablos veered the wagon horses a hard left, then a hard right, trying to avoid the great tangle of horses and humans in the middle of the dusty street. The wagon tipped high onto two wheels and slung three stiff, naked corpses from its bed into the scrambling crowd. It came down only to rise on its other two wheels and repeat the performance. Cinco grabbed Uncle Andy Fill and kept him from flying off with the dead.

"*Yeeeiiii hiiiiii!* Let 'er rip!" Jessup Earles shouted, shooting randomly now at the fleeing townsfolk, enjoying the melee. The church bell fell silent, as if in submission to the relentless gunfire. In seconds the scalp hunters' horses high-stepped among the dead and dying. Running out of targets, the riders held their fire. "Damn bunch of cowards!" Earles called out to the sound of slamming doors and frightened running footsteps. "Don't come back till we're finished here, else we'll kill every damn one of you!"

A half a block away, Cinco Diablos circled the wagon in the middle of the street and came driving it back. Morton Toller jumped down from his saddle and, holding his horses' reins, quickly bent down and sliced the scalp off one of the newly fallen. Raising it in his hand toward Jessup Earles, he hooted aloud, "See? I knew I couldn't keep myself from lifting one! It's in my blood!"

"*Loco bastardo!*" Cinco Diablos said under his breath, drawing the wagon to a halt. He spit and gave Toller a dirty look.

"All right, everybody!" said Haddon Marr. "Let's start over at that bank building and work our way from store to store! Leave no money behind!" The child cringed on Marr's lap, hiding her face.

"Now that's the spirit, Haddon," Earles said with a grin. Standing in his stirrups he called out to the hidden townsfolk: "All of you listen to me! You're being robbed, in case you don't have sense enough to already know it! Stay where you are, keep your heads down and you won't get killed. Stick your heads out and we'll chop them off. That's as clear as I can make it." He turned to Haddon Marr and said quietly, "We should have started doing this a *long* time ago. It's almost too damned easy."

"We ain't done it yet," said Marr in a cautioning tone. He stepped his horse over toward the bank, adjusting the child on his lap, his big Colt up and cocked as he looked back and forth along the body-littered street.

"But we're doing it now!" Earles called, sounding a bit put out. "You've been acting peculiar ever since you started packing that hairless whelp around with you. Am I going to have to take her away from you?" He made sure to offer a stiff nervous grin.

"Don't worry about me, Earles," said Marr with a trace of warning in his voice. "I'm up for whatever comes my way." He stopped and turned his horse facing Jessup Earles, his pistol loosely pointed in his direction. "You might want to think long and hard before you go trying to take *anything* from me." He nodded toward the bank building. "You coming or not?"

# Chapter 5

In the blacksmith shop, Jacob Evans and Dick Tyson had hurriedly loaded their guns while the shooting raged in the street. By the time they were prepared for battle the street fell silent, except for the cries from the wounded and dying. The two looked at one another for a second. Then the blacksmith said, "I'm still going out there. They're not getting away with this!" He snapped a shotgun shut and headed for the door. Dick Tyson quickly spun the cylinder on a big Russian revolver and hurried along with him.

"But, Mister Evans!" he said. "If we rush out there like this, won't they just shoot us down?"

The blacksmith stopped before opening the door. "In all likelihood, yes. But that's what fate has offered us this day, Dick. We have no choice but to accept it."

"I'm not so sure," said Dick, scratching his head. "I mean if the fighting is about done, wouldn't we do just as much good staying here, making sure they don't hurt anybody else?"

"And let them ride on after what they've done here?" said Evans, not agreeing, yet seeing some merit in what the young man said. He waited for an answer with his hand on the door latch.

"It's too late to stop what they've done," said the

young helper, "but we can get up on the roofs, keep out of sight. Make sure they don't try hurting nobody else. Don't you think?"

"Lad, I believe you're right," said Jacob Evans. Turning from the front door he hurried toward a smaller door at the rear of the shop, saying, "Follow me! We'll get atop the saloon!"

The pair slipped soundlessly from the blacksmith shop, along a rutted alley, until they huddled against the back wall of the Mergan's Paradise Saloon. Evans looked up the clapboard siding, then at a rain barrel sitting beneath a tall wooden downspout. "All right, up we go," he whispered.

Out in the street, Taos Charlie carried a large leather valise out of the bank and did a little jig on the boardwalk, laughing aloud as he held the valise up and shook it back and forth for the hiding towns-folk to see. *"Whooooie! Folks, the Lord truly loves a generous giver!"* he called out along the street.

Standing watch on the boardwalk, one hand down holding the girl pressed to his side, Haddon Marr hissed, "Damn it, Charlie! Don't taunt these people. Take the money and go! We've still got lots to do here!"

"Oh!" Taos Charlie laughed, "I see! We don't want to make these folks angry at us? Is that it?"

Marr gave him a cold stare. Charlie stopped laughing and walked away shaking his head toward the sound of glass breaking inside the mercantile store, where Cinco Diablos and Jessup Earles had gone to clean out the cash box and take whatever supplies and ammunition they needed. Inside the store a clerk had ducked down and taken refuge behind a table filled with bolts of fabric. He'd waited until the two scalp hunters busied themselves at the gun case. Now he arose and darted toward the door only to run head-long into Taos Charlie.

"Well now, what have we here," said Charlie, "a troublemaker I bet?" Catching the young clerk, hold-ing him out at arm's length, the scalp hunter dropped the leather valise and pointed a cocked gun at his nose. Earles and Cinco Diablos turned from pillaging the ammunition case and stared.

"Please, mister!" cried the frightened clerk. "I just wanted to get out of here! I'm not a troublemaker, I swear!"

"I believe you are a troublemaker!" said Taos Char-lie, tormenting the terrified young man. He kicked the valise, causing it to slide across the plank floor toward Earles and Cinco. "What do you think, Earles? Should I lift his scalp while he's still alive and kicking, or poke a bullet through his eye first?" He pulled the clerk in close and jammed the gun barrel against his eye.

"Suit yourself," said Earles, eyeing the bulging va-lise, "but me and Cinco both are going to get real testy if you pull that trigger and spray his brains all over us."

"Don't kill me, please!" the clerk pleaded, his voice breaking down tearfully.

"Hey, now, buck up!" said Taos Charlie, shaking him roughly. "I hate a damn whiner worse than anything!"

Earles and Cinco walked over to the leather valise stuffing wax-coated boxes of ammunition into their pockets. Earles picked up the valise, opened it and ran a hand down into the loose bills and coins. "Shove him outside if you're going to shoot him," he said. Hefting the bag he added, "Damn this looks like a lot of money!"

Grinning, Charlie said, "It is a lot of money." Then turning back to the frightened clerk, he asked, "What's your name, boy?"

"Jimmy Philson," the clerk replied in a voice weak with fear.

"Well, Jimmy," said Taos, "are you sure you want to live?"

"Ye—Yes sir," the clerk stammered, "I do want to live."

"All right, let me think about it a little," Taos taunted him. "Is there a doctor in this dung hole of a town?"

"Yes, sir," said Jimmy Philson, "there is, Doctor Rasmussen! He's been here the past two years!"

"I see . . ." Nodding, Taos lowered his gun and said, "Think you can go find him and get him over here real quick like?"

"Yes, sir," said the clerk.

"Then get going," Taos Charlie demanded, "before I change my mind and shoot holes in your head!" He gave the young man a hard shove and watched him scramble through the open door and down off the boardwalk. Stepping out behind the clerk, Taos called out, "Hurry up, damn it! I'm watching you!" He raised his pistol and fired a shot in the air, laughing, watching the clerk run across the rutted dirt street.

"Damn, this is a powerful lot of money!" Earles said, raising a handful of money and letting it fall back into the valise. "You made sure this was all of it?"

"I didn't see any more," said Taos Charlie. "I made the bank teller open the safe and this was everything in it."

"All right." Earles grinned, snapping the valise shut. "Toller and Stowl went to the livery barn to look for horses, then to the saloon to bring us something to

drink. If that doctor shows up, get him to patch Uncle
Andy up and let's get out of here. I've got a hankering
to do some more of this kind of work!"

"You mean instead of riding on to Mexico?" Taos
Charlie asked.

"Hell, yes instead of going to Mexico!" said Earles.
"We've saddled this big horse, I say we ride it till we
wear it *too thin.*"

Cinco and Taos nodded and grinned at one another.
"Suits the hell out of me," said Taos.

"*Si,* me too!" said Cinco.

The three walked out onto the boardwalk and stood
abreast, looking back and forth along the blood-
stained street. A wounded man had struggled up onto
his knees and rocked back and forth, moaning loudly.
"Why didn't you shoot that loud-mouthed sonsabitch,
Haddon?" Earles asked, raising his pistol and cocking
it as he spoke.

"He's not going anywhere," Haddon Marr said, un-
concerned, his gloved hand cupping the back of the
young girl's sheared head. She stood with her face
hidden against his side.

Earles looked Marr and the girl up and down curiously. Then he fired a quick shot and the wounded
man in the street fell backwards dead in the dirt.
"There," said Earles, holstering his gun. "That wasn't
so hard, was it?"

Haddon Marr stared at him in silence for a moment,
then, stroking the back of the trembling child's head,
he asked, nodding at the mercantile store, "Did you
see any rock candy in there?"

"No," said Earles, looking away, shaking his head,
"but I can't say I was really looking for any."

Without another word Marr turned and walked inside, the girl pressed against his side. Earles saw Cinco and Taos Charlie looking at him and he shrugged it off. Across the street he saw the young clerk returning with a squat, elderly man hurrying alongside him. In the street, Uncle Andy sat rocking back and forth in the wooden wagon seat. Behind him flies swarmed above the stiff, swollen corpses. As the doctor and the clerk approached the wagon, the doctor slowed down, staring in disbelief at the wagonload of death and the bodies of townsfolk lying in the street.

Earles called out along the street, "All right, people! We're about done here. You can come out, so long as you behave yourselves."

The doctor climbed up into the wagon seat beside Uncle Andy and began examining his wound carefully. Jimmy Philson stood in the street, afraid to leave and afraid to stay.

Seeing no one come forward out of hiding at his urging, Earles called out louder, saying, "Damn it to hell! I mean get your scared-to-death asses out here *right now*! Before I burn this town to a cinder! Does anybody hear me?"

Slowly townsfolk appeared from doorways and alleyways. They came forward fearfully, as if with the slightest encouragement they were ready to bolt away in every direction. As they gathered in front of the boardwalk where Jessup Earles stood, the doctor straightened up from examining Uncle Andy Fill. He looked at the bodies in the wagon, then said to Earles, "Who are you people? Where is Kirby Romans, and our sheriff?"

Earles stared at the doctor. "Who the hell is Kirby Romans?"

The short, stocky doctor put his fists on his waist in

defiance and replied, "Kirby Romans is the gentleman whose hat and coat you're wearing, sir! Now where is he?"

"Oh, *that* poor fellow?" Earles grinned. "He's laying out there in the dirt where I left him! Any other questions?"

"Yes," said the doctor. "What about our sheriff? What about the rest of the posse who rode out to Clifton Wells?"

"They're dead," Earles shrugged. "We killed them all. Now get that man's wound dressed or we'll kill you too!"

The doctor seethed for a moment, but then returned to attending Uncle Andy's bloody chest.

Standing with his hands raised chest high, the town's newspaper owner, Cornelius Beakly, asked Earles in a shaky voice, "You mean Sheriff Tackett is dead? You killed our sheriff?"

Earles gave him a cold look. "We didn't exactly ask their names first. We just sort of shot them down and left them laying, if you can picture that."

From across the street Morton Toller and Crosseyed Burton Stowl walked out of the saloon carrying bottles of whiskey stuck up under their arms and cigars sticking out from their shirt pockets. Toller's middle bulged with the cash he'd taken from the bartender and stuffed inside his shirt. "It's about damn time," said Earles, watching them step down from the boardwalk and walk toward him. "Did you find any good horses?"

Toller shook his head. "None worth feeding," he said. "It looks like the ones we took off the posse was the best this town had to offer."

"All right then, to hell with it," Earles grumbled, "we got what we came here for." He turned and walked inside the mercantile door. "Haddon," he called out, "let's get out of here. There's another town forty miles on. We'll hit it the same way."

"We'll be along in a minute," said Marr.

"Damned if this don't beat all," Earles whispered under his breath. In the far corner of the store he saw Haddon Marr stooped down in front of the girl, tying the sash of a new yellow and white checkered sun bonnet beneath her chin. Earles said aloud, sounding impatient, "Come on, Had, we ain't got time for all this."

"I'm going to wash her face," said Marr, without looking toward him.

"Stick its head in the water trough out front if you want to," said Earles. "But let's get going!"

Marr straightened up slowly and faced him with a flat stare. "I said we'll be right along."

"So you did," said Earles, turning and stomping out the door. On the boardwalk he called out to the doctor, "Are you getting on with that wound?"

In the wagon, the doctor stood up with a roll of surgical gauze in his bloody hands and called out, "Yes, I about have it bandaged. But this isn't enough. He needs nursing. Medicine for infection . . . and he needs bed rest. He's going to die if he keeps riding!"

"Hear that, Uncle Andy?" Earles called out to Andy Fill who sat slumped with his shirt off and his belly wrapped in bloody gauze. He held a shiny whiskey flask he'd taken from the doctor's black bag in his left hand. His right hand held his pistol resting in his lap.

"Yeah, I heard him," Uncle Andy said flatly, his voice sounded thick and wet with his own blood.

"He says you're going to *die*, Uncle Andy," Earles said with a nasty grin. "What do you think?"

"Ha! I bet I outlive this red-handed poltroon," said Uncle Andy, taking all of his strength to lift his pistol toward the doctor. The doctor tried to duck, but the blast of fire lifted him from the wagon and flung him dead in the street. Andy raised the shiny flask in his left hand and sipped from it, coughing painfully as he swallowed. "See what I mean?" he growled.

The townsfolk stood stunned at the sight of Doctor Rasmussen lying dead with blood pooling beneath him in the dirt.

On the roof of the saloon, Jacob Evans and Dick Tyson had watched the senseless killing, first of the wounded townsman, now of the town's elderly doctor. "That's enough!" shouted the blacksmith. "I can't take any more!" He stood up and aimed the shotgun down over the top edge of the saloon's facade and triggered a blast of buckshot at Uncle Andy Fill.

"Up there, get 'em!" shouted Jessup Earles, raising his gun and firing toward the saloon roofline as Uncle Andy Fill flew sideways off the wagon seat and landed atop the dead doctor.

Townsfolk scattered, taking cover anywhere they could find. Another shotgun blast took a bite out of a post near Jessup Earles' head. He jumped off the boardwalk, grabbed a woman who had fallen in her haste to get away and held her up in front of him as a shield. "Fire away, you *shotgunning* sonsabitches!" he bellowed at the roofline, firing his pistol rapidly.

In the dirt Uncle Andy squirmed away from the doctor and crawled under the wagon full of bodies. Toller, Cinco and Burton Stowls dived behind a stack of freight crates out front of the mercantile. They fired heavily at the saloon roof, but Dick Tyson kept the big pistol firing while Jacob Evans reloaded the shotgun, then fired toward the freight crates, avoiding hitting the screaming woman in Earles' arms. Earles hooted and cursed as he reloaded his pistol, the woman struggling and kicking but to no avail.

Inside the mercantile store, Haddon Marr had jerked the girl back by a length of thin rope he'd tied around her neck, as if she were a dog on a leash. But at least the rope had kept her from walking out into the shotgun's blast when the fighting started. She stood frozen in place, her eyes wide and blank. Haddon snatched her up under his arm and backed farther away from the open door. "Don't you worry, I ain't letting nobody hurt you," he said.

With her under his arm he ran to the rear of the mercantile, out the back door and up a set of steep wooden stairs leading to the roof. Atop the stairs he stepped over onto the roof as gunfire raged on the street below and from the roof of the saloon straight across the street. He hastily tied the end of the girl's lead rope to the rough wooden handrail and jerked the knot too tight for her to possibly loosen. "Don't you try getting away from me," he said, stooping down and staring deep into her frightened eyes. He shook her slightly by her shoulders. "You're *my* little girl now. Mine and nobody else's! You better do like I tell you, or I'll give you over to Taos Charlie and he'll eat you up like a wolf! Do you hear me? Do you want that?"

She tried to speak but couldn't make her words come out. Instead she gasped and nodded her head vigorously, wild-eyed with terror.

"Good," said Marr, tipping her chin up gently, causing her to settle down a bit. His voice turned gentle, soothing. "I'm going to go kill these fools so's they can't hurt you. Then we'll take you away from all this." He leaned forward and kissed her softly on her moist forehead, the kiss of a father.

She stood trembling, watching him move across the flat tin roof in a crouch, his pistol in his hand, until he reached the facade and peeped over the edge toward the two men on the roof of the saloon. She raised her hands to the rope looped around her neck and felt the hard tight knots. She watched Marr to make sure he wasn't looking her way, then she examined the knots in the rope where he'd tied the end to the handrail. She couldn't loosen the knots. Even if she could have, she kept seeing his face up close to hers, telling her what he would do if she tried to run away—*You're my little girl now. You belong to me and nobody else.* . . .

She swallowed hard, her mouth having turned dry with fear. She watched Marr fire his pistol at the roof straight across from them. Then she heard a man scream in pain. She cringed and raised her hands to cover her eyes. She wasn't going to try to get away. She didn't want to die! Marr had turned and came walking back toward her now. She couldn't see him but could hear his footsteps come across the tin roof. When she opened her eyes he was only a few feet from her. The shooting had stopped on the street, and Marr walked upright now, as if there was nothing more to worry about.

"There," he said, offering her a smile. "You don't have to be scared now. I killed them for you."

For her? she thought. But she couldn't speak. She only nodded and watched him untie the rope from the handrail. First he looked closely at the knot, as if he could tell whether she had tried to loosen the rope.

After a second he turned his smile back to her and said, "Good girl. You done just like I told you."

She breathed a sigh of relief and followed along behind him when he'd loosened the rope and led her down the long stairs to the alley behind the mercantile. As they walked around to the street, Earles and the others were mounting up and getting ready to ride out. "Hurry up!" said Earles. "These folks are starting to get restless on us. They'll soon be hard to handle!"

Haddon Marr gathered the girl's lead rope and tucked the child up under his arm. Heading to his horse, he said to Jessup Earles, "I'm sure I hit one of them on the saloon roof. Don't know if I killed him or not."

"It makes no difference right now!" said Earles. "Whoever is over there has stopped shooting, but somebody else will soon take it up. Let's get going!"

"I'm right behind you," said Marr, stepping up into his saddle and swinging the girl around onto his lap. In the street where Uncle Andy had fallen there remained only a puddle of blood. Marr looked back and forth but didn't see Uncle Andy anywhere. "Where's Andy's body?" he asked, giving his horse a kick to keep up with Earles.

"His body? Hell, it's right up there in the stirrups!" Earles gave a nod toward Cinco Diablos a few yards ahead, riding out onto the dirt street leading a horse with Uncle Andy Fill lying slumped in the saddle, bloodier than ever yet still alive. "He is one hard sonsabitch to kill," Earles laughed, heeling his horse out of town.

As quickly as they had arrived the scalp hunters vanished, leaving the wagon full of dead, along with the dead lying in the streets of Wakely. As townsfolk

gathered in the settling dust and stared after the riders
and walked among the dead, Jacob Evans came limping from an alley with Dick Tyson's arm looped over
his shoulder. "Somebody give us a hand here," he
pleaded.

"Lord God, Jacob!" said Cornelius Beakly, hurrying
to assist him with Tyson, "we thought for sure you
two were dead!"

"We came very near to being," said Evans, the two
of them sitting Tyson down on the edge of a boardwalk. "This young man has shown tremendous
courage!"

Tyson just gave a weak smile. Then looking around
the street at the dead, he stared at the doctor's body
and said, "What will we do without Doctor
Rasmussen?"

"We'll just have to do the best we can," said
Beakly. "They also murdered poor Sheriff Tackett,
Kirby Romans and the rest of the town posse."

"We better get prepared in case they turn around
and come back on us," said Jacob Evans.

"Why would they come back? They've already
taken everything a bunch like that would be interested
in," said Beakly.

"Who knows what they're apt to do?" said Evans,
standing up slowly, staring off at the lingering dust of
the scalp hunters on the horizon. "They're brute savages. We better be ready for anything."

# Chapter 6

———

Darkness had set in by the time the ranger and Sheriff Tackett rode up on the town and stopped at a distance of a hundred yards. "I swear," Sheriff Tackett said in a lowered voice, "I feel like a dog sneaking up on my own town this way."

"You'd feel worse if we rode straight in and ran smack into those scalp hunters," the ranger replied. As he spoke he drew his rifle from his rifle boot, checked it and held it in his left hand. "Give me a three-minute head start. I'll circle wide and come into town from the other end. I'll stick to the alleys until I see that everything's all right. If the least thing looks wrong, you haul out of there quick. Don't get yourself killed."

"Don't worry," said Tackett. "I want to live long enough to see these birds dead. I don't plan on dying before they do." He jerked his own rifle from his boot and checked it as the ranger heeled his horse away silently in the darkness. "Three minutes," he said almost to himself.

At the far edge of town the ranger rode in through an alley behind the saloon. The first thing he noted was the lack of music or laughter coming from the saloon's dim-lit interior. But that gave him no cause for alarm, only an idea that the scalp hunters had hit

and gone. He rode the Appaloosa stallion down a
shorter alley that connected to the main street. From
within the shadows he saw two men with rifles walking
back and forth along the boardwalk across the dark
street. No street lamps had been lit. Rough planks had
been nailed up to cover broken windows and doors
along the boardwalk. Across from him the ranger saw
two bullet holes in the bank window. The scalp hunters were gone, he was certain of it. He waited until
he saw the dark silhouette of Sheriff Tackett and his
horse venture forward slowly in the middle of the
street.

"Who goes there?" a shaky voice called out from
the boardwalk where the two men patrolled with their
rifles. Hearing the voice confirmed it for the ranger.
These men were there to protect the town.

"It's me, Sheriff Tackett," the ranger heard Tackett
say, seeing him stop his horse in the street.

"Sher—Sheriff Tackett?" the voice said, sounding
stunned and even more shaky.

"Yes, it's me," said Tackett. "I've got a ranger with
me. Don't shoot at us."

Another voice called out. "Sheriff! It's me, Cornelius Beakly! They told us you were dead! You and
Kirby and all the rest!"

"Who told you that?" asked Tackett, nudging his
horse over closer to the boardwalk as the men stepped
down and came forward toward him.

"The killers who did all this!" said Beakly. "Thank
God they were lying!"

"They weren't lying altogether," said Tackett. "I'm
afraid the rest of the posse is dead, except for Kirby."
He paused, then added, "I'd be surprised if he's still
alive by now. We left him with a fellow so we could

hurry back here. These killers have a little girl they're holding hostage."

"We know," said Beakly. "We saw that poor child. She looked scared to death all the while they were here."

As they spoke the ranger eased the big Appaloosa forward. The townsmen turned quickly toward him.

"Easy, fellows," said Tackett, "that's the ranger I was telling you about." He waited for a second while the ranger drew closer, then he asked Beakly, "How did they seem to be treating the girl? Did she look to be holding up all right?"

"I can't say," Beakly replied. "Had it not been for the dress she wore, I wouldn't have known she was a girl child at all. Her hair had been hacked off something awful."

"We figured somebody done that to keep them from scalping her," said Tackett. Other townsmen gathered from out of the darkness, from the saloon, from doorways. Tackett looked back and forth, then said, "We're going after her. I intend on dogging their trail until I get her away from them." He swung down from his saddle and stretched his back.

"You're going after them?" Beakly asked, sounding astonished. He and Otis Townsend gave one another a look in the darkness, then Beakly said, "Sheriff, I believe you're most needed right here in Wakely. I'm afraid we must insist you stay here and protect us. I daresay, had you been here in the first place, this nev—"

"Don't finish that statement, Cornelius," said Tackett, cutting him off. "Not if you ever plan on you and me being friends again."

Beakly caught himself and let out a breath. "I'm

sorry, Sheriff. I didn't mean that. It was just raw nervous talking. But the fact remains, we need you *here,*
in case these men come back!"

The ranger stepped down from his saddle and
stood listening.

"All the way back here," said Sheriff Tackett, "I've
been running things through my mind. Part of me says
I was only doing my job riding to Clifton Wells. But
part of me says I left this town unprotected to ride
out and see about the woman who was coming here
to be my wife. I don't know which part of me is
right—might be that both are. But that's done and I
can't change it. That little girl is still alive though, and
I can't draw an easy breath thinking of her being with
those killers."

Jacob Evans had walked up and stood next to Cornelius Beakly. Seeing where Tackett's conversation
might be headed, he said, "Sheriff, nobody here is
doubting you. You didn't let us down: We were caught
off guard. Who can say it would have been any different had you been here?"

"Obliged, Evans," said Tackett. "But the fact remains that I'm going after that little girl. I owe her
poor mama that much. I can't serve this town and go
after her at the same time. . . ." As he spoke he
unpinned the sheriff's badge from his chest, reached
out and pinned it on Evans' chest. "So, Jacob, I'm
handing you the office. I don't think any of the town
leaders will object." He looked around in the darkness
from face to face and added, "If this town wants me
back once this is over, I'd be honored to resume office.
But for now, I've got to go. Any unfinished business
I've got here, I'll have to clear up tonight. Come day-
break I'll be back on their trail."

The gathered townsmen looked at the ranger.

Beakly said, "What about you, Ranger, are you going with him?"

"As far as it takes," said Burrack.

"Will the Badlands outpost approve of you going after these men without any other rangers joining you?" Evans asked.

"I'm used to working alone," said the ranger. "And I don't have time to stop and go explain this to my captain. It's most important that we don't break away from their trail."

"Then I'll telegraph your captain as soon as we get our lines repaired," said Evans, already rising to his position as sheriff. He turned to Tackett. "Anything else I can do, let me know."

"Thanks, Jacob, there's plenty," said Tackett. "We've got bodies laying out there that will need to be brought here." He lowered his voice in privacy to Evans. "The critters will have made quick work of them by now, I expect. But their families will want them brought back and buried proper."

"Of course," said Jacob Evans, looking back and forth between Tackett and the ranger. "And what about Kirby Romans? Who did you leave him with?"

"We'll tell you all about it in the office," said Tackett, turning, leading his horse away in the darkness.

Evans gave Beakly and the townsmen a look of uncertainty. "Well, go on," said Beakly. "You're the sheriff now. You don't need our permission to do your job."

Evans nodded, turned and walked alongside the ranger toward the sheriff's office.

Ted Riley had no idea exactly when Kirby Romans had died. In the night, Riley had reached over every hour or so, placed his fingertips on Kirby's wrist and

searched for a pulse. The first time he'd found the
wounded man's pulse to be weaker than it had been
during the day, but the second time it had turned
weaker still. The third time he checked the pulse was
gone. Kirby's skin was cold. That was that, Riley told
himself. He laid in the dark beside Kirby without ben-
efit of a fire until first silver light mantled the horizon.
Then he stood up, wrapped the body in its blanket
and carried it over to the horse. Once he'd prepared
the horse for the trail, he laid the body over the animal's rump behind the saddle.

He could have left the body behind, he told himself,
but he'd said he would bring the man to Wakely, and
that was what he intended to do. Besides, bringing the
body to town for everyone to see would quiet any
rumblings about what had killed the man. The only
wound showing on Kirby Romans would be the one
the ranger and Sheriff Tackett had already seen. He
looked at the body with a sad half-smile and murmured to himself. "Riley, you really are a mess.
There's nothing to keep you from going away now
with a clear conscience. But then stepping up into the
saddle and heeling the horse along a high ridgeline,
he silently rebuked himself. You gave your word. If
your word's not good *here and now,* when was it ever?
More importantly, he thought, when would it ever
be again?

"All right, that's enough of that!" he said aloud to
the vast, empty land. He rode on in the direction of
Wakely through a hot whirring wind.

Only an hour had passed when he rode into a short
stretch of hills where the trail snaked between two tall
mounds of rock and headed downward toward flatter
land. Rounding a blind turn in the trail, he didn't see
any sign of the horseman until he sat facing him less

than fifteen feet away. Riley's horse grew nervous and high-hoofed beneath him, and he had to settle it with one hand while placing his other hand back to steady Kirby Romans' body. As he regained control of the skittish animal, the rider's eyes fixed on the Remington pistol on Riley's hip. A smile came to the man's dust-caked face.

*"Buenos dias, señor!"* Taos Charlie said, a pistol coming out of his harness quickly, already cocked and pointed before Riley had time to respond.

Seeing the string of scalps hanging from Taos Charlie's saddle horn, Riley realized at once the terrible spot he was in. But he stayed calm, lifted his hand from steadying the body and let it fall loosely to his side. "Good morning to you too," he replied.

"That's a mighty fine-looking Remington you're strapped to, amigo," Charlie said, gesturing a short nod without taking his eyes off Riley's.

"It'll do," said Riley, flatly, already getting an idea where this was headed.

"It's mine," said Taos Charlie, his smile disappearing, "take it up with two fingers and pitch it." His glove stretched tight across the knuckles of his gun hand.

"I found it back at the relay station," said Riley, stalling, trying to get the man to ease down a little. As he spoke, his eyes searched the trail behind Taos Charlie for any sign of the others.

"I didn't ask where you got it," said Charlie. "I said lift it and pitch it here."

"Anything you say," said Ted Riley, placing his thumb and finger on the pistol grip. "I don't want any trouble over it." Instead of lifting the Remington, he stepped his horse closer. "But I can't pitch it that far with two fingers."

Taos Charlie sized him up, the soft Southern accent, the easy manner of the man, the way he'd already rolled over and showed his belly, saying he wanted no trouble. He hadn't even questioned what Charlie had said about it being his pistol. This man was soft, too clean, too gentle, Taos thought. His glove turned less tight on his knuckles. His pistol slumped a fraction. "Then just *hand* it over, mister," said Charlie, sounding disgusted with him, knowing he would kill this man as soon as he got his Remington back from him. "I don't want trouble either."

"Thank goodness!" said Riley, looking relieved. "There's so much violence these days. A person never knows who they'll come upon riding along these trails."

"Yeah, yeah, I suppose so," said Taos Charlie, not wanting to talk with him. "Just give it here." He reached out for the Remington with his free hand, seeing Riley struggle to lift it with two fingers.

The pistol looked wobbly, too heavy for the man, Charlie thought, watching him hand it over toward him. But suddenly, in a move almost too quick to be seen, the man's fingers opened; his hand snatched forward around the pistol butt, the thumb snapping expertly over the hammer, taking it back effortlessly. All this in a split second, the suddenness of it causing Taos Charlie to freeze. "Wait!" he shouted, as if to call the whole thing off.

The shot exploded less than a foot from his face, fire from the barrel leaving burnt, blackened flesh around the bullet hole between Taos Charlie's eyes. Behind Charlie a mist of blood and smoke stood in the air. A redder streak of blood and matter splattered heavily on the face of a large boulder.

Both horses reared. Kirby Romans' body slid to the

ground, landing a few feet away from Taos Charlie. Ted Riley grabbed the reins to Charlie's horse before it had time to turn and bolt away. He settled both animals quickly, then jumped down from his saddle, wiping the back-blast of Taos Charlie's blood from his cheek. Looking down at himself he saw more of the scalp hunter's blood splattered across his chest. But that didn't bother him; he was alive. With the sound of the gunshot still ringing in his ears, he took a careful look along the trail and down toward the flatland. He didn't want to get caught down there by the rest of the scalp hunters, especially after killing one of them.

In the distance he saw the six riders headed away from the direction of Wakely. They stopped in a flurry of dust and stared toward the hills in his direction. He swallowed hard, knowing they had heard the shot. From this distance he doubted if they could see him, but once he rode down onto the flatlands his tracks would be easy to find and follow. "A bad piece of luck . . ." he murmured to himself. But maybe this was for the best.

He realized that now with two good horses to keep him moving and without the body of Kirby Romans to slow him down, he had a fast, clean ride to Wakely. Given the twist of circumstances, the ranger would just have to take his word for Kirby's death. He tied both horses to a stub of juniper and turned to the bodies on the ground. He carried Kirby off the trail into a narrow rock crevice and leaned him against the rock wall, making it as easy as he could for someone to find the body—what the coyotes and other creatures left of it. Then he dragged Taos Charlie off the edge of the trail and gave him a shove, watching his body tumble downward among rock and scrub brush.

When he returned to the spot where he could look

out across the flatlands below, he saw the riders again; this time they rode toward the hills surrounding him. With two horses he could get ahead of them and stay ahead he thought. But just as he started to turn back to the horses to leave, he caught sight of a rider he hadn't noticed before. He watched this rider grow closer, the missing child huddled against his chest. Riley winced and backed away a step as if in regret for having noticed the rider and child. For a moment he stood transfixed, staring at the scalp hunter and the child as if the other had vanished and only these two remained.

He whispered to himself, "This gets worse every turn in the road." Stepping over to the horses, he untied their reins and stepped up into the saddle of the one nearest him, the one he had been riding all along. He led Taos Charlie's horse by its reins, seeing a streak of Charlie's blood down its side as he turned both horses to the trail. "Ted Riley, you'll never learn," he said to himself, nudging the horses forward, taking his time now.

On the flatlands Jessup Earles rode at the head of the riders, all of them racing abreast toward the hill line, in the direction of the gunshot. Sidling up to Earles in a full run, Cinco Diablos asked above the roar of hoofbeats, "Do you think Taos has gotten himself into a shoot-out with some other posse?"

"One shot don't make a shoot-out," Earles called out in reply.

They rode on at a fast clip until they began ascending the rocky trail leading into the hills. Once on the steep, narrow trail, they had no choice but to slow down rather than to risk losing a horse. "I saw a rider awhile ago right after we heard the shot, up along that far ledge." Cinco pointed, speaking to the others over his shoulder. "He was looking our way. If he's killed ole Taos and he seen us coming, he's long gone out of here by now."

But before they had gone another fifty yards, Earles threw up his hand and brought the others to halt behind him. "What the hell is this?" he asked, dumbfounded. Higher up another fifty yards around a turn in the trail, a spiral of gray brush smoke curled upward. "This sonsabitch has built a fire!"

"Guess he must want to be seen as well as heard," Morton Toller said. "Want me to slip on ahead and scout this out?"

"Why do that?" said Earles. "It's pretty plain he's calling us in to him."

"Maybe it's Taos after all," said Cinco. "Maybe he is hurt and calling out to us with the smoke."

"Yeah, I'm satisfied that's it," said Earles, skeptically. Then he growled almost to himself, "The damn fool *had* to ride on ahead to look for that gun. I'm betting he's laying up there dead right now. This is no business to be in if you have to go backtracking yourself."

They slowed the horses to a walk, then started around the turn in the trail where the smoke lay just beyond a tall wall of solid rock. As they eased cautiously around the turn, prepared to catch someone by surprise, the riders taken aback by the sight of Ted Riley standing in the center of the trail, his feet spread shoulder-width apart, his left hand holding the reins to both horses, his right hand resting on the butt of Taos Charlie's big Remington revolver.

Stopping and spreading out abreast in front of him, the riders stared, first at the pistol, then at Taos Charlie's horse, then at the string of scalps Riley had taken from around the saddle horn and draped over his shoulder.

"Morning, gentlemen," said Riley, a flat, serious look in his eyes. "I thought you'd never get here."

"Oh?" said Earles. "You've been waiting for us, when you could have gotten away? Wearing our *amigo's* gun, leading his horse?"

"That's right," said Ted Riley. He shrugged. "I could have gotten away . . . but where was I going to go?"

Noting the splattered blood on Riley's shirt, Earles eyed him up and down then asked pointedly, "Just where is our *amigo,* Taos Charlie?"

"Oh, he's dead," said Riley, bluntly.

"Dead, huh?" said Earles, his hand poised close to his gun.

"That's right," said Riley. "I killed him and rolled him off the trail."

"You? All by yourself? You killed Taos Charlie?" asked Earles.

"Yep," said Riley.

"That's awfully hard to believe," Earles said, looking as if at any second his hand would snatch the gun from his holster and start firing.

"You can believe it all right," said Ted Riley in a calm, level voice. "Do you think I'd be wearing his scalps if he was alive?"

"The only way you could have killed Taos Charlie is if you're a bushwhacking, back-shooting sonsabitch," Earles growled, his hand still poised, the other men in similar intense positions.

A thin, mirthless smile came to Riley's lips. "So? Everybody's got their own way of doing things."

For a second the riders sat as if frozen in place. Then a thin ripple of laughter stirred among them. "Well, by God," said Earles at length. "You got me there. I can't argue with that." He let his gun hand

ease a bit, then said, "So what is it you want? Are
you here looking for a fight?"

"No," said Riley, "not if I can keep from it. I saw
you coming from out on the flatlands. I wanted to
clear the air between us. I don't want you dogging my
trail while I'm getting away from the law."

"Getting away from the law?" Earles raised an eye-
brow in curiosity. "You mean you are a fugitive
from justice?"

"That's right," said Ted Riley, taking a step back
as if preparing to mount and ride away. "I was a prisoner on my way to territorial prison—until you fellows
showed up at Clifton Wells and started lifting scalps."
He offered a thin smile. "You might say it was *you*
who set me free."

Haddon Marr stepped his horse forward from the
line of riders and cocked one of his big Walker Colts
at Riley, the sound of it causing Riley to freeze with
a hand on his saddle horn, ready to swing up. "Nobody said you could leave," Marr growled.

Riley looked at Marr's gun, ignoring the child
seated on his lap with her face hidden. Then he cut
his attention to Jessup Earles. "Is that right, I can't
leave? I thought I was talking to the boss. But if we're
going to have ourselves a shoot-out—"

Earles cut him off with a gesture of his hand. "Forget all that . . . tell us how we caused you to be
set free."

Riley looked back and forth between Earles and
Marr. "I don't talk well with a gun cocked at me."

"Let down, Haddon," said Earles, "I want to hear
what this convict has to say."

# Chapter 7

The scalp hunters had moved off the trail into the shade of a cliff overhang, listening to Ted Riley tell his story about being the ranger's prisoner, about finding Kirby Romans wandering among the dead with the back of his head missing, his plaid duster and bowler hat having been stripped from him. At that point Earles grinned with satisfaction and ran a hand up and down the front of the plaid duster. "Well, when a man wears something as proud and dashing as this, he ought to realize somebody's apt to shoot him for it. But I didn't know he was still alive when I took it off him. I could see clear inside the back of his skull!"

"He's right up the trail there," said Riley, giving a point in the direction where he'd left the two bodies, "so is Taos Charlie. Want to go see for yourself?"

"Naw," Earles brushed it away. "If we didn't believe what you're telling us, you wouldn't be alive this long. Right hombres?" He looked around at the men. They nodded in agreement, except for Haddon Marr, who sat silent, the child standing near him, facing away from Riley with the lead rope around her neck. Riley made no mention of the child in his story, other than the fact that the sheriff and the ranger knew the scalp hunters had her. But that had been enough to cause Marr to stare coldly at him ever since.

"So what if his story *is* true?" said Marr. As he spoke he stood up, took a step toward Riley and closed a hand around the string of scalps hanging from his shoulder as if he were about to take them.

But Ted Riley closed a hand over his, stopping him. "Taos Charlie was my kill. That makes these *my* scalps," he said firmly, staring straight into Marr's eyes. "Isn't that the way you men always call it?"

"Yeah, we call it that way," said Haddon Marr, his other hand holding the child's lead rope, "but we also say that if you're wildcat enough to take something from a man it's yours until he's wildcat enough to take it back."

Riley looked past Marr, and at the girl, making sure Marr saw him do it. "I can live with that way of thinking."

Marr's eyes smoldered with rage. "You ain't one of us. Don't suppose to include yourself. The fact is I don't believe one damn word you've said."

"Aw, hell, Had," said Earles, "look at his wrists!" When Riley had clasped his hand over Marr's hand, his shirt cuff had risen an inch, exposing the chafed skin where the handcuffs had been. Earles stepped in and shoved Riley's shirt cuff up farther, giving the men a better look. "He didn't get like this singing in a church choir!"

Haddon Marr turned loose of the scalps and pulled his hand away roughly. "That cuts nothing far as I'm concerned." He turned and walked away, giving a short jerk on the child's lead rope to bring her along with him.

Riley stared after him. "What's got his bark on so tight?" he asked Earles.

"He's been that way ever since I've known him," said Earles, "but he's a good man, any way you stack him up."

Stowl cut in, giving Riley a cross-eyed stare, "He's got worse since he started totting that girl around though."

Riley gave Earles a questioning look regarding the girl. Earles shrugged. "He's got her stuck in his craw. We ain't figured if he's going to make her his wife, his daughter or his supper." He cackled under his breath. Then, dismissing the matter, he said, "You took a big chance standing up to Had that way, Ambush. I'm surprised he didn't kill you."

Riley caught the way Earles had already given him a name, calling him *Ambush*. That was a good sign he thought. Giving Earles a level stare, Riley said, "You mean the same way you were surprised your friend Taos Charlie didn't kill me?" He studied Earles' eyes for a second. "Maybe I'm not as easy to kill as you might think."

"Maybe you're not," said Earles. "But I know you had to have ambushed Taos Charlie; he was faster than any of us, except maybe for Haddon."

Without commenting further on the matter, Riley made mental note of it. It was good to know that he'd already killed one of the best gunmen in the group. He didn't care how Earles thought he'd done it. "However fast he might have been," said Riley, "he's as alive now as he'll ever be."

Earles looked him up and down appraisingly. "Why don't you ride along with us for a spell, Ambush? We'll see how much of you is hard salt and how much is hot air. It would be safer for you riding with us than alone, if the law gets too close to your tail."

"You're right, it would be safer," said Riley. "But

I don't ride for free. If I ride *with* you. I ride *for* you . . . If I ride *for* you, I get paid the same as the next man." He shook the string of scalps. "I took down one of your top men. If I fill his boots I want the same share as he got."

Earles looked around at the others and saw no objections. "You caught us at a time when we're short on help." He nodded toward Uncle Andy Fill, lying on a blanket on the ground where Cinco Diablos had put him. "I've got a man wounded, and now Taos Charlie is dead. Play your hand right, you're in with us, Ambush." He grinned. "In scalp hunting, a man keeps what he lifts. It keeps everybody working their best." He raised a finger for emphasis. "But right now we ain't lifting any more scalps for awhile. We're hitting towns for everything they've got, banks, stores, everything—all the way to the border. Then we'll split the take, go redeem our scalp bounties and take it easy all winter. Does that sound good to you?"

"It sure beats where I was headed," said Riley.

Burton Stowl asked, "What was you sentenced for?"

"You don't want to know," said Riley, playing it off. "What if I told you it was chicken stealing?"

"That figures," said Earles with a laugh. "How come those lawmen ever trust you to bring in their wounded man for them?"

"Because I gave them my word?" said Riley. He stared at Earles, waiting for his reaction.

Earles grinned. "Your word, huh? That's a good one!"

"Yeah," said Riley, "I thought so too."

"As soon as the lawmen got out of sight, I bet you poked a stick inside his head and scrambled his brain, didn't you?"

Riley shook his head slowly. "No, he died on his own, in his sleep." He returned Earles' grin. "So it turns out I didn't have to take him to town anyway."

"Then you didn't really break your word, did you, Ambush?" Earles asked.

"No," said Riley. "When I saw you fellows riding across the flatlands after I killed Taos, I thought to myself, where would be the *best* place for me to go? On into town, then on to prison?" He cut a glance to where the child stood beside Haddon Marr, on the end of the lead rope over beside Marr's horse. "Or, should I stick around out here, just to see how things go?"

"You made the right choice wanting to hook up with us," said Earles. "We're on a winning streak. There's a town called Sheldon twenty-eight miles from here. I've always wanted to split that place apart and see what's inside it. I can't think of a better time to hit it than now." Watching Riley's eyes for a reaction, he said, "We ride in shooting, take what we can grab, then ride out the same way. Kill anybody that gets in our path. How does that sound to you, Ambush?"

Riley nodded. "It sounds like a good day's work to me." He looked all around at the others, then past them to where Haddon Marr stood beside his horse, the animal's reins in one hand, the little girl's lead rope in his other. "I'm ready when you are," he said to Jessup Earles. He started to step over to his horse, but Cinco Diablos stepped in, blocking his way. "Oh, I meant to tell you, Ambush," said Earles in an offhand manner, "the Mexican here will be riding *beside* you for awhile . . . just till I feel like it's safe having you riding *behind* me." He grinned, turning to his horse and stepping up in his stirrup. The others laughed.

"Once I see that your hands are as bloody as ours, we'll all feel lots better about you."

Ted Riley got the message. He watched Jessup Earles' horse turn and step away from him. The rest of the men had mounted and began following Earles, except for Haddon Marr, who stood in the same spot, staring coldly at him. "What did you think, *amigo*?" Cinco Diablos asked. "That you could throw in with us and do as you please?" He wore a slight smile beneath his thin wisp of a mustache.

Without answering, Riley stepped around him and up atop his horse. Cinco mounted and gestured toward the trail. "I will ride behind you for a little while, eh?"

"Suit yourself," said Riley. Giving a nod toward Marr, he said to Cinco, "It looks like he's going to ride behind both of us."

"*Si*, he rides where he chooses to ride," said Cinco, turning his horse slightly behind Riley's. "I think he does not like you so much, eh?"

"Yes," said Riley, "I'm starting to think that myself." He heeled the horse forward and tried to relax. He'd done what he set out to do, he'd gotten in with the gang. Now he had to see where it would take him.

The town of Sheldon had been laid out no differently than Wakely or countless other towns across the desert frontier. The desert trail led in off the flatlands onto one long street that ran the length of the town. Sheriff Artimus Fitch stood out front of his office with his hands spread, resting on a hitch rail. He looked back and forth along the empty street at the row of businesses, shops and offices, most of them with boarded up windows and doors. On almost every corner of the boardwalk stood a closed-down saloon.

Only the Lucky Jackrabbit Saloon remained, and only one dusty horse stood reined to a hitch rail out front of the faded drinking and gambling establishment.

"Leonard, I'm afraid I have some bad news for you from the town council," said Sheriff Artimus Fitch to his deputy, Leonard Peck.

"What's that, Sheriff?" Leonard asked.

Fitch thought about it for a moment longer, still looking for the best way to tell the deputy that his job was over. "Leonard," said Sheriff Fitch, starting over, "if this town doesn't turn around pretty damn soon, we both just as well pull up stakes and leave here, go find us another place to make a living. Don't you think so?"

"Maybe you, Sheriff," said Leonard Peck, "but not me. This is as far as I ever got from Ohio. I ain't going back and I ain't going no farther. I've reached what my pa always called 'a happy spot.'"

Fitch shook his head. "Well, how happy are you going to be when I tell you the town board doesn't have enough money to pay us this month?"

Leonard chuckled. "Hell, they never paid *me* last month, remember?"

"Yeah, I remember, Leonard," said Fitch. "You got cut out last month, this month they're cutting us both out." He spit in the dirt at his feet and stared at the spot in contemplation for a moment. "Are you going to take the hint, or make them hit you with a hammer?"

"I ain't stepping down from my badge until you tell me I have to, Sheriff," Leonard replied. "You told me back when I first took this job that law work ain't all about money."

Sheriff Fitch let out a breath of exasperation. "Leonard, I told you that because I wanted you to take the job cheap. I didn't really mean it."

"Oh, so you lied?" Leonard asked flatly.

"I don't like to call it lying, Leonard," said Fitch. "It wasn't intended to deceive you. It was intended to *inspire* you."

*"Inspire* me?" Leonard looked away with his jaw set firmly.

"Yeah, you know, get you to take a deeper inter- est," said the sheriff. "This place was a boomtown then. I said it to make sure you got *involved* in your work."

"Well, it must've worked." Leonard ran his hand up under his hat. "I've jumped in and broke up so many fights the top of my head looks like an Arkansas road map." His hand came down from under his hat and felt around on various places, on his stomach, his hip, his shoulders. "I've been shot, cut, set fire to, strangled by a length of barbed wire and more than once nearly drowned in a horse trough! I believe I have been more than just a little *involved* in my work."

"I know that, Leonard," said Fitch, looking out across the land at a rise of dust forming on the horizon as he spoke. "That's why I'm talking to you the way I am. You've been a good deputy. I think you deserve to be set straight regarding your future here—which is to say, as kindly as I can, that you don't have one."

In the distance seven riders seemed to rise up from the ground, coming toward town in a hard gallop.

"What are you saying, Sheriff? Are you telling me I'm fired?" Leonard asked, still needing it made more clear to him.

" 'Fired' is a harsh way of putting it," said Fitch,

craning his neck a bit now, trying to get a better look at the horsemen. "Let's say that there just isn't enough business in this town to make it worth you staying on here."

"So, I *am* fired, to put it bluntly," Leonard said. "Well, thanks a hell of a lot then!" He started to reach up and unpin the badge from his shirt pocket. "I've put my life on the firing line every day for this town . . . got myself a limp here that'll be with me the rest of my life! Now that things have slowed down a little, I'm thrown out like last night's stove ashes!"

"Hold on, Leonard . . ." Still staring at the approaching riders, sensing something bad heading his way, Fitch said without turning to face Leonard, "Did I say *fired*? Hell no! There you go jumping to conclusions. You know how bad I hate for somebody to put words in my mouth."

"But you just said—" Leonard had begun staring out at the riders too, seeing them riding hard and fast, closing down onto the town like a band of hungry animals.

"You mistook what I was saying, Leonard." Sheriff Fitch straightened up from leaning on the hitch rail.

"I don't know how I could have mistook it," said the deputy. "You made it pretty plain—"

"Shhh, not now, Leonard," said Fitch, cutting him off again. "We'll talk more about it later. What do you suppose we've got coming here?" He gestured toward the riders as he adjusted his gun belt out of habit.

"Beats me," said Leonard warily. "They don't look familiar. Think I ought to go grab us both a shotgun?"

"Yes, I believe you better," said Sheriff Fitch. "And hurry it up, they'll be here any minute the way they're riding."

"Yes, sir, Sheriff!" Leonard limped hurriedly onto the boardwalk and into the sheriff's office. On the street, Sheriff Fitch waited, growing more and more anxious as the riders drew nearer.

"Leonard!" he called out over his shoulder, growing nervous as the ground beneath his feet began to tremble with the thunder of horses' hoofs. But he heard no reply from the office. He waited a moment longer, then called out, "Leonard, damn it to hell! What's going on in there? Hurry up!" The horses had almost reached the far edge of town. Sheriff Fitch couldn't wait another second. "He's run off and left me!" he cried out, turning, running into the office. But just as he entered the door, Leonard looked up from loading a shotgun. Another shotgun lay on the sheriff's battered oak desk. "Jesus, Leonard!" Fitch gasped, hearing the increasing rumble of hoofs, "I thought for sure you'd run out the back door on me!"

"Is that what you think of me, Sheriff?" Leonard asked with a hurt expression. "That I would quit you in the midst of trouble on the stir?" He shook his head, snapped the shotgun closed and pitched it to the sheriff. "I ain't that kind of man, Sheriff!"

Sheriff Fitch caught the shotgun, looking ashamed of himself. "Hell, I know it, Leonard." He watched the deputy pick up the other shotgun from the desk and limp quickly toward the front door.

But before Leonard stepped out onto the boardwalk, Sheriff Fitch grabbed his arm and pulled him back. "Hold it, Leonard, they've stopped!"

"They sure have," Leonard said almost in a whisper. The two stood for a second in the silence.

"Stay here, Leonard," said Fitch, "cover me from the window!" He waited only a second longer while the deputy stepped over to a dusty window ledge.

Then he stepped out onto the boardwalk and looked along the street, seeing seven horsemen spread abreast, sitting atop their horses less than twenty yards away.

At the center of the riders, Jessup Earles looked all around at the closed businesses, and the bank building with the wooden planks covering its door and windows. "What the hell is this?" he growled under his breath, his pistol in hand, still raised for action. Uncocking it, he let it slump as he looked back and forth in amazement.

"There's the sheriff," said Cinco Diablos, "why don't you ask him?"

"By God I will!" said Earles, feeling embarrassed at having told Ted Riley about all the money they were going to make raiding the town. He gigged his horse forward roughly. "Come on, follow me!" he said over his shoulder to the others. "We'll get to the bottom of this!"

On the boardwalk, Sheriff Fitch watched the horsemen come toward him slowly. Without turning to look at the window, he said quietly, "You all set in there, Leonard?"

"You're covered, Sheriff," Leonard said.

Fitch stood silent until the riders were only thirty feet away, then he said, "That's close enough, boys! Rein 'em down."

The horsemen stopped, except for Earles, who came one step closer than the rest. He stopped and turned his horse sideways in the street. "I reckon you saw what we came here to do, lawman."

"It'd be hard to miss," said Fitch, "but the pickings are awfully slim here, as you can see." He gestured along the boarded-up stores with his shotgun, keeping both hands on the sawed-off double-barrel.

"There appears to be a few places still open," said Earles. "We can still do ourselves some good."

"Not enough to make it worth what it'll cost you, scalp hunter," said Fitch, making no effort to conceal his contempt as he eyed Earles' string of scalps and gruesome neckless of finger bones. "You're sitting just about right for us to empty four loads of nail heads into you." He gave a short nod toward Uncle Andy Fill, who sat stooped over in his saddle, buckshot marks all over his blood-splattered clothes. "You'll look worse than that poor devil."

"That 'poor devil' needs some serious doctoring," said Earles. "I suppose we can at least stay long enough to get him looked at, can't we?"

"No," said the sheriff. "I don't know how he got buckshotted and I don't care. Take him somewhere else."

"You won't even allow a man medical treatment? What kind of town is this? You ain't charitable, I can tell that much!" said Earles.

"Not to the likes of you we ain't," said Fitch. "Now turn and ride."

Earles' eyes moved from Fitch to the window, where he saw the second double-barrel ease out above the ledge. "We rode all this way, we're taking something for our trouble," he said.

As Fitch listened to Earles, he looked among the riders, seeing the child hiding its face against Haddon Marr's chest. "Whose child is that?" he asked boldly.

"It's his," said Earles, gesturing with a nod toward Haddon Marr. He quickly went on to say, "You'd be doing the smart thing, giving us what we want . . . get us to ride on out of here."

As he listened to Earles, the sheriff's eyes went to Ted Riley, noting that this man looked out of place.

He wore no collection of bones, no necklace of dried ears, teeth or fingers. Only a string of scalps hanging from his saddle horn signified any connection to this coarse-looking group of men. "What about it, mister," he asked Riley, "does this child belong to anybody in this bunch?"

Riley only stared blankly at Fitch without answering, yet Fitch thought he saw something in the man's eyes. Was this man's silence trying to tell him something?

"Sheriff," said Earles, cutting in, "you do want us to ride on out of here peaceably, don't you?"

"That's up to you," said Fitch. "But you're not taking a damn thing from here as long as I'm standing behind this badge. And the longer I talk, the more I'm tempted to drop these hammers and let hell fly."

Undaunted by the sheriff's threat, Earles offered a slight grin. "Come on, Sheriff," Earles said with a shrugg. "You mean you're willing to die for a town that's about dead itself?"

"Everybody dies sometime or other," said Fitch. "Now back out and ride."

# PART 2

PART 2

# Chapter 8

Leonard Peck stepped out onto the boardwalk beside Sheriff Fitch as the riders rode farther away from town. "That was a close one," said Leonard, breaking his shotgun down and pulling out one of the loads. "I'm glad it's over."

"Don't lay that scattergun to rest just yet, Deputy," said Fitch, staring after the boiling dust along the trail. "Let's make sure they're gone."

"You figure they might come back?" Even as he asked, he shoved the load back into the chamber and clicked the gun shut.

"They're like a pack of dogs," said the sheriff. "You never know what might catch their attention," said Fitch. "Just stay on guard awhile longer. Till we see if it's over with them."

Two men in suits came walking over from the saloon. One wore a bowler hat, the other a black flat-crowned Stetson with a silver Mexican medallion pinned to it. They stopped in the street and looked up at the sheriff and the deputy. "Excuse me, Sheriff," said the one wearing the bowler hat, "did I just see what I *think* I saw?"

"I've got no idea what you *think* you saw, Landers," said the sheriff, already knowing that Phillip Landers was somehow displeased with what had happened.

"I believe I just saw you run *eight* thirsty travelers out of town!" said Landers, placing a fist on his hip.

Fitch gave a thin smile. "Then I reckon you saw exactly what you *think* you saw," he replied. "But take my word for it, you didn't want these thirsty customers. They're scalp hunters, the lowest form of trash ever to seep up out of hell."

"That's quite dramatic, Sheriff," said Landers. "All the same, I shouldn't have to remind you that we've got a bad economic situation here. We can't afford to chase business away! So they're scalp hunters." He shrugged. "That takes place on the other side of the border. Let Mexico settle it. Meanwhile, if they've got money to drink on while they're here, I say let's serve them!"

"They didn't come here to *buy* anything, Landers," Sheriff Fitch said, scowling at the saloon owner. "They came to take whatever they wanted! Their first stop was the bank. Seeing it closed down, they came to me . . . wanted us to give them some whiskey or horses to get them to leave town without tearing it apart."

"Oh?" said Landers, looking skeptical. "And I suppose you and this so-called deputy ran them off. Just told them 'Skedaddle,' and they did, eh?"

"What do you mean, 'so-called' deputy?" Leonard Peck asked, bristling a bit. "I've stuck my neck out too many times for this town to be talked down to by a four-flushing whiskey slinger like you!"

"Easy, both of you," said Fitch. "If you two want to do some fighting, just wait awhile. These scalpers will go mull things over, realize how far it is to the next town, and decide it might be worth riding back in here and turning this town upside down!"

Leonard Peck and Phillip Landers settled down. But Landers still doubted the sheriff. "I hope this isn't something you two have concocted, hoping to make yourselves look needed here."

"Landers," said Fitch, "you'd be greatly surprised to know just how little time I spend making myself look *needed* here." He looked at the other man and said, "Finley, can you make this man understand what I'm trying to tell him about that bunch?"

Marlon Finley turned to Landers, saying, "Come on, Phillip. You wanted to know what's going on, he told you. Let's go back to the saloon. The sheriff knows how to do his job."

"You're damn right I do," Fitch whispered almost to himself.

Landers gave a sour expression, but turned and walked away with Marlon Finley. Halfway across the street, Landers said, "For two cents I'd ride out and invite those men back for a drink. One can't exclude folks simply because they dress a bit peculiar or make their living in an objectionable manner."

"You wouldn't really go and do something that stupid, would you, Phillip?" Finley asked as they neared the saloon. "After Sheriff Fitch warning you about those kind of men?"

"Ha!" said Landers. "We're talking about a sheriff who knows he's on his way out, a town that's on its last breath. . . . Damn right! If I thought it would make me some money to get out of here without losing my shirt, I'd bring them back here and set the first round up on the house, just for spite. Bet me I wouldn't!"

"Careful now," Finley cautioned him, patting the lapel of his coat, with the leather wallet full of cash under it, "you're talking to a gambling man."

"So are you, Marlon." Landers smiled. "What say we dig into this thing and make some sport of it. There's nothing else to do in this short-dog town."

The two stepped onto the boardwalk out front of the saloon and turned, looking back at Sheriff Fitch and Deputy Leonard Peck.

Seeing the two look their way, the sheriff said to Leonard, "Better keep a close eye on Landers."

"Yeah, I will." Leonard looked over at the two men as he spoke. "What's wrong with him anyway?"

"He knows he's going broke here," said Fitch. "It's making him itchy and looking for some trouble to get himself into." He let out a breath. "Hell, I understand how he feels, but it ain't you and me causing this town's problems. Some towns make it, some don't. It looks like Sheldon is going to be one of the don'ts."

"What about those scalp hunters?" Leonard asked.

"What about them?" the sheriff replied.

"Shouldn't we be getting prepared, in case they *do* decide to come back?" Leonard asked.

"Not much preparing to do," said Fitch. "We're loaded and ready. That's about all we can do. Let's hope they mull it over and keep moving. Their main weapon is the element of surprise. They know they've already lost that here."

"Should we try to telegraph out, warn the nearby towns?" Leonard asked, a concerned look on his face.

"Good luck getting through," said Fitch. "I'd bet a month's pay—since I ain't getting paid anyway—that they cut the telegraph lines on their way here. Not that it mattered any. Every town out here is too far apart to do one another any good with a bunch like this on the loose." He shook his head. "I'd sure like to know more about that child they've got with them."

In the midst of a sandy stretch of cactus, cholla and scrub juniper, the scalp hunters passed around canteens of tepid water and cursed back and forth in their disappointment. "That's about as poorly as I've ever been received," said Jessup Earles, sitting atop his horse. Staring back toward the town in the distance, he spit and ran the back of his hand across his mouth. "I say we ride on, find us a place where the sheriff ain't so skittish to begin with. I don't like riding in and finding shotguns staring me in the face."

Ted Riley had breathed a sigh of relief as they'd turned and left Sheldon. Now that it appeared they were going to ride on, he looked at Cinco Diablos sitting beside him and said between the two of them, "Think there's any chance of us riding clear on across the border?" He glanced over at Earles sitting twenty feet away, making sure he wasn't being overheard.

"No, we will go on to another town," the Mexican replied quietly. Looking Riley up and down, he added, "But why do you ask? I thought you were all set to make some big money. Or was that all just some big talk when all you really want is to ride with us bad hombres so the law will think twice before trying to capture you?"

"Don't concern yourself with *my* reasons for what I do," said Riley. "I came face to face with all of you and spoke my piece. If you didn't like what I had to say, you should've told me so right then."

Cinco considered his words for a moment, then said, *"Si,* you are right. It took lots of courage to come face to face with all of us. Still, I am the kind of person who *wonders,* and I wonder what other choice you might have had. This is all I have to say on the matter." He turned his face away from Ted Riley and looked out across the flatlands.

Cross-eyed Burton Stowl raised a canteen to his lips,

swished around a mouthful of water and squirted it out. "I hate getting all set for some killing and some whiskey then missing out on both!"

"That ain't the only town in these parts, Stowl," said Earles. "You'll still get your fill of both." He gazed back along the trail toward Sheldon, seeing a thin rise of dust.

"What have we got coming now?" asked Toller.

Crossed-eyed Burton Stowl stood in his stirrups and craned his neck, looking along the trail. "Two riders," he said, sounding a bit uncertain. "Both of them dressed just alike, riding roan horses."

"Cinco?" said Earles, giving Stowl a disgusted look. The Mexican stood in his stirrups and looked along the trail. *"One* rider on a *roan* horse," he said confidently. "He sees us, too. . . ." He studied the rider for a moment, then said, "It looks like he is coming to us." He settled back into his saddle, staring at Earles.

"Then let's just see what he wants. Everybody spread out in a little half circle." Earles drew a big pistol, cocked it and lay it across his lap. As the rider drew closer, he took off the bowler hat and laid it over his pistol as he raised a bandanna and wiped it back and forth across his sweaty forehead. "Good day to you, pilgrim," he called out with a wide, broken-toothed grin.

Reining his horse down slower, Phillip Landers returned the grin and tipped his hat to the men as he rode in closer to Jessup Earles. Before he realized what the scalp hunters were doing, they had closed the half circle around him tightly. He looked around dubiously, then back at Earles. "Sir, I'm glad I caught up to you!"

"Oh? Why?" Earles asked, unused to anybody deliberately seeking out him and his scalp hunters.

Landers' eyes went to the necklace of finger bones around Earles' throat, hanging beneath the plaid riding duster. "Gentlemen, I am the owner of the Lucky Jackrabbit Saloon in Sheldon. I'm afraid you left town without getting your complimentary drink at the bar!" He looked around at the men, grinning at each in turn. "I can't let that happen, now can I?" He looked at the young girl and her roughly sheared head. The child had ventured a look toward Landers, but now, upon seeing his eyes on her, she turned her face away, raising her hand to her face.

The men sat silent, staring at Landers as if he had just dropped to earth from some plane of existence foreign to them. Finally Earles said, "We weren't made welcome in your town, mister. I don't mind telling you I was troubled by it. We all were." He nodded toward the others, keeping the bowler hat over his cocked pistol.

"That was our sheriff's fault, gentlemen," said Landers, reaching back to his saddlebags, pulling out a tall bottle of whiskey as he spoke. "I wouldn't want you thinking we other townsfolk condone that sort of behavior." He passed the bottle forward to Earles, who took it without raising his right hand from the bowler hat.

"Well, damn now!" Earles grinned again, looked at the bottle closely, then pulled the cork and spit it away as if it would be of no further use. "This does a lot to restore my faith in human kind." He threw back a long swallow, then passed the bottle on to Burton Stowl.

"The thing is, gentlemen," said Landers, "since our sheriff has given you such a bad impression of our town, on behalf of the Lucky Jackrabbit, I feel it's both my pleasure and my obligation to extend you all a warm, heartfelt welcome to Sheldon! In short, I want to buy you all a drink at my saloon!"

"You mean . . . you *want* us to ride back to town with you?" Earles asked, feeling a warm surge in his chest from the whiskey.

"I most certainly do." Landers beamed.

"After the sheriff running us off?" said Haddon Marr. "It sounds like you're trying to start trouble."

"Not at all, sir," said Landers. "But let me explain something to you. Unlike the sheriff, I don't judge a man by how he dresses, what he does for a living or how he treats his horse!"

"Treats his horse?" said Stowl, looking confused.

"That is just a figure of speech, sir." Landers smiled. "But the point is, Sheriff Fitch has already decided that you men are not welcome in Sheldon simply because you . . . well, because he thinks you're scalp hunters."

"No fooling?" said Earles, flatly.

"No fooling," said Landers. Then catching himself, he said, "Not that it would make me any difference if you really were, you understand. I'm far too broadminded to let that sort of thing form my opinion of you."

"I always admired a liberal attitude," Earles said.

"It still sounds like you're trying to start trouble to me," Haddon Marr cut in. "Soon as that sheriff sees us, he's gonna go for his shotgun; so's his deputy."

"Not if you slip into town unnoticed," said Landers. "I can show you a way into Sheldon that is impossible to see from the sheriff's office."

"A secret way into town?" said Earles. "Now ain't that something!"

"I knew you would enjoy hearing about it," Landers grinned. "It's a trail only us locals are familiar with.

The good thing about it is that it leads right to the back door of the Lucky Jackrabbit!"

"And you would do all that just for us?" Earles asked, sounding touched by Landers' offer.

"Yes, that's why I came all this way," Landers replied.

The men just stared. Riley felt like telling the man to turn and ride away as quickly as he could. But he doubted that Landers would follow such sound advice. He took the bottle as it came around to him, and stared at Landers as he raised it to his lips and took a modest sip.

"And what's in this for you, mister?" Earles asked, his expression changing, turning hard all of a sudden.

Landers took a deep breath, considering it, then decide to tell them. "All right, can I be honest with you?"

"I admire honesty more than anything," said Earles.

"A fellow in town has bet me a considerable amount of money that I won't bring you to town against the sheriff's wishes and set you up a drink at my saloon. Isn't that the raspberries?" Landers chuckled as he told them.

"It sure is," said Jessup Earles, giving Haddon Marr a quick glance. Then with a grin and a wink, he said to Landers, "What say we all just ride right in on that *secret* trail of yours and have that drink you're talking about?"

"That's the spirit!" said Phillip Landers. "I knew you men would be good sports about this!"

"Well, hell, yes we are," said Earles. "You'll find that I'm somewhat of a sporting man myself."

"Oh, really?" said Landers. Then brushing Earles' words aside, he raised a finger for emphasis, saying, "Remember though, just one drink . . . enough for me to win the wager. Of course, we'll see to it you leave with another bottle of whiskey under your arm."

"Sure enough?" said Earles. "A whole bottle, up under my arm? *Whooiee!*" He turned in his saddle and said to the rest of the men, "What are we waiting for! Let's ride!"

The circle of riders expanded and put Jessup Earles, Phillip Landers and Haddon Marr at its head. Landers was forced to ride at a hard gallop pressed between the two men until they slowed to a walk then stopped at a fork in the main trail a mile outside of town. "This way," said Landers, out of breath, pointing along a thinner path that led down into a dry creek bed. "This time of year, you can follow this bed right around the town dump and up into an alleyway behind my saloon."

"Who would have thought it!" Earles beamed, him and Marr nudging their horses along, keeping Landers in the lead. Evening shadows had grown long across the land as they rode on toward Sheldon. It had turned dark by the time they rode up out of the creek bed again and circled wide around the dump and up into a narrow alleyway.

"Now this is more like it!" Burton Stowl whispered. "I knew if there was any kind of God in heaven we wasn't going to have to ride all the way to the next town to do our drinking."

"Before you do any drinking," said Earles, "I want you to go find the doctor and bring him to the saloon. See what he can do for Uncle Andy."

Burton Stowl let out a low groan in protest, but Earles cut him off, saying, "Don't worry, Stowl, you've got the rest of the night to catch up on your drinking when you get back."

Hearing the conversation, Phillip Landers flashed

Earles a glance, saying, "But we agreed only one round of drinks, just to win my bet, remember?"

"You might have agreed to it, mister. I didn't," said Earles.

# Chapter 9

Inside the Lucky Jackrabbit, only Marlon Finley and the bartender, Herbert Doyle, stood at the dim-lit bar. "When Landers told me to close early," said the bartender, "I just figured it was because we're not doing any business anyway. I didn't know anything about you two having a bet going."

Finely smiled, raising a shot of whiskey. "Well, I wouldn't be concerned if I was you. I doubt if he was able to reach those men. Just between you and me, I doubt if he really tried that hard to catch up to them."

"No," said the bartender, disagreeing, "if there's money involved, he tried to catch up to them. I just hope he wasn't able to. I'd rather see him lose the bet."

"Well, it looks like he has," said Finley, finishing his whiskey shot and reaching for his mug of beer.

But no sooner than he'd raised the frothy mug to his lips, they both heard footsteps on the rear walk planks. Turning toward the sound, Finley was the first to see Landers and the scalp hunters enter through the rear door. "Well, I'll be damned. . . ." Finley set his mug of beer down and stared, as if lost for words.

"Oh, no," the bartender murmured under his breath as the men came forward leading their horses right into the saloon. They appeared out of the shadows like wild apparitions from some unholy realm.

"Well . . . pay up, Finley!" Landers laughed, seeing the incredulous look on Marlon Finley's face. Then without a pause he said to the bartender, "Doyle, pour each of these gentlemen a drink. We don't wish to detain them any longer than absolutely necessary."

"Poor smartly until I tell you to quit," said Jessup Earles, stepping in close to the bar. He picked a half-full bottle that the bartender had been pouring shots from for Marlon Finley. "I've never been detained in my life unless it was by my own choosing." Wiping a hand around the rim of the bottle, Earles grinned, looking at Haddon Marr, who stood at the bar with the child on the end of the lead rope. "Ain't that right, men?"

"Damn right it's right," said Marr, giving the bartender a flat, level stare, "keep it pouring; we'll tell you when to whoa."

While the rest of scalp hunters stood drinking, Burton Stowl had stayed outside and walked along the alley to the empty street. He crept along the deserted boardwalk in the shadows until he found the doctor's office. As he approached the door it swung open from the inside and a woman stepped out carrying a baby wrapped in a blanket. "Keep him salved and warm," the white-haired doctor said. "I'll be by come morning to check on him."

"Thank you, Doctor Turner," the woman said.

Stowl stepped back and watched quietly as the woman walked away along the boardwalk. Then the portly doctor turned to Stowl and asked, "Are you here to see me, lad?"

"Yes, I am," said Stowl. Stepping inside, he added, "But it's not for me, Doc, it's a friend of mine." Inside the office he turned, facing the doctor with his hand on his pistol butt. "He's over at the saloon. Somebody accidently loaded him full of buckshot."

"Accidently?" The doctor looked skeptical.

"Yeah, more or less," Stowl said with a shrug. "Anyway, he's also got a bullet wound. He's in bad shape."

"Buckshot and a bullet wound?" The doctor looked Stowl up and down, noting his ragged clothes, the gruesome souvenirs hanging around his neck. "Both of these are accidental wounds?" He looked into Stowl's severely crossed eyes.

"Damn it, Doctor, we're talking too much!" said Stowl, snatching his pistol from his holster. "Get whatever you need and let's go, before I bash your head in!"

"Don't threaten me, lad!" said the old doctor. "I treat the ill and injured because it is my profession, not because some saddle tramp threatens me!"

"Don't call me no saddle tramp!" Stowl cocked the pistol and poked it into the doctor's soft round belly. "I'll blow daylight through you!"

"Oh?" The old doctor remained defiant. "And then who will treat your friend's unfortunate *accidental* gunshot wounds?"

"I don't care if the sonsabitch lives or dies!" said Stowl. "I was sent to get a doctor and that's what I'm doing. Now hurry up, so I can get back and drink me some whiskey."

"All right then, lad," said the doctor, sensing that Stowl wouldn't give a second thought to shooting him dead on the spot. "Just calm down. Let me get my hat and my bag. We'll go attend to the poor fellow."

Deep in the night Sheriff Fitch awakened in his room behind the jail to the sound of gunfire coming from the Lucky Jackrabbit Saloon. No sooner than he had swung up onto the side of his bed and planted his bare feet on the cold plank floor, he heard Leonard Peck banging on the door with his gun barrel. "Sheriff! Wake up! Open the door!" he called out.

Fitch sighed, hurriedly pulling his trousers on. "It's not locked, Leonard! Come on in!" He jerked the galluses up over his shoulders and grabbed his boots from beneath the edge of the bed.

The door swung open. "Sheriff, we better hurry, there's shooting going on at the Lucky Jackrabbit!"

"I heard it, Leonard," said Fitch, stepping into his boots one at a time and stamping them into place. He picked up his gun holster as another round of gunshots erupted from the direction of the saloon.

"Good Lord!" said Leonard. "It sounds like a war has broke out!"

"Yeah," said Fitch, hurriedly strapping the gun belt around his waist. "I hope it ain't who I think it is."

"Those scalp hunters?" Leonard asked. He had one of the shotguns cradled in his left arm.

"That's right, Leonard," said Fitch. "If it's them and they've gotten themselves inside the Lucky Jackrabbit, we'll have our hands full."

The two hurried from the sheriff's room along a row of empty jail cells and into the office. Grabbing his hat and the other sawed-off shotgun, Sheriff Fitch and the deputy ran from the office toward the Lucky Jackrabbit as breaking glass, drunken laughter and gunfire resounded in the night. "Wait!" said the sheriff, grabbing Leonard's arm, stopping him in the middle of the street. He saw that the big wooden doors of the saloon were closed, concealing the swinging bat wing doors. Only Marlon Finley's dun horse stood at the hitch rail out front of the saloon. Thinking quickly, the sheriff said, "Let's go around back first, see if we can find out what we're dealing with here."

They crept quickly along the alley beside the saloon while gunshots still erupted inside. When they stopped at the rear edge of the building, they saw the scalp hunters' string of spare horses standing tied to a hitch post. Fitch cursed in a whisper. "Damn it! It's them all right! Landers had a hand in them coming back here, I'm certain of it." He looked into the darkness in the direction of the dry creek bed that led out onto the flatlands, getting a good idea of what had happened. "For two cents I'd be tempted to let that cock-proud bastard deal with them the best he can." Fitch slipped over to the rear door and tried it, finding it locked. Then he released the string of spare horses and shooed them away quietly.

The two stood in silence for a second, then Leonard said, "What do you want me to do, Sheriff?"

"Just back me, Deputy," said Fitch, "and be careful you don't get yourself killed. This town won't be here a month from now. Let's try our best to outlive it."

They slipped back along the alley to the main street. Out front of the saloon a couple of the few remaining townsmen had ventured forward from their warm beds to see what was going on. Seeing them standing in the middle of the street, Sheriff Fitch waved them aside, saying in a muffled tone, "Get out of here, both of you! These men are dangerous."

"We thought you might need some help," one of them answered in a whisper. "George has a pistol; so do I."

"Much obliged, Nelson," said Fitch, "but Leonard and I work better by ourselves. Now get back out of the way."

"Well, all right then," said Nelson Embry, the local

land surveyor. Looking back over their shoulders, he
and George Brunder moved away quietly.

Once the two townsmen were out of the street, Leonard said, "Want me to go check, see if those big
doors are locked?"

"No," said Fitch, "save yourself a trip. The doors
are locked, you can count on it." As he spoke, three
more shots rang out from inside.

"Then what will we do?" Leonard asked.

"Stay right here and keep me covered, Leonard,"
said Fitch. "I'm going to see if I can take a peek in
through the windows."

Sheriff Fitch slipped along the boardwalk in front
of the saloon in a crouch until he reached the edge of
a large, dusty window where he could look in through
a part in a set of faded red drapes. On the floor he
saw Marlon Finley lying motionless in a dark pool of
blood. From a wide smear of blood lying between Finley and the far wall, Fitch could tell someone had
dragged his body to the middle of the floor. Against
the far wall stood Phillip Landers, shirtless, trembling,
dripping wet, with a full beer mug standing atop his
head. A trickle of blood ran down his cheek from a
swollen bluish gash beneath his right eye.

"Sweet Jesus!" Sheriff Fitch murmured to himself,
looking all around the dim-lit saloon.

In a chair beside a billiard table sat Doctor Turner,
a worried, haggard look on his face as he washed his
hands in a pan of water on his lap. Fitch watched the
doctor roll down his shirt sleeves. On the billiard table
lay Uncle Andy Fill with gauze covering most of his
chest, all of his right arm, and half of his face and
head. Red blood spots stood out on the white gauze
like polka dots on a clown's shirt. Uncle Andy lay
propped up on one elbow, a bottle of whiskey in his

left hand, his pistol lying beside him on the green felt tabletop.

At the bar stood Jessup Earles, Morton Toller and Burton Stowl. Earles swayed drunkenly. He reloaded his pistol and clicked it shut. "Anybody wants to get a bet down, better do it quick!" Staring at the trembling bar saloon owner he called out to him, "See? I told you, sir! I *am* a sporting man!" He laughed aloud, raised his pistol and took aim. But before he started squeezing the trigger, his hand wobbled slightly.

"Hold it," said Ted Riley, standing a few feet away beside Cinco Diablos at the long bar. "When do I get my turn?"

"I thought you didn't want none of this, Ambush!" Earles said drunkenly, letting his cocked pistol sag in his hand.

"That was awhile ago." Ted Riley grinned. "I seen how much money you made off the other man until you missed and nailed him in the forehead."

"Oh, so now you figure you can shoot just as good as me?" Earles asked, uncocking his pistol, staggering in place.

"I can't do any worse," said Riley, teasing a bit, but not too much.

The scalp hunters laughed, including Jessup Earles, who lowered his pistol into his holster. "All right, Ambush, show us what you've got. Are you going to have him turn his back to you, make it feel more natural?"

"No," said Riley, going along with Earles' little joke. "I've always wondered how it felt shooting at a man from the front." Again the men all laughed.

A few more feet away along the bar, Haddon Marr stood holding the child's lead rope. On the other end of the rope the child was standing very close to the ornately carved bar front, facing it from only inches away as if being forced to stand there in punishment. In a far corner the saddled horses milled and huddled. As Fitch stared, he saw the doctor turn his eyes toward the front window as if sensing someone was there. Seeing the doctor's tired, worried eyes look in his direction did not bother the sheriff. But when suddenly Haddon Marr flashed his eyes toward the window, Fitch dropped down flat on his belly and crawled backward quickly.

"What happened?" Leonard asked as the sheriff came back and stood around the corner of the building at his side.

"It's bad," said Fitch, dusting the front of himself and taking the shotgun Leonard had held for him. "These devils have themselves set up in there, horses and all. They've got Doc Turner, and they're taking turns shooting beer mugs off Landers' head." He gave Leonard a grim look. "It looks like they've already killed Marlon Finley."

"Oh, Lord," said Leonard, "this is all we need, right now when this town is dying in the dirt anyway!"

From inside came a pistol shot followed by a drunken round of laughter and hooraying. "I hope Landers didn't just get his brains splattered all over the wall," said Sheriff Fitch. He winced, then said, "We've got to get him and Doc out of there. I've got a feeling these men knew we'd be coming, but since they've got Doc Turner and Landers as hostages, they know they've got us where they want us."

"I've got no idea what to do, Sheriff," said Leonard. "But whatever you decide, I'll back till we're cleaning these snakes off our boot heels."

"I know, Leonard, and I appreciate your help," said Fitch. He paused for a second, then said, "Well, I don't know nothing to do but call them out, see what happens next."

The two walked cautiously to the other side of the street, where they took cover behind a dusty stack of empty shipping crates out front of the closed-down mercantile store. Nelson Embry and George Brunder crept in closer from out of the shadows along the street. Seeing them unexpectedly startled the sheriff. "Damn it! What are you two doing back here? I told you to stay back out of the way!"

"Sheriff, we want to help!" said Nelson Embry. "Don't tell us you don't need us. We heard all that shooting. It sounds like there's a dozen wild men in there!"

"Yeah," said George Brunder, "you can use our help! We're men just like you fellows are! We ain't afraid!"

"All right," said Fitch. "Both of you keep covered. I'll go get their attention, find out what they're up to here."

Inside the saloon, Burton Stowl carried another full mug of beer over to where Landers stood shaking uncontrollably against the wall. Beer and broken glass streamed down Landers' face and chest. He sobbed. "Please! I can't stand any more of this!"

"I don't know what you're griping about, I'm the one lost a dollar, betting he couldn't do it!"

In front of the bar, Ted Riley stood with his feet shoulder-width apart, the Remington pistol still curling smoke in his hand, a dead-serious expression on his face. "I'm tired of this," he said. "Let's find some other entertainment."

"Well, now, Ambush, what have you got in mind?" Earles asked with a half-drunken grin.

"Yeah," said Cinco Diablos. "Tell us what we should do, since we are only here to amuse you."

The others laughed. But Ted Riley gave everyone a look in turn, then said, "If we're really *sporting* men the way you told this fool you are," he said to Earles, giving a nod toward Landers, "we'd at least make the bet more interesting by taking turns against that wall."

"Ha!" said Earles. "Do you want to be the *first* to stand there, Ambush?"

"Not after seeing what you did to that one," Riley said, making a gesture at the body of Marlon Finley lying on the floor. "I say we cut the cards for it," said Riley. "High card shoots; low card stands against the wall."

Earles laughed and threw back a long swig of whiskey. He looked at Haddon Marr, asking, "What do you say, Had? Will you participate if we do it this way?"

"Shoot each other to hell, if that's what you've a mind to do," said Haddon, giving Riley a harsh stare as he spoke to Earles. "I got better things to do." He jerked on the lead rope and walked the child to the far corner where the horses stood.

Riley watched Marr to see what his intentions were. When he saw him open his saddlebags, take out a strip of jerked meat and hand it down to the child, he breathed a little easier and turned his attention back to Earles. "What's it going to be? I brought up the idea. Has it backed everybody down?"

"Hell, no," said Morton Toller, sitting his bottle of whiskey on the bar. "I don't back down from nothing! Somebody get a deck of cards, let's cut and see who's first to stand against the wall."

"That's the spirit," said Riley. Turning to Landers,

he said, "Get away from there barkeep. You're shaking too bad to play in a man's game!"

The men laughed drunkenly as Landers scurried away from the wall and toward the rear door. But then he stopped suddenly as he reached for the door handle and a shot exploded from Earles' gun. Splinters stung Landers' face as the bullet thumped into the thick door only inches from his head. "Nobody said leave!" Earles shouted. "Get back here behind the bar! You and the good doctor are staying till the last waltz is over."

Seeing Haddon Marr lead his horse and the girl toward the rear of the saloon, Earles called out, "Where you going, Had?"

"I'm going to check on the rest of the horses," Haddon replied, "since nobody else has done it."

Taking note of Haddon Marr walking out the back door, Ted Riley reloaded the big Remington and looked at Morton Toller, who staggered forward, taking a deck of cards that Cinco Diablos held out to him. "Let's get the cards cut," said Riley. "I hear nature calling me."

# Chapter 10

From behind the stack of freight crates, Sheriff Fitch called out to the Lucky Jackrabbit Saloon, "You men in there! This is Sheriff Artimus Fitch! Throw out your guns, and come out with your hands raised! You're all under arrest!"

A silence passed, then Jessup Earles called out, "*Hola,* Sheriff! I've been wondering when you'd show your face. What are you proposing to arrest us for?"

"For the murder of Marlon Finley, the man lying dead on the floor! I want you and your band to throw out your guns right now, scalp hunter, then step out the door!" said Sheriff Fitch.

"We never murdered this man, Sheriff," said Earles with a drunken chuckle. "He died in the midst of a legitimate sporting contest. It's nothing to get all worked up about!"

"Toss the guns, then come out," said Fitch, firmly.

"Aw, come on, Sheriff," said Earles, "let's talk about this for a minute. I believe we can reconcile any differences we might—"

"There's nothing to talk about, and we both know it," said Sheriff Fitch, cutting him off. "If you don't toss your guns and come out, we're coming in and dragging you out by the heels."

"That's unfriendly of you, Sheriff," Earles shouted.

"And unwise too, seeing as how we've got your doctor in here, and this bartender and Landers. You've gotten close enough to see what I did to this man laying here on the floor—is there any doubt in your mind that I won't do the same to these three?" He paused long enough to chuckle aloud, then he said, "Sheriff, it's time you start acting the way I want you to act. Quit thinking you've got the upper hand here."

"Damn it," Fitch said over his shoulder to Leonard. "I figured he'd hold them as hostages. All he did was just confirm it."

"Are we really going to rush the place?" Leonard asked.

"Not if it means we get innocent people killed," said Fitch. "I left the back door unguarded, hoping him and his bunch would make a run for it. I hope they're not too drunk and kill-crazy to make a run for it. I'd rather them ride away than leave a string of bodies on the floor."

"Then just *tell* them to take the back door and get out of here," Nelson Embry whispered from behind the freight crates.

"It doesn't work that way, Nelson," said Fitch. "These men might go if they think it's because we forgot to guard the back door, but the sonsabitches won't budge if they think that's what I want them to do." He let out a breath and said, "It's time I see what they want."

"Surely you're not thinking about going along with anything these low-down *scalp hunters* ask you to do?" asked George Brunder.

Sheriff Fitch only gave Brunder a look over his shoulder, then he said to the Lucky Jackrabbit, "All right, scalp hunter. What do you want?"

"Now that's more like it," Earles laughed. "First

off, you better stop calling me *scalp hunter*. My name is Jessup Earles, and I don't care who knows it. You can call me 'Mister Earles,' law dog!"

"All right, Mister Earles, that's what I'll call you," said the sheriff. To Leonard, Fitch said quietly, "He's dangerous, Deputy. He ain't even trying to hide his identity."

"I hear you," said Leonard.

"What I want you to do, law dog," said Earles, is to start gathering anything left in this town that's worth anything. Not just money either. I want guns, horses, watches, rings, tie pins, everything!" I want it all loaded into a big wagon right out front here where I can see it, first thing in the morning."

"How do I know you won't go ahead and kill those people once you get everything you want?" asked Sheriff Fitch.

"You don't know it." Earles laughed. "You're just going to have to take my word for it. Now don't make me think you don't trust me. That would hurt my feelings something awful."

Fitch looked at Leonard. "He'll kill all three of them as soon as we give him everything he wants." Then he called out to Earles, "All right, we're getting started. But if anything happens to those men, the deal is off. Are we both clear on that?"

"Clear as summer rain," said Earles.

While Earles and Sheriff Fitch spoke back and forth to each other, Ted Riley had eased to the rear door and slipped outside without being noticed. He stood wary for a moment until he realized there were no guns pointed at him. Seeing that the string of horses had been freed, he looked all around for Haddon Marr. In the moonlight he saw a dark figure on horseback, leading another horse behind him. But he caught only a quick glimpse just as the horses stepped out of sight around the corner of a woodshed. Riley raced along the alley after the rider, but in a moment he slowed to a halt as man and horse disappeared down into the dry creek bed. He looked around wildly in the dark and saw the large wooden doors of what looked like a livery barn only a few yards away.

Running to a smaller side door, Riley found it unlocked and hurried inside and along a row of empty stalls until he saw a big paint horse standing back against the wall. The horse stared and nickered under its breath. "Easy now," said Riley, jerking a saddle and blanket from atop a feed bin as he stepped over and opened the stall door. "We're going to have to take a little ride, you and me."

But as he stepped in and pitched the blanket onto the horse's back, a voice said in the darkness as a hammer cocked, "Hold it right there, mister, you're not taking that horse nowhere."

Riley turned slowly, his hands chest high, still holding the saddle and bridle. He watched a hand reach over to the wall and throw open a window to the outside, allowing moonlight to fill the stall, illuminating Riley's face and the face of the livery hostler holding the gun on him.

"I heard all the shooting," said the grimy hostler, bits of straw entwined in his tangled gray beard. "I figured some jackleg might come snooping around looking to steal himself a horse."

"Well, you got me, mister," said Riley with a sigh, "just don't shoot. Tell me what you want me to do."

The old hostler stepped around to the side and motioned with his pistol toward the stall door. "Drop the saddle and step out there."

"All right," said Riley. He dropped the saddle, but

as he did so he gave the bridle in his other hand a sharp swing and knocked the pistol barrel away from himself and the horse. A shot exploded. But Riley jumped in and caught the old man's wrist before he could collect himself.

"Turn it loose!" said Riley, wrenching the gun back and forth in the strong, knurled hand until he managed to get it free.

"Lord God! I reckon I'm a dead man now!" the old hostler called out.

"Shut up!" said Riley. He gave the man a shove, then stuck the pistol down in his belt. "Sit down and stay down!"

Riley hurriedly bridled the big paint horse, picked up the saddle and swung it over the horse's back. "If I hear you yelling out," he said, "I'll turn around and ride back here. Do you hear me?"

"I hear you, mister!" said the hostler. "I don't want to die!"

"Then do like I told you!" said Riley, jerking the horse toward the stall door.

The hostler spit and touched his thick fingertips to his lips. "You know you busted my dang mouth with that bridle!"

"Are you going to be able to shut up?" said Riley, stopping for a second, looking down at him.

"Yeah, I will, just don't shoot me!" the old hostler said.

Ted Riley hurried out the door and swung up onto the paint horse's back. He gave the big horse a solid tap with his boot heels and felt the animal snap forward beneath him—a good strong horse, he told himself. That was a stroke of good luck just when he needed it. He reined the horse down a bit as they circled the barn back to the alley. Then he put the animal forward toward the dry creek bed, lying low on its back, racing along in the moonlight.

Across the street from the Lucky Jackrabbit, Sheriff Fitch and Leonard listened to the sound of a horse's hoofs speeding away from the livery barn, right after having heard the single gunshot. Standing watch on the saloon from their cover behind the empty wooden crates, Fitch said to George Brunder and Nelson Embry, "Why don't you two go see what that was about?"

George and Nelson looked at each other, then Brunder asked the sheriff, "Do you mean it?"

"Hell, yes, I wouldn't have said it if I didn't mean it, George! Just be real careful in case some of this bunch is in there."

"Sure thing, Sheriff!" said Brunder, getting excited at being involved in helping Fitch and his deputy. "Come on, Nelson, you and me will just go check this thing out real proper like!"

Fitch shook his head and murmured something under his breath, watching the two run toward the livery barn in the darkness.

Inside the Lucky Jackrabbit Saloon, Jessup Earles and the others had also heard the single pistol shot resound in the night. Looking around, Earles had asked anyone listening, "Where the hell is Ambush? Where the hell is Haddon?" He shot a whiskey-blurred glance at the horses in the corner.

"Haddon went to check on the spare horses out back, remember?" said Cinco Diablos, checking his rifle, getting prepared for a fight.

"And Ambush?" Earles asked.

"I have not seen him," said Cinco.

"Didn't I say for you to keep an eye on him?" said Earles.

"Yes, you did," said the Mexican. "But you two

were acting like such amigos, I thought everything was all right."

"It's all right when I tell you it's all right!" said Earles, drunkenly. "Now get to the back door, see what's happened to them two! Haddon's been gone too long to be checking on the horses!"

While Cinco eased the rear door open and inched cautiously outside, Earles stepped over in front of the doctor, who sat with his big pale-white hands folded on his large stomach. Staring at the doctor with his pistol pointed loosely at his stomach, Earles asked Uncle Andy Fill lying on the billiards table, "Has this sawbones done you any good, Uncle Andy?"

"Hell, I reckon so; I'm still alive," said Uncle Andy, heavily bandaged, his blood spot having grown only slightly larger. "I can sure enough ride, if that's what you're wanting to know."

"Ride hell," said Earles, "I want to know can you fight?"

"I can always fight," said Uncle Andy.

"Good," said Earles. Cutting a drunken scowl at the others, he continued, "Because, as far as I'm concerned, we're taking everything we can get our hands on, then we're shooting this sheriff and this town to hell on our way out!"

The old doctor stared up into Earles' drunken, bloodshot eyes and said, "So this is all a lie, about you getting what you want and leaving peacefully?"

"Well, of course it's all been a damn lie!" Earles laughed insanely. "I just wanted the good sheriff and his deputy to do all the gathering up for us before we reveal our true intentions."

"So, we're all three going to die, I expect?" The doctor gestured a nod toward Landers and the bartender.

"Oh, I'd say so for certain," Earles grinned, reaching down and poking the pistol barrel playfully into the doctor's paunch. "But you've got nothing to complain about. It looks like you've lived a good, prosperous life for yourself."

"I'm not complaining," said Doctor Turner. "In fact, I look at something like you crawling around in your own scum, and it makes me grateful that for most of my life I've had to have little to do with anything so foul."

Earles' eyes filled with white-hot rage. He cocked the pistol and jammed it more firmly into the doctor's belly. "You don't know what put me on the path I'm on, you smug sonsabitch! I've done without in my life! While you've never wanted for nothing!"

"So what if you've *done without*?" the old doctor said, coming right back at him, grunting slightly at the gun barrel jammed into his soft belly. "What makes you so important that your doing *without* is a bill the rest of the world has to pay? You came to this life as nothing and you've only become something less as time wore on. Pull that trigger, you sorry, worthless bastard."

"Doc, please, shut up!" Landers sobbed. Then he said to Earles, "He doesn't mean it! Even if he did, he isn't speaking for me! You don't have to kill us! Take whatever you want . . . everything here! Just don't kill us!"

Landers words distracted Earles for the moment. Earles eased the pistol barrel out of the doctor's belly and looked toward the sobbing bar owner. "Oh?" he said, turning the pistol barrel in Landers' direction. Landers stood behind the bar, still naked from the waist up, dried beer and blood streaked down his face and chest, his hair filled with sharp bits of broken glass. "You mean I can leave here with more than just *one* bottle of whiskey tucked up under my arm?"

"I meant no offense when I said that!" Landers pleaded. "It was a token of my gratitude! I thought a bottle of whiskey was what you would want!"

"Mister, you have no idea what I want," said Earles. He raised the pistol and fired one shot, putting the bullet dead center of Landers' forehead. The shot shattered the mirror behind Phillip Landers, splattered it with blood as it slammed him against the wall of whiskey bottles and let him sink out of sight behind the bar. Doyle, the bartender, who had been standing beside Landers, raised his hands instinctively, shielding himself. Then he stood trembling, blood-spattered, his mouth agape, staring wide-eyed at the smoking pistol in Jessup Earles' hand.

Seeing Earles cock the pistol in the bartender's direction, the doctor said quietly, weighing his words, "That's the way. Go ahead and shoot him next. Then hurry up and shoot me."

"Jesus, Doc, shut up!" said the bartender.

"No . . . if he's going to kill us, it's best he kills us now. We're all he's got." His eyes stared coldly up at Earles. "The quicker you kill us, the quicker that sheriff and his men can come in here and kill you . . . you and the rest of this foul-smelling heap of dung."

Earles turned the cocked pistol back toward the doctor.

"*Sante Madre,* Earles!" said Cinco Diablos, having hurried inside the rear door at the sound of the gunshot. "He is right! Don't be a fool and get us all killed! Wait until we are out of here, then kill them!"

A tense silence passed, then Earles lowered the pistol and eased the hammer down on it. He grinned at the doctor. "You are a real fireball, ain't you though."

He took a step back, hearing the sheriff's voice call out from across the street.

"What was that shot, Mister Earles?" Fitch shouted.

Taking a step closer to the locked front doors, Earles shouted in reply, "That was nothing, Sheriff! Just your bar owner, Landers, getting his brains aired out a little. "Do you want me to toss his scalp out to you, just for a keepsake?"

"God have mercy on him," said Sheriff Fitch, slumping against the wooden crates.

Inside the saloon, Earles turned to Cinco Diablos and asked, "What's going on back there? Where's Haddon and Ambush?"

"They are gone," said Cinco, "so is our string of horses." He looked at Toller, at Uncle Andy, at Cross-eyed Burton Stowl, then at Jessup Earles.

"That damn crazy Marr!" Earles cursed. "He's gone and let that little girl get his mind all twisted around!" He settled himself down, then said, "Well, he'll show back up before long. We won't hold this against him."

"What about the other one . . . Ambush?" asked Cinco. But he already knew the answer.

"That son of a bitch!" said Earles. "I don't know what to think of him. Just shoot him if we run into him!"

"*Si,* I will," said Cinco. Then he went on to say, "There is nobody out there guarding the way out of town. We can still make a run for it to that dry creek bed if we choose to."

"What?" said Earles, acting surprised at such a suggestion. "And miss all this fun?"

When Nelson Embry and George Brunder returned from the livery barn, they brought the hostler with them. Before Fitch could ask them anything, George

Brunder said, "We heard a shot from the saloon! What happened?"

"They've killed Phillip Landers," said Sheriff Fitch with a grim expression.

"I'll be dogged," replied Brunder, staring toward the saloon.

"He was a ne'er-do-well, but he didn't deserve to die I don't reckon," said Nelson Embry. "Looks like that'll be the end of the Lucky Jackrabbit." He shook his head slowly.

Nodding toward the livery barn, Fitch asked, "What was *that* gunshot about? Was it anything to do with this bunch?" He pointed at the saloon.

"Yes, Sheriff, it was!" said Brunder. "We found Denver here in the livery barn with his lip busted—"

"I'll tell it," said Denver Heath, cutting Brunder off. "Sheriff, I had the man dead to rights! He was stealing your horse, Monty! I put a gun on him and was fixin' to bring him to you. Then danged if he didn't trick me, busted me in the face with a bridle and lit out, big as you please!"

Sheriff Fitch gave him a flat stare. "Then he *did* steal my horse? You let him ride away on Monty?"

"What could I do?" said the old hostler. "He took my gun, pointed it at me. Said I'll kill you deader than hell if you try to stop me! Then he rode off!"

"Jesus," Fitch murmured. Then he said to Leonard, "All right, at least that's one more we won't have to deal with, even if I will never see Monty again." He nodded toward a buckboard wagon sitting half a block up the street. "Go get that wagon. You and Denver get some horses hitched to it—not the best horses you can find, mind you. Just something that'll get these men out of here. Maybe we can catch up to them somewhere along the trail."

"I understand, Sheriff, said Leonard. Turning to Denver Heath he said, "Let's go see what kind of wagon horses you've got on hand."

"Who's paying for them?" the old hostler asked.

"The town will pay for them, Denver!" the sheriff cut in.

"Ha!" said Denver. "The town is about broke, is what I've heard!"

"All right then," said Fitch, "I'll stand good for the horses. Does that suit you?"

"Don't be cross with me, Sheriff," said Denver. "I'm just looking out for the livery barn's interest."

"Is the livery barn going to pay me for my horse being stolen right out of its stall?" asked Fitch.

"All right, Deputy, let's go get some wagon horses," said Denver Heath without answering the sheriff.

# Chapter 11

———

Ted Riley ran the big paint horse along the dry creek bed, the horse finding its footing in the loose soil and rock by the light of the moon. He knew that the man he was chasing would hear him coming, but that was something he couldn't help. His intentions were to ride him down and take the girl from him, whatever the risk, whatever the cost. The horse pressed forward as if it knew the urgency of the situation. Riley rode with the Remington pistol in his right hand, ready for any surprise Haddon Marr might spring upon him.

When he reached the spot where the creek bank cut up onto the trail, he reined the horse to a halt and listened intently for a moment until he heard the slightest sound of hoofbeats on the trail Phillip Landers had led them in on. "Gidup!" he said, giving the paint horse the flat sides of his boot, sending it forward at a run on the hard, flat trail.

Two hundred yards ahead of Riley, Haddon Marr had stopped long enough to catch the sound of hoofs on the trail. He rode with the girl on his lap, leading a spare horse behind him. Upon hearing the hoofbeats of a single rider, he looked down at the girl and said, "Hold tight, child. We can't let him get you. He's a killer, that one." Then, feeling the girl tighten her hold on him, he booted the horse sharply and cut off the trail across a stretch of rough, rocky ground strewn with thorny brush and upthrust boulders. "Let's see how Ambush likes this kind of riding," he said grinning to himself.

But a half an hour later when Marr stopped to switch horses, he heard the hoofbeats following close behind him, Riley having lost no ground in spite of the harshness underfoot. "You're no easy piece of work, Ambush," Marr said aloud to himself, loosening the cinch on the saddle in order to switch it over to the fresh horse. To the child standing beside him he said in a consoling tone, "Don't you worry, I won't let him get you. You'll be safe so along as you're with me." Tossing the saddle and blanket over onto the other horse, he quickly cinched it, then stooped down to the girl and with his hands on her shoulders said, "You believe me, don't you?"

Hilda avoided looking into his eyes, but he tipped her chin up, forcing her. She trembled slightly and said in a barely audible voice, "Yes, I do."

"That's good," he said, and he hugged her to him for a moment, then stood up and hurriedly finished preparing the fresh horse for the trail. "When we get to where we're going I'll take the lead rope off you. But if I do, you have to promise not to make a fuss or try running away. All right?"

"All right," she said quietly.

"There's some mean people where we're headed. If you stray away from me, they're apt to kill you and not think twice about it. They'll lop your head right off and stick it on a fence pole! You understand?"

"Yes," she said, and her voice sounded frightened at the terrible images his words provoked.

"Then you're going to be all right." Haddon Marr smiled to himself, lifted her up and onto the saddle.

"I'll have to tell you how it was when I was a kid. You think you've got it bad? This ain't nothing, nothing at all." He swung up behind her, lifting her onto his lap as he slid beneath her onto the saddle. "Grab ahold of that saddle horn and hang on. We're going to be riding fast till we reach them hills up ahead." Heeling the fresh horse forward, leading the tired horse behind him, Marr looked back in the moonlight and said to himself, "Keep coming, mister, I'll have a little something waiting for you."

It took nearly a solid hour of riding before Marr reached the rocky slope reaching up into the rugged cliffs and hill lines. He'd almost switched horses again before reaching the hills, but when he'd stopped the sound of hoofs had grown closer behind him, so he'd pushed on. Now the horse beneath him had gotten more worn than Marr would have liked. But at least he'd made it to the shelter of the hills. He looked up into the dark rock labyrinth. From up there he would take care of Riley and be on his way. In three days he would be across the border and headed deep into Mexico. Whether or not Earles and the others made it out of Sheldon alive meant nothing to him. He had the girl and himself to think about, no one else.

Marr and the girl stayed atop the horse as long as they could on the steep upward-winding trail. When the trail grew too difficult, he stepped down, helped the girl down and pressed on afoot, leading her by her rope in one hand, the horses' reins in his other, until they reached a rugged cliff overhang that loomed in the darkness above one side of the trail. "There's where we'll stop and rest," he said, giving an extra little tug on her rope.

They circled around and up to the flat crest of the cliff. Marr tied the horses to a dry stand of juniper and led the girl over close to the edge where he could look down and see the thin trail in the moonlight forty feet below. Lying down on the flat stone surface he drew his pistol and laid it on his chest. He gave a tug on the lead rope and said in a whisper to the girl, "Sit down here, beside me."

She hesitated, but only for a second. When he gave another, harder tug on the rope, she sat straight down, mechanically, facing away from him.

He laughed quietly, then said, still in a whisper, "You are one funny-*looking,* funny-*acting* child. I don't know what I ought to do with you." He looked her up and down, then took her by her slender arm and gave her a turn until she faced toward him, the single strand of hair hanging down the side of her closely cropped head. "What's your name anyway?"

She sat in silence.

"Come on now, you can talk some," he said in his whisper. "I'm not going to hurt you. You ought to know that by now."

"Hilda," she said, barely above a whisper.

"Hilda, eh?" Marr nodded. "Well then, Hilda, where did you come from, you and your folks?"

Hesitantly, she replied in a shallow tone, "My mama and I came from that way." She pointed absently.

Haddon Marr chuckled to himself and raised up onto one elbow, his pistol hanging loose in his hand. "Just you and your ma traveling alone? That was foolish."

"We go meet my new papa. He waits for us," Hilda replied.

"I see," said Marr, "your *new* daddy. What about your old daddy?" He offered a slight smile.

"My papa is dead," she whispered, turning her eyes away from him.

"And your ma was about to take herself another man," he said bluntly, still in a whisper, looking at her dirty face in the moonlight. He seemed to think about something for a moment, then he said, "Damn, girl, this place will eat you alive. Didn't your ma know that? Didn't you know it?"

She only stared without answering.

"How old are you anyway?" he asked, first taking a glance down along the trail.

"I am twelve," Hilda said.

"Twelve years old . . . ain't that something," he said. As he spoke he raised up into a crouch, his face close to hers. He took another quick glance at the trail below, then said, "If I take this rope off, are you going to give me any trouble?"

"No," Hilda said.

"Because you know if it wasn't for me, them men would have had their way with you and killed you dead. You know that, don't you?"

She nodded her head.

"All right then. Here, I'm taking the rope off," he said. "But you sit right there and don't move until I tell you to, all right?"

"Yes," she said quietly.

Marr coiled the short lead rope up and dropped it beside her. "You better hope I stop the man following us. If he was to get past me, there's no telling what he'd do to you. Do you understand what I mean?"

She nodded.

Marr smiled to himself. "I'll be right over there. You sit real still here."

He walked to the horses, drew his rifle from his saddle boot and walked across the cliff overhang, crouching as he neared the edge. He lay down on the hard stone surface, took up a steady prone shooting position and raised the rifle butt to his shoulder, taking a practice aim at a scrub cedar alongside the trail. "All right, Ambush," he whispered to himself, "I'm ready when you are."

A few minutes passed before he heard the click of hoofs on the stone trail. In the moonlit darkness he lay poised, his rifle aiming down, waiting for his target to ride into view. He cocked the hammer back on the rifle and breathed evenly. At first sight of the horse he started to fire, but then he realized that there was only the horse. The saddle was empty. He cut a quick glance back and forth, searching the rocks and scrub brush alongside trail, raising slightly as he did so. Suddenly he saw the figure stand up in the darkness behind a rock. He swung his rifle to fire, but before he could get a shot off, he saw the blue streak of fire from the pistol barrel below.

Marr jerked back away from the edge of the cliff, but not quick enough to keep three rapidly fired shots from kicking slivers of stone up into his face, one bullet grazing the side of his forehead, lifting his hat from his head.

"*Ayiieee!* Damn it!" Marr shouted, snapping a quick shot down at the muzzle flashes, then dropping flat to take cover. Blood ran down his face. He wiped it from his eyes. His left eye felt gritty and wrong as he opened and closed it. Blinking, rubbing his hand back and forth, he realized that a chip of stone had nicked his good eye, narrowing his already impaired vision through a watery veil. "To hell with it," he told himself, blinking and levering a round into the rifle. He called out to the trail below, "Come on out, Ambush! I knew you was going to be trouble the first time I laid eyes on you!"

From alongside the trail, Riley shouted up to him,

"All I want is the girl, Marr! Send her down and ride away!"

"Not until I leave you laying dead, Ambush!" Marr bellowed, still wiping blood from his good eye, trying to focus toward the direction of Riley's voice. "I *know* what you'll do if you get your hands on her! I won't stand for it! You're no different than the rest of them!" He fired wildly, the bullet not even coming close to where Riley hunkered down behind the rock.

Ted Riley thought about Haddon Marr's words for a moment, trying to understand why he had said such a thing. Finally he called, "Is that what you're telling that little girl, Marr? That she can't trust anybody but you? That everybody else is out to harm her?"

"I'm telling her the *truth*!" Marr shouted. "And she knows it!" He sent another shot down, the bullet ricocheting off the large rock protecting Ted Riley.

"Marr, you dirty no-good bastard!" shouted Riley. "The only person out to harm her is you! Send her down here. Let me take her back to her family! Do something decent for once in your rotten life. Don't hurt that child!"

Marr's reply was another explosion of fire, the bullet whining across the top of the rock and thumping into a scrub juniper.

"Listen to me, little girl!" Riley yelled. *"That* man is the only person you have to fear. He's been lying to you, deceiving you!"

"Shut up, Ambush!" Marr shouted like a wild man. Two more rifle shots exploded, one going wide, but one hitting the rock. "I *know* what men do! I'll protect her from all of you!"

"Marr, listen to yourself," said Riley. "Either you're lying to her to keep her under your control, or else you're so afraid of what you might do, that you're seeing the rest of the world to be as low-down and crazy as you are! If there's any decency in you, send that child down here!"

Marr started to shout something then pull the trigger. But before he could respond in either manner, Hilda ran over beside him and screamed down at Riley, "Go away! Leave me alone!"

Riley stood stunned behind the rock, unable to believe what he'd heard.

Marr raised into a crouch and hurried back from the edge, grabbing Hilda by her forearm and pulling her with him. He stared at her with his good eye, his wounded eye watery and blurred. Blood ran down his face. But he paid no attention to his condition. He too had been stunned by Hilda's words. With his hand on her forearm, he felt her tremble uncontrollably. She sobbed loudly, nearly hysterical. "Shhh! No, don't cry, Hilda! Don't be afraid!" said Marr, holding her to him tightly. "I promised I won't let anybody hurt you, and I meant it!" He stood up, holding her, and staggered in place, his vision blurred. "Guide me to the horses!" he said. "I'll get us out of here! I swear I will!"

"But you can't see anything!" Hilda said in a trembling voice. "Your eyes are bleeding!"

"Hush crying, child," said Marr, his voice sounding almost consoling, "and do like I told you! I won't let you down."

Alongside the trail below, Ted Riley waited a few minutes wondering what to think of the girl crying out that way. When he realized that Haddon Marr seemed to have stopped firing, he ventured from behind the rock and hurried to where the big paint horse stood a few yards away from the firing, as if waiting for him. "Somebody trained you good, big fellow," he whispered to the horse, slipping up into the saddle and nudging the horse along, following the two horses' hoofprints to the path leading upward. A few yards up the path he started getting a hunch that Marr and the girl had ridden on. But he couldn't afford to get foolish and take a chance on running right into the man's gun sights.

Near the top, where the path began to wind around the cliff overhang, he stepped down from his saddle and led his horse the rest of the way, keeping the Remington cocked and ready. At the crest of the flat stone overhang, he let the pistol slump in his hand as he looked down at the hoofprints leading away across a flat stretch of land. Then his eyes lifted from the ground and he stared out in the moonlight through a drifting rise of dust. On the other side of the hills he knew there lay a scattering of small settlements and a handful of one-hand ranches, and some goatherds. Beyond that lay the border and an endless land where a man like Haddon Marr could keep the girl and himself from ever being seen again.

Riley shoved the Remington into the holster and took stock of himself. He had two pistols and a belt nearly full of bullets, a good horse and an empty canteen hanging from the saddle horn. Somewhere along the trail he'd have to find water. He would have to take on food and grain for the horse if he planned on sticking to Marr's trail. But for now he'd have to make do with what he had. Stepping up into the saddle, he gave the horse a nudge with his boot heels. "Let's go, big fellow," he said.

On the main street of Sheldon, Sheriff Fitch, George Brunder, Nelson Embry and Denver Heath had taken up the same position behind the freight crates. As a thin silver wreath of sunlight mantled the horizon, the four men stood watching as Leonard Peck pulled the loaded wagon up in the middle of the street out front of the Lucky Jackrabbit Saloon. "Easy, Leonard," Fitch whispered, knowing full well that the deputy couldn't hear him. Fitch kept his shotgun aimed and cocked, not knowing what to expect from the scalp hunters.

Leonard Peck had been sitting stooped low in the driver's seat, a pistol in his hand. Now that he'd stopped the wagon and wound the reins around the brake handle, he slipped quickly down and hurried across the street in a crouch. "Good work, Deputy," said Sheriff Fitch, handing him the other shotgun as Leonard ducked in beside him.

Holstering his pistol now that he had the shotgun, Leonard said, "I took all the flour, coffee, and airtights of beans left at the mercantile."

"What about ammunition?" asked Fitch, looking out at the wagon and the string of horses tied to the tailgate.

"Yep, bad as I hated to, I gave them everything they asked for, guns, bullets and supplies," said Leonard. "Most of those horses are the ones you cut loose last night out back of the saloon. But the fact is this'll leave us with only a couple of horses in town, neither one of them fit for hard riding."

"Just the way Earles likes it." Sheriff Fitch winced. "What about money?"

"The most money I could come up with is the seventeen dollars we've kept on hand for emergencies," said Leonard. "It's in a tobacco bag under the wagon seat."

"Well, this is an emergency if ever I've seen one," said Fitch. He said over his shoulder to Denver Heath,

"Looks like you'll have to wait to get paid for the wagon horses."

"Aw, to hell with it," said Denver, brushing it off. "Just consider them stolen like all the others, I reckon."

"Seventeen dollars doesn't sound like a lot of money," said Leonard. "Think it's enough to get Doc Turner and the bartender out of there alive?"

"Let's just *pray* it is," said Fitch. He stepped to the edge of the freight crates and called out to the saloon, "Mister Earles! There's the wagon and the things you asked for! It's nearly daylight. . . . Turn those men loose!"

Earles shouted, "What about money, Sheriff? How much money did you scrape up out of the busted mud hole?"

"See?" Leonard whispered. "Seventeen ain't going to get them freed."

"They're both dead, sure enough," George Brunder whispered.

"Quiet back there!" Fitch warned Brunder. Then he called out to the saloon, "Mister Earles, the money is in a tobacco bag under the seat. It ain't a lot, but you see the shape this town is in."

Earles called out, "We're bringing out whiskey, Sheriff. Now that Landers is dead, I don't reckon anybody will object, do you?"

"No," said Fitch, sounding defeated, "I reckon not. Take what you want; let's just get on with this."

In the Lucky Jackrabbit, Jessup Earles turned to the others with a grin, then to Doctor Turner. "Hear that, sawbones? The sheriff is jumping out of his johns to see to it you don't get harmed." He turned his grin to Doyle, the bartender. "If it wasn't for the good doctor here, I bet the sheriff wouldn't lift a finger to get you off the spot. Hell, everybody knows that a soft-handed *doctor* is worth more than a *bartender* any day of the week! Ain't that the way it's looked at?"

The bartender didn't dare say a word, but the expression on his face told Doctor Turner that he knew what Earles said was true. Earles looked back and forth between the two hostages and laughed smugly. "Looks like I sure struck the right vein that time, didn't I?"

Without responding to Earles, Doctor Turner stepped over to the billiard table and leaned in for a closer look at the blood-spotted bandages wrapped around most of Uncle Andy's torso. "If we've got time, we need to change these dressings again before you leave."

Uncle Andy gave the old doctor a shove. "Get away from me. I'm feeling spry as a summer goose! I don't need you no more!"

"If you get infection in those wounds, you'll think *summer goose,*" said Doctor Turner. "You'll be begging your friends here to put a bullet in your head!"

"Like this you mean?" said Uncle Andy, his hand coming up from his lap, cocking a Colt, pointing the tip of the barrel beneath the old doctor's double chin. *"Bang!"* he said loudly. Then he lowered the gun, chuckling in the doctor's face. Doctor Turner only stared flatly at him.

Laughing, Jessup Earles said, "All right, everybody grab up some whiskey. Let's get out of here."

Uncle Andy Fill stepped stiffly down off the billiard table and grabbed the back of a chair, using it as a walking cane. Cinco Diablos and Morton Toller quickly hopped over the bar and shoved bottle after bottle of whiskey down into their clothes, anywhere they could stick them. "Careful, men," said Earles, watching them with his strange grin. "You might want to be able to move around enough to fire a gun if we have to."

Cross-eyed Burton Stowl in his haste grabbed a bottle of horse liniment tonic sitting beneath the bar. But Cinco saw his error and stopped him from shoving it down into his waist. "Stowl, if you drink this it will kill you!" he said.

"Oh . . ." Stowl only slowed down for a second, then continued grabbing bottles of whiskey.

Earles stepped over behind the doctor and wrapped an arm around his neck. He placed his cocked Colt to the doctor's head, then shouted to the street, "Sheriff, we're coming out! Don't do nothing stupid or I'll be wearing your doctor all over the front of my shirt!"

"All right, Mister Earles," Fitch replied, "come on out. Nobody is going to try to stop you."

"Cinco, get the bartender," said Earles. He gave the doctor a nudge forward, the two moving as one to the large doors. "Toller, unlock the doors. Stowl, Uncle Andy, get over here. Let's keep in a tight circle going to the wagon."

On the street, Sheriff Fitch said quietly over his shoulder as he saw the big doors open slowly, "All right, here they come. Everybody stay calm. Don't get these hostages killed."

Burton Stowl stepped out first, warily, his Colt fanning back and forth as he searched the empty street in the grainy dawn light. Pressing behind him came Doctor Turner, held tight against Jessup Earles' chest. Then came Cinco Diablos with the bartender in the same position as the doctor, followed by Toller assisting Uncle Andy Fill.

"I hate being stuck helpless like this," Leonard whispered to Fitch.

"Easy, Deputy," Fitch whispered in reply, studying the scalp hunters, and realizing that two were missing. One had stolen his paint horse and already left town; he had no idea about the other one, the man who had carried the child on his lap.

At the wagon Earles began to give the doctor a shove upward toward the seat. Fitch called out, "All right, Mister Earles, let the hostages go. We did everything you asked of us."

"You wait here an *hour,* Sheriff. I'll let them go down the trail a ways," said Earles. He grinned, shoving the doctor upward with one hand, keeping the pistol pointed at his back with the other. "You surely didn't think I was stupid enough to turn them loose right here, did you?"

Sheriff Fitch didn't answer. He stood with Leonard and the three townsmen, watching helplessly as the scalp hunters loaded the two hostages onto the wagon. Aboard the wagon, Earles sat beside the doctor and waited while Toller and Stowl ran back inside and brought out the horses.

Once mounted and ready to ride, Earles put the reins in Doctor Turner's hands, "You get to drive the wagon, Doctor," he said.

Sheriff Fitch and his deputy stood in front of the townsmen and watched the strange-looking procession move away along the dirt street, the wagon rolling forward in the midst of the riders, followed by the large string of horses.

Fitch said to Leonard Peck, "Do you suppose those two horses we've got left will hold out long enough for us to ride out and get the hostages?"

"They might do that much," said Leonard, "but that's about the whole of it."

Sheriff Fitch shook his head in disgust. "Times like

this I feel like sailing this tin badge as far as I can and forget I ever pinned it on."

"You ain't quitting are you, Sheriff?" George Brunder asked, looking alarmed.

"No, I ain't quitting," said Fitch. "I reckon I ain't got enough sense to quit this kind of work, or I would have long ago!"

# Chapter 12

———

Ten miles from Sheldon on an upward-winding trail, Jessup Earles reached over, took the reins from Doctor Turner's hands and brought the wagon to a halt. Looking down along the side of the trail at a drop of forty feet into rock, scrub brush and cactus, Doctor Turner commented, "This is probably the worst trail you could have chosen for horse or wagon."

"No fooling?" said Jessup Earles, the two of them stepping down onto the rough, rutted trail. "Lucky for us you came along to tell us how to travel," he said with a sarcastic grin.

Morton Toller pulled his horse in close and spoke down to the doctor, "We like riding the rough trail. It keeps us ahead of the rest of the world." He had his Colt in his hand and he pointed it down at the doctor, closing one eye as if taking close aim. "You should be more worried about where *you're* going than where we are."

The others laughed grimly.

Doctor Turner stood silent, a sinking feeling coming to his stomach. He watched Herbert Doyle and Cinco Diablos step down from the wagon bed at the same time, Cinco with his gun in Doyle's ribs. Cinco shoved Doyle over close to the edge of the trail and turned him facing out into the morning air. "You get over there too, Sawbones," said Jessup Earles.

"You're going to kill us, aren't you?" Doctor Turner said flatly, without following Earles' order. "Even after giving your word that you would set us free."

Earles and the men chuckled. "Now what could have given you that idea?" said Earles.

Morton Toller said to Turner, "You people ought to know better than take the word of a bunch of low-down murdering scalp hunters! What the hell is wrong with you anyway?"

Again the dark laughter.

At the rear of the wagon Crossed-eyed Burton Stowl had unhitched Earles' horse and walked it forward. But not seeing clearly, he almost walked right past Earles.

"Damn it, Stowl!" said Earles, stepping a few feet over, stopping him and taking the horse's reins. "Why don't you get yourself another eye patch so you can quit seeing double?" He jerked the horse away from him. Irritated now, Earles looked back at Doctor Turner, saying, "Get your fat ass over there where I told you!"

"So you can kill us both at once?" said Doctor Turner, defiantly shaking his head. "I don't think so." As he spoke he caught Doyle's eye. Shaking violently, Doyle still managed to see that the doctor was trying to tell him something with his eyes.

"Well, hell then," Earles said to the doctor, drawing his pistol, "it makes me no never-mind. I can kill you where you're standing."

"God have mercy on me!" Doctor Turner shouted quickly as his hand streaked inside his coat and jerked out a two-shot derringer. Catching everybody by surprise, he fired both shots at Earles. One of the bullets hit Earles, drawing everybody's attention for a second. "Run, Doyle! *Run!*" the doctor turned and shouted.

Earles fired his Colt instinctively, his shot nailing the doctor in the center of his chest, knocking him backward, leaving him lying beside the wagon.

"That sneaking son of a bitch shot me!" shouted Earles in surprise. He pressed his hand to his upper chest beneath his collarbone, where he felt the hole in his buckskin shirt. "Shot me with a damn hideaway!" He brought his hand away from his shirt covered with blood. "I'll be damned!"

"Where the hell did he get a gun?" Cinco Diablos asked, stepping forward toward where Uncle Andy Fill had climbed stiffly down from the wagon. Cinco shoved his hand down into Uncle Andy's boot.

"Get away from me, Cinco, damn you!" shouted Uncle Andy, jerking his boot away from him.

"Just like I thought!" said Cinco. "Uncle Andy's derringer is gone!" He glowered at Uncle Andy.

"This is Uncle Andy's all right," said Morton Toller, who had stepped down from his horse and snatched the derringer up from the ground, smoke still curling from the short barrel. He held the small pistol up for everybody to see.

"Damn it all, Uncle Andy," said Earles, stepping closer, his Colt still in his hand, half pointed at Uncle Andy's chest, "you, of all people, letting a soft-handed doctor take your hideaway pistol?" Earles asked, as if in disbelief.

"Well, hell yes, of course I *let* him take my gun!" said Andy, his eyes full of fear, anger and humiliation. "How *else* could I make sure he shot you with it?" He turned to Cinco Diablos. "And you! Don't you ever stick your hand down into my boot, or anything of mine!" He trembled in his rage.

"Where's the bartender?" Toller asked, looking all around.

"There they are!" shouted Cross-eyed Burton Stowl pointing at a short cedar on the other side of the trail.

"Damn it, Stowl! There's only *one* bartender!" shouted Earles, blood seeping down the front of his buckskin shirt.

"The fool is pointing at a *tree*!" said Cinco. The men rushed to the edge of the trail and looked down, except for Uncle Andy, who stood steadying himself with one hand on the wagon.

Loose dirt and rock still trickled down the side of the drop-off where Doyle had gone over the edge. Forty feet below on a narrow ledge lay one of his boots. "Well, adios, bartender," said Earles, giving a cavalier salute with his good arm. "Damn coward would rather leap to his death than face a bullet I reckon."

"He might still be alive," said Toller, spitting downward.

"Yeah," said Earles, "he might. Why don't you just climb right there on a rope and look around some, make sure he's dead, then climb back up?"

Toller spit again, staring down intently, as if considering Earles' request. After a moment of silence he said sidelong to Earles, "You're joking, right?"

"If he's alive after a fall like that, he must be blessed by the devil himself," said Cinco. He also spit down. Then he added, "To hell with him."

"*Was* you joking, Earles?" asked Toller, still concerned about climbing down on a rope.

Without answering, Earles turned away with his hand to his bleeding wound and walked back to the wagon. Looking down at the doctor, he said, "I just *killed* the one man who could have done me some good getting this little bullet out of me."

"Yeah," said Uncle Andy, "but don't forget he's the same sumbitch that put it in you in the first place."

Earles glared at him. "And I ain't forgetting whose gun he used doing it."

Uncle Andy grumbled under his breath and started to climb stiffly back up into the wagon.

But Earles stopped him, saying, "Stay down here, Andy. Get over by the edge of the trail with Stowl."

Uncle Andy froze. He looked over at Stowl, who stood with his hand on his gun. Then he gave Jessup Earles a frightened look, saying, "Now wait a damn minute, Earles, you know damn well what happened with that gun could have happened to anybody!"

Wearing his strange grin, Earles stared at him in silence for a moment. The others stood stone-faced, until finally Cinco began to laugh quietly. Then the others broke down and laughed also.

"Uncle Andy," said Earles, "I just wanted you to get out of the way so we can unhitch the wagon."

Uncle Andy looked relieved but embarrassed. "How the hell was I supposed to know that?"

The men all laughed aloud. *"Sante Madre!"* said Cinco Diablos. "He thought you were going to tell Stowl to shoot him!"

"Tell Stowl? That wouldn't be real smart," said Earles. "Stowl would be lucky if he didn't shoot himself and half the horses."

The men laughed, except for Burton Stowl. "That ain't funny," he said, giving them his off-centered stare.

"Neither is you thinking that bartender was a tree,"

said Earles. Then he said to everybody, "Let's quit wasting time. We're going to split up everything we took from town and get moving. As soon as that sheriff and his deputy get mounted they'll be on our tails like stink on a bear's ass."

"Are we splitting up?" asked Stowl.

"Jesus, Stowl!" said Earles, "ain't that what I just *said*? Yes, we're splitting up. We're all riding out in different directions." He looked around at everybody. "We're going to drive the sheriff crazy wondering which one of us to follow. One week from today we'll all meet up just across the border at Piedra Negra and see what we're going to do next. If any of you run into Haddon Marr on the trail, tell him I said to get himself straightened out on what he's going to do about that snot-nosed kid. . . . I can use some help." He grinned. "And tell him I've got his share of everything. That ought to get his attention."

In moments the team of unhitched wagon horses stepped away from the wagon tongue and joined the string of horses standing behind Cinco Diablos and Jessup Earles, who sat atop their horses awaiting the others. Morton Toller hurried over to the edge of the trail and looked down again, searching for any sign of Herbert Doyle. "I'd feel better if I saw that bartender's brain splattered all over a rock."

Pressing a faded bandanna to his wounded upper chest where the bullet lay lodged just under the skin beneath his collarbone, Earles said, "Well, that's the sad thing about life, Toller, you can't just see a man's brains splattered out any time it suits you." He nudged his horse forward, saying over his shoulder, "Follow in these tracks until you see the string split up. Then go your own way like I told you to."

The men nodded, then fell in behind Earles and Cinco and followed the string of horses along the winding trail.

Sheriff Fitch and Leonard Peck had to be careful not to push the weak and aged horses too hard. They kept the animals at a walk until they started up the winding trail. When they'd only gone a few yards before the horses began to wheeze and blow and struggle for breath, Fitch shook his head and the two stepped down and walked the next mile and a half before seeing the empty wagon in the middle of the trail ahead. Stopping and moving quietly off the trail behind a rock, Leonard asked Fitch, "What do you suppose happened, Sheriff? Think the wagon horses gave out on them, they had to leave the wagon sitting?"

"No, Leonard," said Fitch. "What I think is that they've tricked us. They didn't care about most of the stuff we loaded up for them. They wanted guns, money and horses, maybe some things small enough to pack in their saddlebags. But they just wanted us to think they'd be traveling with that big, slow wagon. They've more than likely split up here." As he talked he took down his canteen, uncapped it and took a sip. "I dread thinking about what we'll probably find awaiting us at the wagon."

"You mean . . . ?" Leonard's words trailed.

"Yep," said Fitch. "I've got a feeling if Doc Turner or Herbert Doyle were still alive, we would have already met them back along the trail."

Leonard considered it for a moment, then said in a resolved tone, "You're right. Those damn, lying, murdering dogs! We never should have trusted them to do what they said they would."

"We didn't trust them, Leonard," said the sheriff.

"They just had us in a position where we had no choice but to go along with them and hope they might keep their word." He capped the canteen and hung it back around his saddle horn. "An honest man is always at a disadvantage dealing with men like Earles and his bunch."

They stepped out from behind the rock and led their horses forward, walking closer to the wagon with caution. But before they'd gone ten yards they both stopped abruptly, seeing Herbert Doyle sitting against the front wheel of the wagon with Doc Turner's head in his lap. Doyle's torn shirt clung to his chest, wet with blood. "There's the answer to any question we might have had about Earles' intentions," said Fitch, the two of them looking around warily then rushing to Herbert Doyle.

Herbert Doyle looked up at the two lawmen, his face bruised and scraped from tumbling down over rock and through sharp, thorny brush. "Ole Doc got himself killed saving my life," he said to Fitch with a bemused look. He sat stroking the dead doctor's silver hair back over his head. "Why you suppose he did a thing like that, Sheriff?" he asked, seeming to be in a daze.

"I reckon that's just the kind of man he was, Doyle," Fitch said quietly. Then just as quietly he said to Leonard, "Get your canteen, and find us a clean rag."

While Leonard stepped over to the worn-out horses, Sheriff Fitch stooped down and examined Herbert Doyle carefully. "What happened to you, Doyle?" he asked, holding his torn shirt open and taking a look at Doyle's bloody belly. He saw a large bruise with a deep cut across it.

"I jumped over the edge of the trail, Sheriff," he

said dreamily. "I don't know how come I'm still alive. It just wasn't my time to go." He kept stroking the old doctor's hair. "They was getting set to kill us both and Ole Doc here come up with a little gun and shot the leader. He told me to run, knowing he was going to die." Doyle stopped for a moment, then said, "I should have stayed and tried to save him, the way he did me."

Fitch shook his head. "No, you did the right thing, Doyle. Doc wanted you to take a chance getting away, otherwise he would've figured he shot Earles for nothing. That's the way Doc would have looked at it. And that's how you've got to look at it too." He reached down and stopped Doyle from stroking the dead doctor's hair. Then he looked closely and saw the large knot on the side of Doyle's head, scrapes and cuts down the side of his neck.

"Back in the saloon, Earles said everybody knows that a doctor is more important than a bartender. I reckon if Doc Turner felt that way, I wouldn't be sitting here alive right now." He looked down at the doctor's face as if in apology.

Returning with his canteen uncapped, Leonard poured a trickle of water on a wadded-up bandanna and handed it down to Sheriff Fitch. Fitch pulled the doctor's body out of Doyle's lap and said to Leonard as he began wiping Doyle's face, "At least Doc Turner managed to shoot Earles for us before he died."

"He did?" Leonard said in surprise. "How'd he get his hands on a gun? He never carried one that I know of."

"It doesn't matter how," said Fitch, smiling down at the old doctor's face. "The main thing is he did it. Maybe Earles will draw an infection and die. That would be some satisfaction."

"Not as much as watching him swing on the end of a rope," said Leonard.

"Yeah, but once they get across the border we might just as well forget about ever seeing them hang," said Fitch, cleaning Doyle up as he spoke.

Standing behind Fitch, Leonard heard the sound of hoofs on the hard trail. "Sheriff! Listen!" he said quickly. He drew his pistol and pulled the tired horses around out of the way.

Fitch had heard the sound too. Dropping the wet bandanna on Doyle's lap, he stood up, drawing his Colt. Looking back toward the spot where they stood behind the large rock only moments ago, they caught a glimpse of a horse. Then a tense silence passed until a voice called out to them, "Hello, the wagon. We're lawmen in the pursuit of a gang of scalp hunters. We saw the horse and wagon tracks leading up here and followed them."

Sheriff Fitch and Leonard Peck breathed a little easier, but they still kept their guns in hand. Fitch called, "I'm the sheriff of Sheldon. Show yourselves with your hands raised."

Behind the rock, Tackett looked at the ranger, saying, "It's Artimus Fitch. We never met, but I saw him once at a territory trial."

The ranger nodded and lowered his rifle. "It looks like they've come upon the same bunch we're after." He turned and shoved his rifle loosely into his saddle boot as Sheriff Tackett holstered his pistol.

"Sheriff Fitch?" Tackett called out.

Fitch perked at the sound of his name. "Yes, that's me."

"This is Sheriff Boyd Tackett from Wakely," said Tackett. "I've got a ranger with me. We're coming out."

Fitch and Leonard lowered their guns further, watching Boyd Tackett and the ranger walk toward them, leading their horses, their hands held chest high.

Looking past the ranger at the big Appaloosa walking along behind him, Fitch said quietly to his deputy, "They're all right, Leonard. That's the ranger everybody's been talking about, the one who killed Junior Lake and his bunch."

"That fellow?" Leonard Peck looked the ranger up and down, then said sidelong to Fitch, "He doesn't look like much to me."

Fitch turned a gaze to Leonard. "We're all lawmen here, Deputy. Let's keep that in mind."

Leonard only nodded.

"I'm Sheriff Boyd Tackett and this is Territory Ranger Sam Burrack," said Tackett, touching his hat brim as they stopped a few feet from the two lawmen.

Touching their hat brims in response, Sheriff Fitch holstered his pistol and introduced himself and Leonard Peck. "If you're trailing a gang of scalp hunters, I'm betting it's the same bunch we've had to deal with." He gestured a nod down at Doctor Turner's body and at Herbert Doyle, sitting bloody and battered in the dirt. "This is some of their handiwork. Too bad you didn't get them before they made it to Sheldon."

"Believe me, Sheriff Fitch," said Tackett, "we would if we could have. They've kidnapped a child, murdered her mother and tore my town all to pieces."

"We saw the child," said Fitch. "But she wasn't with them when they left town. She was gone, and so was the man who kept her with him all the time. Another fellow riding with them was missing when they left town. He was more of a clean-cut fellow, didn't look at home with that bunch. But then the sonsabitch stole my paint horse from the livery barn and cut out."

Tackett and the ranger looked at each other. The ranger looked at the wagon, then said to Fitch, "We need you to tell us everything that's happened so we can get on their trail. Will you two be riding with us?"

Fitch slumped a bit. "No," he said, "we're nearly afoot after them taking all of our horses."

Leonard cut in quickly, saying, "But we would go, if we had any horses that is."

"We know you would, Deputy," said Tackett, seeing that the young man wanted them to know he wasn't trying to back away from his duty. Tackett nodded down at Doyle and Doctor Turner's body. "Even if you had good horses, you've still got these men to look after. We can't wait while you get them back to town. The ranger and I are already on these men's trail. We plan on sticking to them."

"Maybe if we found some good saddle horses we could catch up to you," Leonard offered.

Tackett, the ranger and Fitch all looked at one another. "Yes, I suppose that's something to consider," Burrack replied, knowing the deputy was only trying to remain a part of the hunt.

Fitch stepped forward and stooped down to Doyle, saying to the deputy, "First things first, Leonard. Help me get Doyle up and out of the sun."

The two lawmen carried Doyle to the shade of a rock and when Fitch returned, he took his hat off and dusted it against his leg. "Gentlemen, along with Sheldon, Leonard and I have suffered a bad loss from this bunch. You know as well as I do that we're not going to be able to catch up to you and bring them in."

"We understand that, Sheriff," said the ranger. "Now tell us everything you can about theses snakes."

While Leonard cleaned up Herbert Doyle and prepared him for the ride back to Sheldon, the ranger and Tackett talked to Fitch about the scalp hunters and everything that had happened in Sheldon. When they were through talking, Burrack and Tackett rode away, following the tracks of Earles and his men. Farther along the trail, Tackett said to the ranger, "Do you suppose that clean-cut fellow Fitch talked about could be your prisoner, Riley?"

"I've been wondering that myself," said the ranger. "I can't picture Riley riding with Earles and his bunch."

"He's on the run," said Tackett. "A man will do whatever he needs to do to keep from going to prison. I probably would myself if I was in his shoes."

"Me too," said the ranger, "but we've got no time for wondering about Riley right now. He'll show up one way or the other."

They rode on in silence until they reached a spot where the hoofprints bunched up then broke off into several directions. "This is what I've been afraid they'd do," said Tackett. "They've split up."

The ranger's eyes fixed on the gathering of hoofprints for a moment then followed each set of tracks off into the distance. "They won't be split up for long," he said. "They didn't get enough to satisfy them in Sheldon. They'll have to get back together real soon and pull another raid. It appears that Earles has taken a liking to it."

"Meanwhile, where's the girl?" said Tackett, looking back and forth across the endless land.

"They'll be meeting up somewhere everybody's familiar with. Someplace they know is safe," said the ranger. "My guess is it'll be somewhere across the border. What we've got to do is run any one of them down and find out when and where they're getting back together."

Tackett gave him a flat look. "You make that sound easy, Ranger."

"Did I?" said Burrack, nudging his big Appaloosa forward. "I sure didn't mean to."

"Which one do we pick?" Tackett asked, looking down at all the tracks to choose from.

As if having already made his selection, the ranger looked back over his shoulder and said, "There's less water in this direction. Let's pick the man who didn't know the land as well as the others."

"Makes sense to me," said Tackett, considering it. He gave his horse a nudge with his boot heels and they rode on.

# Chapter 13

Ted Riley knew better than to push the big horse any harder. He'd kept the horse at almost a run since daylight. He'd only stopped once, long enough to water the animal and cool it out for a couple of minutes at a small watering hole at the edge of a cactus-covered desert. There he had filled his canteen, wet his head and face, and pushed on. Now he drew the tired horse into the thin shade of a tall saguaro and gazed through swirling heat toward what appeared to be a place where land ended and hell began. Looking down at the fresh tracks he'd been following all morning, he stepped down from the saddle and rubbed his eyes. Beyond this arid furnace lay the border. Haddon Marr and his hostage were on their way to Mexico, provided Marr hadn't stopped long enough to first ambush him somewhere out there.

A hot blast of wind swept in off the desert floor and lifted his hat brim. Then so be it, Riley told himself, tugging his hat down tighter on his head. The only advantage Marr had out there would be the advantage of the first shot. Once Marr fired that first shot, if he missed, Riley would know his position. "That's about as fair as you can ask for, isn't it?" he said to the big, sweaty paint horse, rubbing its wet muzzle. The horse blew out a breath and lifted its head into the hot wind.

Moments later Riley stepped up into the saddle and heeled the horse forward. He rode for an hour, then stopped for ten minutes, then rode on again. The next time he stopped the sun was at its peak and the heat had caused him to reel slightly in his saddle before concentrating hard and turning the horse with deliberation to the shelter of a low rise of sand mantled by a line of barrel cactus along it stony crest. In the thin shade he poured a trickle of water on his head and into his dry mouth. He wet the horse's muzzle, cupped a puddle of tepid water in his hand and raised it to the horse's lips. "We ought to stay here till evening," he said to the tired horse. "But we can't stop that long. Just long enough to shake the fire out of our heads."

This time when he continued on he led the horse, resting it as much as he could in the hottest part of the day, leading it from the shade of one cactus or stand of brush to the next. As the heat began to lessen in the late afternoon, he had reached a stretch of land where stone protruded from the sand more and more until walking alongside a rise of sand soon grew into walking alongside a broken wall of rock. Soon that wall of rock towered above him, offering dark, cool shade that he no longer needed. Feeling the heat loosen its grip on him and the horse, Riley stepped up into the saddle and let the horse's senses take him to a small water hole farther along at the base of the rock wall.

While the horse drew water, Riley looked closely at the hoofprints in the soft ground at the edge of the water hole. An hour and a half at the most, he told

himself, stooping down and touching his fingertips to
the soft, wet ground. Realizing he had to push on
through the night to put this stretch of land behind
him before the sun came up boiling again, he slumped
on his haunches with his eyes closed and the reins in
his hand until the horse drank its fill and he felt it
straighten up and shake out its mane. Then Riley
stood up wearily and looked all around at the sunken
valley of rock and sand. He hadn't eaten since the day
before, but with no prospect of food in sight, he put
aside any thought of it and stepped back up into the
saddle. Food wasn't important, he told himself. Not
yet anyway. He had water, and that was the main
thing for now.

He traveled into the chilled desert night wishing for
just a few degrees of the heat that had tortured him
throughout the day. Most of the desert basin now lay
behind him. In the night he noted that the hoofprints
he followed had turned sharply toward a line of rocks
less than fifty yards to his right. No sooner than he
had turned the paint horse and continued to follow
the prints than a shot exploded in the night. He felt
it zip past his head, and instinctively he dropped from
the saddle and hurried along in a crouch, still following the hoofprints.

Another shot rang out. Riley saw the fiery blossom
of muzzle flash in a low shelf of rock less than a hundred yards away. He heard the bullet slice through
the air above the saddle, realizing that had he stayed
mounted, this shot would have caught him dead center. He looked all around for cover for himself and
the horse. Seeing none, he hurried along in a zigzag
across sand mixed with rock and heard another shot
resound, this one not as well placed as the one before.

As soon as the shot exploded, he jumped back up atop the horse and gave it his boot heels, sending it forward in a run toward the dark line of rock. He veered the paint horse back and forth. Knowing that Marr was aiming at a shadow in moonlight, Riley kept that shadow moving illusively until the darker shadow of the line of rocky hills engulfed him and the horse.

Another shot exploded as Riley stopped his horse and dropped from the saddle behind a broken boulder embedded in the hillside. He breathed a sigh of relief, hearing the shot ricochet off another rock a long ways off. Good! Marr had lost the shadow. He had missed that first shot that Riley knew was so important. "Now we're back to even," Riley whispered to himself. He drew the Remington and began leading the horse forward quietly across the sloping ground littered with broken stone.

Less than seventy yards away, Haddon Marr lowered his rifle an inch from his shoulder and searched the darkness for his lost target, his bandanna-covered eye greatly impeding his search. He rubbed his good eye and cursed in a whisper. Then he turned to the child, who huddled against a rock with her hands pressed to her ears. He started to speak, but then realized she couldn't hear him. Keeping his patience in check, he pulled her hand from her right ear and whispered, "I want you to yell out to him, tell him not to shoot this way. Tell him he might hit you if he does." Marr smiled to himself.

"Mister," shouted Hilda along the dark, sloping hillside. "Go away, do not shoot! You will kill me!"

Riley whispered under his breath, "Marr, you dirty bastard." But he realized that what the girl said was true. He couldn't take a chance on even shooting toward the direction of her voice. It struck him that was exactly the point Marr wanted to make having her call out instead of calling out himself.

"Did you hear me, mister?" Hilda called out.

Riley stared angrily in the direction of the girl's voice, knowing Marr had instructed her to say it. But he wasn't about to answer her. That would tell Marr his exact position and give him the powerful advantage of being able to shoot at him without Riley being able to return fire.

"Do you hear me, mister?" Hilda called out.

Riley gritted his teeth, but still didn't reply.

In a moment Haddon Marr let out a long, taunting laugh. Then silence closed around the cold hillside. Riley anticipated Marr's next move. It stood to reason, he thought, that Marr was at that moment quietly moving up the hillside to claim higher ground and be ready for him come daylight. If that wasn't Marr's plan it should be, Riley said to himself. It was certainly what *he* intended to do. He quietly raised the horse's reins and gave a gentle pull forward, getting the horse to walk along behind him up the long, sloping hillside.

Inch by inch, it seemed, Riley kept the horse silent and measured each of his own steps, careful to not make the slightest sound. He had no idea how long it took to reach the summit of the hill, but he knew he'd gotten there when he saw the starry sky stretch before him instead of the dark images of rock and dried brush.

When he'd found a safe place for himself and the paint horse in a shelter of surrounding rocks atop the hillside, Riley lay quietly and realized it had taken him half the night to work his way up the rocky slope without making a sound loud enough to draw gunfire. The cover of night had kept each man waiting for the other to make the next move. Now the darkness was slowing fading behind them. Riley gazed steadily through the grainy dawn light in the direction he felt Haddon Marr and the girl had taken. Yet, before the first rays of sunlight broke above the horizon, he heard the slightest nicker of a horse a few yards away, in the opposite direction. He turned around quickly and listened for any further sound.

"Damn it!" he whispered to himself.

In spite of his vigilance, somehow it appeared that Marr had circled around him. Even as he considered how Marr had done it, he heard the sound of hoofs begin to move quickly along the crest of the hill. He jumped up from the ground and hurriedly threw himself into the saddle, not about to let Marr make his getaway. But before he could even heel the horse forward, it dawned on him that he'd just made a terrible mistake. He felt the bullet hit his back and drive him forward from his saddle. At the same second he heard the exploding shot shatter the silence. Yet, he hit the ground fully conscious, wondering as he squirmed and struggled across the rocky earth on his belly how Haddon Marr had managed to slip one of the horses past him in the night. He managed to draw the big Remington and get it cocked. He felt foolish and ashamed at having been so easily tricked.

Riley made it halfway behind a rock, but then he stopped and lay as still as stone when he heard the sound of one horse stepping quietly toward him in the grainy morning light. The impact of the bullet had knocked him numb in his back. But he had managed to move his legs. His upper body was working; his lower body was working. Only the middle of him had ceased to function, as if that section of torso between his chest and his hips had fallen asleep suddenly. He wanted to reach his hand around and examine the wound with his fingertips. But he dare not try it now, not with Haddon Marr's horse stepping closer with each slow, soft click of its hoofs.

"Well, well," Marr said softly. "That wasn't a bad shot for a man down to one good eye." Bringing his horse to a stop less than fifteen feet away, he said, "It appears that Ambush just lost this little game of fox and hound."

Lying with his face down in the rough, cold dirt, Riley could not tell if Marr was talking to the girl or to himself. He heard no reply. He strained to hear the slightest sound of the child, to know whether or not she was sitting perched on Marr's lap the way she had been most times Riley had seen her. But there came no such sound, and it left Riley with a hard choice. Should he turn his upper body quickly enough and get the Remington pointed at Marr in time to catch him by surprise? Not with the girl in his lap, Riley told himself—he couldn't risk it. He lay tensed, waiting, the Remington cocked and ready. Could he even pull this off if the girl wasn't there? He had no idea. But if he didn't, he knew he was dead.

"Can you hear me, Ambush?" Marr asked. "I know you was alive when you hit the ground, I can see where you've dragged yourself, you poor wretch." A second passed, then he said with a soft, cruel chuckle in his voice, "Say, that's some wound you've got there."

Riley waited, listened, his senses like a coiled rattle-snake, ready to strike.

"What I'm going to do now is what you might call a mercy killing," said Marr.

Riley heard a gun hammer cock. Was the girl there? He couldn't tell, he couldn't guess. He tried to picture her there, the way she usually rode, slightly on Marr's left side. Is that what he would see when he made his move? Riley asked himself. He hoped so. God, he hoped so.

"You never should have come after me, Ambush," said Marr. "You saw this girl and wanted her for yourself. I know it. I saw it the first time I laid eyes on you. But you didn't get her. Nobody is going to get her. . . . Nobody is taking her away from me. I reckon you know that now. So long, Ambush."

Riley put everything he had into the move, all his strength, all his reflexes, every muscle and nerve in his body that would and *could* respond to his will. He flipped over quickly, seeing the child right there where he'd always seen her, on Marr's left side, Marr holding his reins in his left hand, the pointed pistol in his right. Even hesitating long enough to see if the child was there had cost Riley a precious split second. But he was all right. He saw the surprise on Haddon Marr's face. But he also saw Marr recover from it fast as he started to squeeze the trigger.

Making the quick move, Riley felt the pain in his wound come alive like the stab of a white-hot knife blade. He almost yelled out in pain as he pulled the trigger and watched Haddon Marr fly backwards off the horse and land on the rocky ground.

The girl fell with him and rolled away like a rag doll. Riley collapsed onto his back and stared upward at the dawn-streaked sky, hoping that his shot had done its job. The pain in his back had tightened around him like a steel corset. That one shot was all he had, he thought to himself, feeling a heavy darkness close in around him and pull him down.

Fifteen feet away, Hilda pulled herself to her feet against a rock and looked around, blinking in an at-

tempt to clear the blurriness from her mind. A large
knot had sprang up on her forehead. She touched it
carefully, feeling her head throb, and started to walk
toward Haddon Marr's horse standing a few yards
away. Then she heard Marr's broken-sounding voice
call out to her weakly from where he lay sprawled out
on the ground. "Hilda . . . help me," he rasped.

She only hesitated and stared at Marr for a moment,
then she started to walk on toward the horse.
"Hilda . . . come help me . . . else I'll die . . . ," he said.

She held her hands over her ears as if to block out
his voice. But then she took them down and shook
her head. Marr raised his head enough to see the tur-
moil going on in her mind. He said, "Hilda, you can't
leave me this way. . . . I never left *you*."

She had started once again to walk to the horse,
but once again she stopped. This time she turned and
stared at him. She looked over at Ted Riley lying in
the dirt, blood puddling beneath him. "Hilda, child . . .
I will die," Marr said. "If you . . . leave me, you just
as well . . . put a bullet in me . . ." He collapsed, his
efforts exhausting him. Blood covered his chest.

Tears ran down her dirty cheeks as Hilda walked
over and picked Marr's gun up off the ground. Using
all of his strength Marr managed to raise his head
again and look at her. "That's a good child. . . . Now
the horse."

Hilda walked as if in a trance to where the horse
stood with its reins dangling to the ground. In a moment Marr looked up and saw her standing over him
holding the reins and his big Colt pistol with both
hands. He saw the gun pointed at him and wasn't sure
how to interpret the strange look in her eyes. "Don't
think about it, child," he wheezed. "You can't . . . kill
me . . . it ain't right."

She only stared blankly at him, as if not hearing his words, but rather fashioning a dark, violent scene in her mind.

Marr stared harder at her. "Look at you. What will become of you . . . with me dead?"

He saw that his words had gotten through to her. She had stopped long enough to consider his question. He acted quickly, nodding toward Ted Riley, saying, "Go over there . . . and shoot him."

She didn't move.

"Hear me, child?" said Marr. "Him . . . that's the one . . . to shoot. Look what he done to me."

Hilda made a low, painful sound under her breath. "Please," she said, tears spilling from her eyes, streaking the dirt on her face.

"He has to die. One of us has to make sure he's dead." He began to try to struggle to his feet. But then he relaxed and almost smiled as he watched Hilda drop the horse's reins and back away from him. He watched her turn mechanically and walk toward Ted Riley with the big gun held out in front of her. "That's the way, child," Marr rasped. He lay staring up at the dawn-streaked sky, feeling warm blood run down his sides from the bullet hole high up in his chest. Moments passed. His smile began to leave his lips. Then the loud roar of the Colt split the morning silence. He relaxed even more. His thin smile returned. "There's a good child," he whispered, as he saw Hilda walk back and stand over him, her eyes filled with tears, smoke curling up from the lowered gun barrel. "Put my hand . . . in the stirrup, child," he said in a weak, faltering voice. "Help me pull up . . . into the saddle."

Hilda struggled and pushed upward against him until he managed to fall over into the saddle. He collapsed forward on the horse's neck and motioned with his arm dangling down the horse's side. "The reins . . ." he said, completely spent and feeling himself slip into unconsciousness.

She picked up the reins but held onto them, seeing that Marr had passed out. Leading the horse past the spot where Ted Riley lay on the ground, she only gave him a passing glance, then pulled her eyes away from all the blood surrounding him in the dirt. Blood seemed to be coming at her from every direction. There was no escaping it. She cringed and led the horse away toward a trail that winded along the top of the hill.

Had she looked closer at Ted Riley in passing, she would have seen his eyes open for just a second and try to focus on her. Then, as if realizing how helpless he was lying there alone, he closed his eyes and let a silent darkness engulf him. When he opened his eyes again the mid-morning sunlight stabbed him. He squinted against the sun's glare and rolled over onto his side, feeling a deep, harsh pain in his lower back. His shirt stuck to him in a wet, clammy paste of blood. It took a second for his memory to come back to him, but when it did he moved very carefully, realizing he had a bullet in him. He tried to sort things out in his mind and get them into their proper order. He remembered Marr shooting him . . . he remembered shooting Haddon Marr. Where was his body . . . ?

He looked all around on the ground as he asked himself. He knew his shot had hit Marr and knocked him from his saddle. But the shot hadn't killed him. And yet if Haddon Marr was still alive, there was no doubt in Riley's mind that the man would have killed him before he left. He shook his head slowly, as if to clear it. Then he ventured up, using the rock beside him to steady himself and keep as much pressure off his wound as he could. On his feet, but unsteadily, he struggled to remember everything. After he'd shot Marr he remembered trying to keep from losing consciousness. But it hadn't worked: He'd passed out anyway. He was certain he hadn't harmed the girl. Knowing that gave him a certain amount of relief. Leaning against the rock, he put a hand behind him and felt around carefully, locating the bullet hole not by actually touching it, but by knowing it lay beneath the thick layer of congealed blood mixed with dirt. The dirt and blood had formed a muddy poultice pressed into place by his shirt. It would have to do until he found help.

Riley caught sight of the hoofprints on the ground leading south. Spots of blood had dried in the dirt where the girl had helped Marr up into the saddle. Twenty yards away the big paint horse stood grazing in a sparse patch of wild grass. Riley's eyes went back the hoofprints, seeing the girl's small shoe prints beside them. Marr had her leading his horse for him, Riley surmised. "You're in no better shape than I am, scalp hunter," he whispered to himself. "I'd just as well play this thing on out."

# Chapter 14

Morton Toller arrived on foot, staggering like a drunkard into the settlement of Noches Frescas. His horse followed thirty feet behind him, its head low, its reins dragging in the dirt. "Can I get some gawdamned water?" Toller shouted in a parched voice thickened by trail dust. He looked back and forth blearily as he meandered along a wide dirt street toward a part adobe, part rough-board shack where a young woman stood in the doorway holding a clay pitcher in her hands, staring at him. "Lord God, woman, I hope you're real," Toller said to himself through cracked lips. On either side of the dirt street he saw faces watching him from doors of a few crumbling adobes, plank shacks and tents. A skinny dog charged out barking and nipped at his boot.

"Is that the best you've got?" Toller growled, giving a loose kick at the dog. He missed the dog but his action sent it away yelping. When he looked back toward the doorway the woman holding the clay pitcher was gone. Toller stopped and staggered in a full circle, his right hand resting on his holstered pistol. "I ain't asking again!" he shouted hoarsely.

"Mister, there's your water . . . at the town well," said a stooped man leaning on a walking cane. He pointed a long, knobby finger toward a two-foot-high stone wall at the far end of the street. Beside the well stood two laborers who had stopped work to look his way. One of the men held a large stone to his chest, having carried it from a pile of stones to add to the wall surrounding the well.

"By God now!" said Toller, sounding out of his head from the heat, thirst and exhaustion. "Looks like you could put up a sign or *something*, to tell somebody!"

"I just told you," said the man with the cane.

Toller gave the man a hard stare. His hand almost pulled up the pistol from his holster. But his thirst was more important. He reeled and turned and staggered forward grumbling under his breath. Nearing the well, instead of walking straight past the laborers, he staggered sideways into the one holding the stone and shouted wildly, "Get out of my gawdamn way!" Then he lunged forward the last few feet, dropped onto his chest across the two-foot wall and plunged his face, hat and all, into the tepid water.

The two laborers stopped their work and stood to the side, the one carrying the stone dropping it and dusting his hands. "Mister, there's lot of silt stirred up right now. If you'd like to drink from—"

"I don't give a damn if it's got a *dead pig* in it!" Toller shouted, spraying water and jerking his wet hat from his head. He dipped the hat, filled it and sat it on the wall beside him for his horse. But the horse stepped in, nosed the hat out of its way and plunged its muzzle into the well.

"Mister, we don't usually allow livestock to drink from the well," said one of the workers in a timid voice.

"What are you calling me?" Toller spluttered, water running down from his hair and beard. He jerked his pistol up, cocking it.

"Nothing, mister!" said the laborer, both of them stepping back. "I was referring to the horse!"

"The *horse*? Oh," said Toller, as if having forgotten the horse was there. "Yeah, he'll be all right." He shrugged, lowered the pistol and plunged his dripping face back into the water.

"We keep a trough full of water for livestock over there," said the laborer, pointing. "And this here dipper for travelers," said the laborer. He stepped forward and held the dipper down close to Toller's face as he raised it from the water.

Toller cut a sidelong glance at the dipper as water ran freely down his face. "Listen fool," he growled, "if you don't want to leave here wearing that dipper like a donkey's tail, you best get it out of my gawdamn face!"

The man backed away quickly, hung the water dipper on a short pole beside the well, and he and the other laborer picked up their tools and walked away. Toller reached out and, after several attempts, snagged his floating hat from the well and slung it back and forth. He put the wet hat on his head, cursing the horse who stood beside him, drawing water in earnest. When Toller turned around his eyes widened at the sight of the double-barreled shotgun only inches from his face. "Whoa?" he said.

"We're just now getting this well cleared and cleaned up from so many pilgrims like yourself fouling it, mister," said the woman holding the cocked shotgun.

"Fouling it, no ma'am," said Toller, talking fast, hoping he could say something to get her to lower the shotgun, "I am a clean man of Virginia breeding! I've never fouled a well in my life."

"You know what I mean," said the woman, giving him a no-nonsense look. "First it's you, then it's a thousand others. . . . Soon the water becomes unfit for women and children."

"Ma'am," said Toller, "perhaps if the good people here would provide a public receptacle for travelers like myself—"

She reached over, snatched the dipper from its spot and pitched it over at his feet. She scowled at him, her finger still wrapped across the triggers.

"Oh . . ." said Toller, meekly. He picked up the dipper and studied it as if it were a rare find. Then he reached over and hung it back in its place.

"There's a water trough for that horse right over there," the woman said, jerking her thumb toward the water trough the laborer had told him about.

"Are you still here?" Toller shouted at the horse drawing water beside him. "Get out of here!" he half stood, giving the horse a slap on its side. The horse grumbled but didn't stop watering. Toller gave the woman a helpless look. "Ma'am, this horse has never been worth a damn as minding goes . . . begging your pardon."

"Soon as he's finished, see to it he doesn't water here again," the woman said firmly, letting the shotgun slump an inch.

But an inch was all Toller needed. He breathed easier, then asked, "Ma'am, to whom do I have the pleasure of speaking?"

The woman gave him a curious glance. "I'm Thellia Jones," she said firmly. She opened the lapel of her dusty men's linen jacket and revealed a crude badge made from the lid of a tin can.

"You're a sheriff?" said Toller, looking stunned. He stepped forward, staring at the badge as if seeing one for the first time.

"That's right, I'm the sheriff," said Thellia Jones, cutting him off. "Leastwise until Noches Frescas gets itself a council and either appoints or elects a full-timer. I'm a part-time sheriff."

"I see." Toller grinned and decided to try joking with her a little. "So, you are *half* of a sheriff?"

Thellia Jones gave him a cold, crushing stare. "Do I look like *half* of anything to you, mister?" The shotgun snapped back up level to his belly.

"No, ma'am!" Toller's grin vanished, replaced by a somber look. He ran his hand over his wet face.

"What are you doing in Noches Frescas anyway?" asked Sheriff Jones. As she spoke she centered her gaze on the string of bones and teeth around his neck.

Toller spoke quickly, saying the first thing that popped into his mind. "I'm a lawman, ma'am. . . . You might say you and me are kindred in our spirit of upholding law and order."

It took her a second to make any sense of Toller's babbling words. But then she asked pointedly, "Where's your badge?"

Toller felt over his chest as if searching for a badge. "Oh, well, the thing is, I don't exactly wear a badge."

"What kind of lawman doesn't wear a badge?" she asked, the shotgun back in place, butted against her hip.

Toller thought quickly and said, "The kind who doesn't always want folks to know he's a lawman, that's what kind."

"What are you, a sheriff, a marshal, a constable, what?" She spoke fast, not giving him time to work up anything believable.

Toller couldn't think quick enough to figure out which lawman he should be. Finally he shrugged, saying, "None of them . . . I'm a different kind of lawman altogether. I hunt down lawbreakers everywhere." He waved an arm as if including the whole world.

"Who pays you?" asked Thellia Jones.

"Who pays me?" Toller hadn't even thought about it. He looked stuck for an answer.

Thellia Jones offered a thin smile. "I bet you only get paid when you bring in the people you're searching for, right?" she asked, helping him along.

"Yes, ma'am, exactly," said Toller, returning her smile. "Sort of a pay upon delivery, you might say."

"I see," said Thellia, as if studying it. "So, you're sort of a bounty hunter, could you say? That's the kind of lawman you are?"

"Well . . . yes, that's close to it," said Toller, realizing that perhaps he hadn't lied so badly that he couldn't straighten it out. He shrugged, spreading his hands. "You don't have anything against bounty hunters, do you? I mean, we're still both serving justice, ain't we?"

Thellia didn't answer. Instead she stared at his gruesome necklace and said, "This bounty you collect, is that for delivering a person, or for just turning in part of that person to prove they're dead?"

Toller winced. "Well, I don't have to bring in the entire person, feed them and board them and all that. You could say what I do is more simple and less costly—"

"You're a scalp hunter, aren't you?" she asked flatly.

Toller stared, stunned. He had tried to lie to her, but she had taken it full circle and seen right through him. "In a broad sense, I reckon you could call it scalp hunting. Although I like to think that even though what I do is—"

"Get out, you lousy scalp hunter," she said, cutting him off, motioning her shotgun toward the trail out of town.

"Get out?" said Toller, suddenly feeling anger rise in his chest. "Ma'am, I don't intend to go anywhere until I'm gawdamn good and ready—"

One of the shotgun's barrels exploded, kicking up dirt only an inch from the toes of Toller's boots. "Jesus, woman!" he shrieked, jumping back, almost toppling over into the well. Beside him the horse reeled away, giving a high, frightened kick. The animal leaped, circled and stopped ten feet away, water dripping from its muzzle.

Thellia stepped in close, leveling the hot, smoking barrel in his face. "My ma died at the hands of Mescalero who got stirred up by a bunch of filthy *scalp hunters*!"

Toller said, in defense of his trade, "Then, by God, you ought to be mad at the Apache, not the scalp hunters. If I had my way I'd kill every murdering, rotten—"

"Get out of Noches Frescas," she said, cutting him off.

"Ma'am, I had planned to spend some time here. . . . Drop some money into this settlement, see if it's the kind of place I can recommend to fellow pilgrims."

She jerked her head toward Toller's horse. "I'll count to three."

"Ma'am, sheriff or not, this is a free country," said Toller. "I don't believe you can just run a man off because of what he does for a living."

"One," she said with resolve.

"All right then! Damn it to hell! I'm leaving!"

Toller spun angrily away from her and stomped toward the horse, making sure to keep his hand up away from his gun butt. Raising his voice for the few bystanders to hear, he shouted, "I hope every gawdamn one of you sonsabitches choke to death on sheep shit! This country's gone to hell, I'm telling you! When a good Virginian-born man—a *veteran,* that's right, a gawdamn *veteran*—can't come to visit bringing nothing but good intentions and brotherly love! You tell *me* this country ain't lost its soul!"

The two laborers stepped back into the street, one of them hurrying out to Thellia Jones, saying, "Sheriff, are you all right?" He looked her up and down, then looked at Toller and his horse leaving the settlement, Toller raving loudly to himself.

"That man was a lunatic, wasn't he?" the laborer commented.

"Yes, Willy," said Thellia Jones, replacing the spent shotgun load, "I believe he's exactly that." She shook her head slowly. "All you asked him to do was use the dipper."

The hottest part of the day had passed when the ranger and Tackett saw the hoofprints stop. Then the prints continued on, this time with a set of boot prints appearing alongside them. For the past two miles the hoofprints had begun to sway back and forth in an uneven line along the dirt trail. Both lawmen read the prints clearly. The rider had pushed his horse too long and too hard without water. Leaning from their saddles, inspecting the prints, Tackett said, "That poor horse must've stopped right here and refused to carry him any farther."

The ranger only gazed along the simmering trail, studying the land, judging the time of evening.

"Smart horse, I'd say," Tackett commented. "Some animals will keep moving until they fall over dead on the trail."

The ranger said, "I expect this man saw that he wasn't gaining any ground, so he stepped down and walked."

"How old do you say these tracks are?" Tackett asked.

"Three, maybe four hours at the most," said the ranger, giving the big Appaloosa a nudge forward.

"Think we better spread out and watch for an ambush?" asked Tackett. "If he's lost his horse, he'll be looking to kill anybody to get back in a saddle."

"Drop back some just to play it safe," said the ranger, "but I believe all this man is interested in is getting on into the settlement and getting some water back into him. If he hasn't fallen dead, he's probably there right now healing up from the heat."

They rode on in silence another seven miles through rock and sand and saguaro cactus until they topped a land swell and saw the settlement of Noches Frescas lying below them. Tackett sidled his horse up to the ranger and leaned with his wrists crossed on his saddle horn. "I'll circle around and come in from the other end of the settlement in case he sees us and makes a run for it," said Tackett.

"I'll give you a few minutes head start," said the ranger, "but I doubt if this man has any *run* left in him right about now."

Drawing his rifle from his saddle boot, Sheriff Tackett heeled his horse forward and down toward Noches Frescas, swinging wide off the trail and circling to the far end of the settlement. The ranger waited and watched until Tackett cut out of sight behind a stand of cottonwood. Then, giving the Appaloosa a nudge,

Burrack rode down through the falling evening shadows and onto the flat stretch of trail leading along a row of tents and adobes.

At the public well, Willy Newman stood cleaning his mason tools with a wet rag when he caught sight of Tackett riding in through the half-light of evening. "Oh, no, Andrew!" he said to the other laborer. "That lunatic is coming back!"

"What?" Andrew Purley asked in disbelief. Then looking at the shadowy figure approaching, he said, "We best go tell Sheriff Thellia. . . . I bet she'll end up shooting this idiot."

The two hurried away toward an adobe where a lamp had already been lit in a window. Tackett watched the two laborers hurry to the door of the adobe and bang on it hard. Seeing it concerned him. When the door opened slightly and the two rushed inside, Tackett nudged his horse over to the well and sat quietly with both hands up away from the rifle lying across his lap. At the other end of town he saw the ranger riding toward him. Tackett raised a hand and waved for him to halt. Burrack not only halted the Appaloosa, he reined the horse off to the side of the trail out of sight in the shadow of a large, ragged tent.

Looking back at the adobe, Tackett saw the woman walking toward him, her shotgun already up and pointed. He raised his hands a bit higher and said, "Ma'am, I hope that double blaster ain't cocked. I'd hate to get blown all to pieces because you stubbed your toe."

"Don't worry about my toe, mister!" said Thellia Jones, still coming forward. She didn't stop until she'd come close enough to see that it wasn't the scalp hunter. Upon realizing this wasn't him, she relaxed the shotgun a little. "What's your business here this late in the day?"

"Ma'am, if you'll permit me . . ." said Tackett, seeing the tin badge on her breast. He slowly lowered a hand to his lapel and pulled his duster open enough to reveal his own badge.

Sheriff Jones cocked her head slightly. "Oh, another lawman. At least you've got a badge." She sounded wary. "And what kind of lawman are you, mister?"

"Ma'am, I'm Sheriff Boyd Tackett, from over in Wakely. Tackett spoke quickly. "Up the street there I've got Ranger Sam Burrack waiting for me to wave him in. We're both up to our ears in a manhunt."

Thellia Jones relaxed the shotgun some more, letting the barrel point down at the ground. "I've heard of you, Sheriff Tackett, and the ranger too," she said. "You'll have to pardon my manners. My day was broken up by a no-account scalp hunter, who thought he could come in here shouting about everybody."

Waving the ranger in, Sheriff Tackett said to her, "Ma'am, didn't nobody kill him, did they?"

She saw the concern in his eyes. "No, but I sure felt like it. Why? Are you wanting him alive?"

"Yes, ma'am," said Tackett, "we need to make him tell us where the rest of his bunch are. They've kidnapped a little girl."

"Lord have mercy," Sheriff Jones whispered. She looked over at the ranger as he came riding toward them. "Had I only known I would've shot him in the leg and held him here for you."

"We understand, Sheriff," Tackett said to her.

"I'm Sheriff Thellia Jones," she replied, giving them a nod.

"Ranger Sam Burrack, ma'am," said the ranger, stopping his horse and tipping his wide sombrero.

Sheriff Jones told them the story, how the scalp hunter had staggered into town afoot. How she had run him out no sooner than he had watered himself and his horse. When she'd finished telling them, she said, "If you want me to, I'll get my horse and ride with you."

Sam didn't answer. Instead he asked, "Did he get to fill his canteen before you ran him off?"

"No, he didn't get a chance," said Sheriff Jones. "He still had his face in the water when I got here."

"Good," said the ranger.

"What about me riding with you?" Sheriff Jones asked again.

"We're obliged, Sheriff, but that won't be necessary," said the ranger.

Thellia Jones gave him a flat stare. "If it's because I'm a woman, Ranger, you've underestimated me."

"It's not because you're a woman, Sheriff," Burrack replied. "If this man left here without taking water with him, I've got a feeling he'll be coming back." He looked at Tackett, then back at Thellia Jones. "It's a long ways to the next water. He's out there somewhere right now thinking about it."

"Then you want to wait here for him?" asked Sheriff Jones.

"If it's all the same with you, Sheriff," said Burrack.

"Then get your horses watered and out of sight," said Thellia Jones, "I'll get on over to my place and rustle you up some grub. Might as well eat and get comfortable while you wait."

# PART 3

PART 3

# Chapter 15

———————

Morton Toller had sat until dark in the thin shade of a tall saguaro cactus, brooding and cursing, and staring in the direction of Noches Frescas, his pistol in his hand. Both he and his horse had drank their fill before leaving the settlement, but knowing that the well in Noches Frescas was now denied to him had him boiling with anger as well as thirst. It was six miles back to Noches Frescas, but he had no idea how far he would have to go to the next water stop in the other direction. He rubbed the back of his hand across his mouth and twirled his pistol. "Sonsabitches," he growled. He looked up at the horse standing over him in the darkness. "You had to drink out of the gawdamn well, didn't you?" he said, chastising the animal. Then he looked back toward Noches Frescas, feeling the first chilled bite of night air.

"I ain't freezing out here all night, and I ain't going hungry and thirsty when there's food and whiskey aplenty."

The horse blew out a breath and scraped a hoof in the dirt.

As if in afterthought, Toller said, "And there ain't no damn woman sheriff going to tell me what to do, either." He thought about it, then asked himself, "What would Earles and the rest of them say if they heard about this?" He stood up and dusted his seat. Jerking the horse by its reins, he said, "Come on . . . we're going to go take whatever the hell we want."

Stepping up into the saddle, Toller batted his boots to the horse's sides and raced back toward the settlement. Within minutes he slowed the horse to a walk on the rise of ground overlooking Noches Frescas.

"There she is, damn her," he said to the horse, drawing his pistol, staring at the glow of a single light in the darkness but seeing the darker outline of tents and adobes in the moonlight. He rode the horse down to the edge of the settlement then stopped again and pointed his pistol up in the air. "Now we're going to find out who's the biggest dog here!"

In Sheriff Thellia Jones' adobe, Tackett threw his blanket aside and sprang to his feet when the single gunshot split the silence of the night. The ranger had been awake, sipping a cup of coffee while Tackett got some needed rest. He sat his cup down on a table and held a hand up toward Tackett, keeping him from going to the door. Tackett stopped with his hand on his pistol, his free hand wiping sleep from his eyes. Sheriff Thellia Jones stepped in from the other room, pulling up her gallows, her shotgun under her arm. She also stopped, seeing the ranger's raised hand. Outside the sound of hoofs raced along the dirt street to the well, then stopped.

"He's got something to say or he wouldn't have fired that shot. Let's hear him out," said the ranger.

Before he even got the words out of his mouth, Morton Toller shouted from the middle of the street, "Sheriff! I'm back! It's me, the man you run off today!" He paused for a second and called out, "Do you hear, *woman* Sheriff?"

"Answer him, Sheriff," Sam whispered to Thellia Jones.

"I hear you," Sheriff Jones called out in reply. "What is it you want?"

"I'm letting you know that I'm back and I'm staying!" Toller bellowed. Along the row of shacks and tents lanterns began to glow.

"Keep him talking while we get around behind him," the ranger whispered to Sheriff Jones.

Thellia Jones nodded and called out to Toller as Burrack and Tackett hurried through her adobe and out the back door, "You can't stay here, mister. I don't allow scalp hunters in Noches Frescas! I already told you why!"

"Maybe you didn't hear me, woman Sheriff!" Toller shouted. "I ain't going no gawdamn place. I'm staying and I'm taking what I want, and I'll shoot any sonsabitch who tries to stop me!"

"Does that include me?" Thellia Jones asked, keeping him talking.

"Woman! That most especially includes you!" Toller raged. "If you show your face out here in the street, I will shoot holes in you until I run out of bullets!"

The ranger watched from the darkness as he slipped across the dirt street and worked his way toward where Toller sat atop his horse at the edge of the well. He knew that Tackett was now advancing on Toller from the opposite side, the two of them moving quietly and quickly to take him alive. But suddenly the ranger saw Toller point his gun at arm's length at the lamplight in Sheriff Jones' window and pull the trigger. Flame exploded from the tip of Toller's barrel. The ranger raced forward, hearing the sound of glass breaking.

"What the hell?" shouted Toller as Tackett grabbed his horse by its bridle. Before Toller could react, the ranger leaped up out of nowhere and dragged him from the saddle. Toller and the ranger rolled on the ground until the barrel of Sam's drawn Colt struck Toller across the side of his head and he went limp and fell to the side with a groan.

"We've got him, Tackett," said the ranger, snatching Toller's gun from the dirt. Tackett was conscious but addled. Burrack pulled him up to his feet. Toller staggered in place as limp as a scarecrow.

Toller said in a groggy voice, "This is the hardest damn town I ever seen on strangers."

"He broke my *only* damn window!" Thellia Jones growled, coming from her adobe with her shotgun in her hands.

Trying to speak in his own defense, Toller said, "The way you've treated me, you lucky these deputies got here before I—"

His words were cut short as Thellia buried the butt of her shotgun in his stomach, jackknifing him forward with his arms wrapped around his middle. She raised the shotgun, ready to slam it down on his head. But the ranger jerked Toller away just in time, saying to her, "Easy, Sheriff, we need to talk to this man, remember?"

Doubled over in a tight ball, Morton Toller asked in a strained voice, "Talk? About what?"

"What's your name, mister?" the ranger asked.

"Toller . . . Morton Toller," he groaned. "Talk about what?"

"About where that little girl is . . . about where Jessup Earles and his bunch have taken her," said Sheriff Tackett, stepping in and replying before the ranger had a chance to speak.

The ranger pulled upward on Toller's collar, forcing

him to straighten up stiffly, still clutching his stomach. "Little girl?" he asked, his voice still sounding strained.

Burrack shook him by his collar. It helped his memory. "Oh, the little girl that belongs to Haddon Marr. What about her?"

"Where is she?" Tackett asked, sounding impatient.

"She's with Haddon, I reckon," Toller shrugged.

"Let me have him, Sam!" said Tackett, gritting his teeth, his fists clenched. Beside him stood Sheriff Jones, gripping her shotgun tightly, ready to smack Toller with it again.

"I'm going to let you both have him if he doesn't answer me pretty quick," said the ranger, shaking Toller again.

"All right!" said Toller. "Haddon Marr cut out with the girl before we left that last town, the one where we took the wagon full of supplies." He looked around at the three faces staring at him.

"You mean Sheldon," said the ranger, prompting Toller.

"Yeah, Sheldon," said Toller. "Haddon had started acting real·strange over that little girl, started getting hard to talk to. He couldn't stand anybody even looking at her. Then he just up and took off with her. Didn't say nothing to nobody about what he was doing!"

"Is the girl all right?" asked Tackett.

"All right in what way?" Toller grinned.

"You know what way I mean," said Tackett, his voice threatening.

"Ain't none of them laid a hand on her, if that's what you're talking about," said Toller. "Haddon Marr would kill them if they did, the crazy way he's been acting over her."

"Where are all of you supposed to meet up again?" Burrack asked.

"Oh, tell you that, so you can get the drop on my friends, mi amigos?" He shook his head vigorously in spite of the ache in his head from the ranger's pistol barrel. "I'm not telling you another damn thing!"

The ranger gave Tackett and Sheriff Jones a look, then said to Toller, "We don't have time to fool around with you. In Sheldon they'll put a rope around your neck and leave you hanging from a cottonwood."

"Or in my town," said Tackett, "we'll try you for murder and kidnapping and get you into the ground before your toes turn cold."

"Nobody can prove murder and kidnapping on me," said Toller, unable to hide his worried look. "The witnesses at that settlement are all dead!"

"We won't have to prove it against you, mister," said Tackett. "All I'll have to do is turn my back for an hour. My townsfolk will have you gutted and ready to boil."

The ranger shook his head slowly. "I don't know if I've ever had so many bad outcomes to choose from."

"Wait a minute, fellows," Toller cut in. "Can I get a drink, maybe something to eat, and think this thing over?"

"You rotten bastard," Sheriff Jones cut in, trying to get past Tackett to bash Toller's head in with her shotgun butt. "A little girl's life is at risk and you want a drink or two to think it over? Leave him here with me!" She growled.

Tackett blocked Sheriff Jones from coming forward.

"No drink . . . no food," said the ranger, "not until I know you're going to take us to the others."

"And what if I do agree to take you there," said Toller, starting to look out for his best interest, "do I get to go free afterwards?"

The ranger looked at Tackett and saw him nod slightly. "If we find the girl there, unharmed . . ." The ranger stopped and took a deep breath, not liking what he was getting ready to agree to. Then he let out his breath in resolve and said, "Yes, then you have our word, you'll go free."

Toller looked back and forth between them, then grinned in surprise at these two hardened lawmen going along with him. "My goodness!" he chuckled, "I should've been a gawdamned lawyer!"

"Do we have a deal, Toller?" asked the ranger.

"Yep," said Toller, "we've got ourselves a deal. Earles and all of us are meeting at Piedra Negra next week. Piedra Negra means 'Black Rock,' if you don't know," he added smugly.

"Black Rock," said Tackett, giving the ranger a look of dread. "It's across the border."

"Yep, it's in old Mex, sure enough," said Toller, "but we won't be holed up there for long. We're going to pull some more raids along the border before we settle in for the winter. Earles is taken with all the easy pickings around here. Said he wished he'd thought of being a marauder years ago. It beats the hell out of lifting scalps." Toller chuckled to himself, saying, "And I have to *ad*-mit, he's right."

"How do you feel about crossing that border, Sam?" Tackett asked. "Because I can't sit around waiting, hoping they come back with that child."

"If we've got to cross the border to save the child," said the ranger, "I'll cross it with you." As he spoke he pulled a pair of handcuffs from his inside vest pocket and snapped them around Toller's wrists. "There's people crossing it every day for lesser reasons."

Tackett breathed a sigh of relief. "I'm glad to hear you say that, otherwise I was going to have to cross it on my own."

Turning to Sheriff Jones, Burrack asked, "Sheriff, do you have a jail?"

"No, I've never needed one," Thellia Jones replied. "I've got a barn you can chain him in. You two can sleep in my house. I've got an extra room you can share."

"Much obliged, Sheriff," said the ranger, "but we're not getting three feet away from this man until we've found that child. We'll sleep in the barn with him."

"I understand," said Sheriff Jones.

"Let's go, Toller," said Burrack, giving him a slight shove. "We'll get you that whiskey I promised."

Walking behind the cuffed prisoner the ranger and Tackett followed Sheriff Jones to a small barn at the back of her adobe. When Sheriff Jones left and returned moments later with a bottle of whiskey, Toller grinned widely and licked his lips. "So far I'm living better as your prisoner than I ever did on my own. What's for supper, boys?" he asked, taunting them.

Having taken the full bottle of rye from Sheriff Jones, the ranger pitched it to Toller, saying, "Don't let it get stuck to your hands. I want you clearheaded when we ride out in the morning."

Catching the bottle, Toller chuckled, "You won't have to worry about me, Ranger, I stay steady as a rock."

The lawmen allowed Toller a couple of shots of whiskey while they attended to his horse. Then they fed him and handcuffed him to a barn post and settled in for the night. They took turns staying awake and keeping an eye on the prisoner while he slept fitfully on a pile of straw. At dawn, Sheriff Jones shoved the barn door open with her boot and stepped inside carrying a steaming pot of coffee and a pan of biscuits. "I knew you men wanted to get an early start," she said, "but I couldn't see you ride out of here with your gullets empty." She smiled and set the coffee and biscuits down atop a feed bin.

Tackett and the ranger stopped preparing for the trail long enough to have breakfast, then they checked their guns, saddled their horses, shoved the handcuffed prisoner into his saddle and rode away. Sheriff Thellia Jones stood in the dirt street near the well and watched them disappear into the wide silver swirl of morning, on the trail headed to Mexico. "I'd give anything to ride that trail with yas," she whispered to herself. Then she hiked her collar against the crisp morning air and walked back to her adobe with her shotgun under her arm.

# Chapter 16

When he regained consciousness, Haddon Marr only raised his head enough to see the girl leading his horse up a thin path toward a stand of cedar. He smiled weakly to himself and laid his head back down on the horse's neck, the pain in his chest throbbing. He had no idea how long he'd been unconscious, but glancing up with his one good eye he noted that the sun lay far over into the afternoon sky. The child had led him all day? Could that be possible? Thinking about it caused him to push himself up stiffly in his saddle. "Hilda? Where are you taking me?" he asked, his voice gravelly, his hand going carefully to the dried blood on his upper chest.

The girl gasped, startled by his voice, shaking for a moment before stopping the horse and turning to look up at him. "In—into the trees," she said, still shaking. Marr saw the canteen hanging by a rawhide strap from her thin shoulder. "Hilda," he said again, struggling to lower himself down off the saddle. "Water . . ."

But she hurried over and pushed upwards on his leg as if to stop him from dismounting. "No, stay up there!" she said, her voice quivering. "Here . . . here is some water." She pulled the canteen from her shoulder and held it up to him.

Haddon Marr settled back into the saddle, the pain

cutting deep in his chest. "You're right," he whispered, taking the canteen, keeping a hand to his chest, "smart girl. It's too hard getting me back up here."

Hilda nodded, staring up at him. She watched him uncap the canteen with his blood-stained hands and take a mouthful of tepid water, swish it around and spit it out. Then he spit onto his palm, looked closely at it and wiped his hand on his buckskin trouser leg. "Good," he commented to himself, "my lung's not busted."

He took another short sip of water and, feeling his strength waning, held the canteen down for Hilda to take from his hand. Looking blearily at his lap, he said, "I seem to have wet myself." Then he managed to lay forward onto the horse's neck before collapsing. But he did not lose consciousness. Instead, he opened his eyes now and then, staying aware of the direction they were headed in. They were headed southwest, in the direction of the border. That was good, he thought. He knew he had to find help soon or he would die. But as soon as he found help, his next move had to be across the border, toward the safety of Jessup Earles and the others, the very ones he had ran out on.

An hour later, as shadows grew long across the land, even though he thought he had been conscious, Marr felt the horse stop beneath him and raised his head to see the girl and a woman hurrying toward him through a few scurrying chickens. He tried to reach for the gun at his hip, yet his hand could not get started before the woman had taken hold of his arm and looped it out over her shoulder as she pulled him down from the saddle. She had him standing upright, his feet on the ground, but his legs felt limp and unruly. He tried once again to grab for his pistol, this

time reaching across his stomach in a cross draw. But
the pain in his chest would have none of it. He let his
arm drop to his side.

"Mister, you're in some awful bad shape," the
woman said, helping him toward a plank shack stuck
in the side of a rugged cliff. His head bobbed back
and forth. He tried to say something, but he couldn't
get the words formed. "You look like you've lost lots
of blood. . . . Good thing your daughter found us
here." She hurried, struggling with the weight of him
against her.

Found us . . . ? Marr drifted back toward unconsciousness wondering how many people he was going
to have to kill here once he got his feet back under
him. But the next time he opened his eyes and tried
reaching for the gun at his hip, instead of feeling the
cold gunmetal he felt something soft against him. As
he became more conscious, his hand groped around
for the gun butt until it finally dawned on him that he
was in a bed, undressed, beneath a soft quilt. He
turned his face to one side and saw the gun belt hanging over a chair back.

"It's all right, mister, you're safe here," said the
woman's voice. Haddon Marr felt the bandage over
his eye as he turned his face in her direction. He
touched a hand to his bandaged chest, then carefully
to his bandaged eye.

"You're going to be fine," the woman said, seeing
him examine his wounds. "Your eye had me worried,
but it cleaned up all right. I didn't see any sign of
infection in it. The bullet in your chest went all the
way through, didn't seem to hit anything vital inside
you. It's already starting to heal over."

"How long have we been here, ma'am?" Marr
asked.

"Two days," she said, realizing he was trying to get some perspective on how long he'd been unconscious.

"Two days?" Marrs looked bewildered.

"Yes, it's been two days," she said. Then she asked, "Who attacked you folks, Indians?"

Haddon Marr weighed his words before speaking, then he said, "Why did you say Indians?"

"I saw how your daughter Hilda's hair has been cropped off. I once heard of a woman doing that to keep Indians from scalping her." She paused, then said, "If you'd rather not talk about it just now, I understand. You and Hilda have been through an awful lot. She's asleep right now. But don't worry about her. She's awfully tired, but otherwise fine."

"What—What has she told you?" Marr asked, getting an idea that he might be all right here, at least long enough to heal and rest for a few days.

"Nothing much," said the woman, "but I've put two and two together. It's plain to see the poor girl has been frightened out of her wits."

"Yeah," said Marr, thinking it over, "she's been through a lot; we both have. You're right, it was Indians, a band of Apache. They must've come from across the border. We weren't expecting a thing. They hit so quick it was hard to fight back."

"But you managed to get your daughter and get away?" the woman said, trying to get him to talk more.

"Yeah, that was it," he said. "We were lucky; the others weren't. That's the long and short of it." He closed his eyes as if to rest, when he was really only avoiding any further conversation right then.

"Well, I can see you're still weak. You lost a lot of blood," she said. "If you awaken and need anything, just let me know. My name is Lenora Lambert."

"Obliged, ma'am," said Marr. "My name is James Haddon."

"I know," said Lenora Lambert, "Hilda told me."

"She did?" Haddon Marr almost sat up in the bed.

"Well, sort of," said Lenora. "She said Haddon, but she didn't say if it was your first or last name."

"Oh," said Marr, relaxing again. "I feel much better knowing she's got a woman to take care of her while we're here." His voice sounded weak and shallow. "Where is your husband, ma'am?"

"I'm a widow, Mister Haddon," she said quietly.

"Oh, then you live here alone?" Marr asked.

"Yes, just Oscar and me," she said.

"Oscar, ma'am?" said Marr.

"Oscar is my dog, Mister Haddon. He was off in the cedars when you two arrived, but now he is sleeping right at Hilda's side."

"Ain't that sweet!" said Marr, drifting slightly as he spoke, realizing he had little to fear here. He would rest awhile longer then get something to eat and find a chance to get Hilda alone and warn her to keep quiet about who they were and how he'd really gotten wounded.

Lenora Lambert stepped back out of the small room and closed the door softly behind her. While Marr and the girl slept, she busied herself preparing a large dinner of beans, roasted chicken and sweat bread, using a bit more sugar than usual owing to there being guests in her home. Dinnertime was still a good ways off, but cooking helped her control her excitement. Lenora had spent too much time alone lately. It felt good having people around her for a change. As she stirred more water into the pot of beans cooking over the open hearth, she heard the girl and Oscar walk into the room and turned, wiping her hands on her apron.

"Well, it began to look like you two were going to sleep the day away," said Lenora with a smile. Oscar came to her wagging his thick tail, but Hilda stayed back and only stared at her. "It's all right, child," Lenora said, "you can come closer. See, even Oscar likes me, as long as I'll scratch his head for him." As she spoke she reached a hand to the dog's big head and scratched behind his drooping hound ears.

Hilda watched in fascination for a moment, then walked closer. "I just finished checking on your father," said Lenora. "He's doing real good. We'll wake him again and check on him at dinnertime. Then you and I will take him a plate. How does that sound?"

Hilda only nodded.

"Hilda, your father told me what happened, how a band of Apache attacked your group and you and he were the only ones to get away." She stooped down and inspected Hilda's close-cropped hair. "Tell me, dear, what about your mother? Was she there? Did the Apache kill her?"

Hilda only stared at Lenora, her eyes and expression revealing nothing. Lenora hugged the girl to her and said, "You poor child, never mind me. You don't want to talk about it right now and I understand." She released her and said, "Come on, let's you, me and Oscar go get some fresh water for dinner."

Lenora picked up a metal water pail from the shelf where it sat with a dipper hanging on the wall beside it, and the three walked out front to the well. Hilda watched while Lenora lowered a wooden bucket into the well by the long rope tied to its wire handle. Filling the bucket, Lenora lifted it by the rope then poured water from it into the metal pail. "Next time I'll have you and Oscar come and get water for us," said Lenora, turning to Hilda standing beside her. She saw the braided necklace of bone, ears and teeth in Hilda's hands and recoiled at the sight of it.

"My goodness, child! What on earth is that thing?" she asked in a stunned tone.

Without saying a word, Hilda held it up for her to see.

Lenora took it and looked it over, knowing what she held in her hand, her skin crawling at the thought of holding such a grizzly trinket. "Is—is this your father's, Hilda?" she asked. "I bet it's something he took off of one of the savages who attacked him. Is that it?"

Hilda saw the concerned look on Lenora Lambert's face, and in order to ease her mind she nodded her head slowly.

Lenora sighed, handed the necklace back to her and wiped her hands on her dress before picking up the water pail. "Well, if he allows you to carry it, I won't question his authority, but it is something I would never allow a child to have. No indeed," she said. "Now put it away, and wash your hands as soon as we get inside."

When supper had been prepared and Hilda sat at the table eating from a tin plate, Oscar sitting on the floor beside her chair with his nose tipped upwards, Lenora Lambert set a wooden bowl of beans, some chicken and a cup of coffee on a wooden tray and carried it into the small bedroom where Marr lay with his pistol on his stomach. Seeing the gun as she closed the door behind her with her foot, Lenora said as she walked to the bed, "Oh, I see you've been up and around. Good for you, Mister Haddon. You must be feeling better."

"I got up for a minute or two," said Marr, laying the gun off his stomach and alongside him. He scooted up in the bed. Lenora set the tray across his legs, then reached behind him and pulled his pillow up for back support. "There now," she said, taking a step back. "Are you too sore to feed yourself, because if you are I don't mind helping you."

"Obliged, ma'am," said Marr, "but I believe I'll do all right."

She nodded, folding her hands in front of her. "Very well then." She watched him pick up the spoon and begin eating the beans.

After a couple of bites he stopped chewing and looked at her, aware of how closely she'd been watching him. "Ma'am," he said, "is there something the matter with how I'm doing this?"

She blushed. "No, of course not. You must forgive me, Mister Haddon. It's been quite awhile since I've watched a man eat. I didn't mean to be rude." She half turned to start for the door, but Marr stopped her.

"Please stay, ma'am. You weren't being rude. I suppose it's been awhile since I've been around many people myself." He caught himself, then said, "Other than my wife and folks on the trail that is."

Lenora stopped and refolded her hands. "Mister Haddon," she said, her expression saying she'd given this much thought before bringing it up, "I don't mean to pry, but Hilda has a necklace that she said you took from one of the Apache who attacked you."

Haddon Marr almost reached a hand up to his chest to see if his gruesome trophy necklace was missing. But he stopped himself and said, "My daughter told you that, did she?"

"Well, not in so many words," said Lenora. "But I asked her if it was something you took from the Apache—"

"Ma'am," said Marr, cutting her short. "It would be best if you ask me any questions you need to have answered. Hilda is an awfully quiet child, as you've already seen for yourself. The necklace didn't come from the Apache." He lowered a hand closer to the pistol beside him. "I've had it for a good long time."

"Oh, my," said Lenora. "Are those really human teeth, human finger bones?" Her expression turned grim.

"Yes, ma'am, I'm afraid they are," Marr said quietly, lowering his eyes. "I'm afraid I haven't been completely honest with you, and I feel ashamed." He laid the spoon down beside the bowl. "You see, ma'am, Hilda and I weren't attacked by Indians. We were attacked by a bunch of scalp hunters. It was them who killed Hilda's ma and did this to me."

"Oh, I see . . ." said Lenora, trying to make sense of why he'd lied to her. Unable to, after a silent moment she asked, "Mister Haddon, why did you feel like you couldn't tell me that?"

"Because, ma'am, the fact is. . . . God forgive me, at one time I myself made my living taking scalps from the Apache and selling them to the Mexican government for bounty."

Lenora Lambert took a tight breath, Marr seeing her expression change to contempt right before his eyes. "Oh, then I understand why you didn't want to tell me the true story."

"Yes, ma'am," said Marr, humbly. "If you want me and Hilda to leave, I'll just manage to get up from here and ride on. But, ma'am, I believe a man can change himself, and that's what I tried to do. When

Hilda and her ma showed up, and I saw that I now had a family, I left the scalp-hunting profession. That's when my trouble started. The men I used to ride with couldn't stand to see me find some happiness for myself. They turned on me. They're the ones who killed Hilda's ma and nearly killed us both. That's why I was forced to cut off Hilda's hair, to keep them from scalping her."

"My God!" said Lenora. She put a trembling hand to her mouth. "But why would they do that to her, her hair is golden yellow?"

"Yes, ma'am, but believe it or not there are folks in this world, foreigners mostly, who pay top dollar for something like a white woman's scalp, the yellower the better." He sighed and shook his head. "There, you see why I had to get out of that profession, away from those kind of people?"

Lenora stood in silence, contemplating everything he'd told her.

"So, ma'am, if you'll just take this tray, I'll get up from here, and me and little Hilda will be on our way. I'm sorry as I can be for deceiving you." He rose slightly from the pillow behind him and seemed to be waiting for her to remove the tray. The pistol lay close to his hand. He wasn't going anywhere and he knew it. If she agreed that he and the girl should leave, he knew what he would have to do.

"Nonsense, Mister Haddon," Lenora said softly, "you are in no condition to travel, and neither is Hilda." She stepped forward and gently pressed him back against the pillow propped up behind him. "What I want you to do is eat your food and get your strength back."

"Are you sure, ma'am?" Marr said, his eyes searching hers.

"Of course I'm sure," Lenora said. She didn't see it, but his hand had just relaxed and moved away from his gun. "I happen to believe that a man can change his way of life too."

"God bless you, ma'am," said Marr, managing a weak, innocent smile.

# Chapter 17

Ted Riley had stayed doggedly on Haddon Marr's trail, having cleaned his wound with canteen water and bandaged it as best he could with strips of cloth he tore from his shirt sleeve. But the pain in his lower back was relentless, and he knew it had cost him precious time. By the end of his second day in the saddle without food and with very little water, Riley had barely reined the big paint horse into shelter beneath a cliff overhang before collapsing to the ground, leaving the horse to stare in wonder at him. The horse scraped at Riley's boot with its hoof, nudged him with its muzzle, then getting no response, turned and walked to a nearby patch of sparse wild grass and grazed itself.

Night came and went, and still Ted Riley lay in the same spot. The paint horse continued to wander away long enough to graze and take water from a thin trickle of water running down out of a crack in the stone. When Riley finally awakened it was dark again, and what stirred him to consciousness was the smell of food cooking. A crackling fire burned beneath the overhang, and the smell of roasting jackrabbit permeated the air. Nearby a gravelly voice said, "You best be wake up, Pilgrim, lest your bones end up sleeping here forever."

Riley reached for his pistol butt as he opened his eyes, to make sure the gun hadn't been lifted in his sleep. But the gun was gone and his trousers had been loosened. The old man standing over by the fire in a ragged duster and a tall, battered silk stovepipe hat, interpreted Riley's move as that of a coiling rattlesnake ready to strike. "Whoa, Pilgrim!" the old man said, jumping back a step, dropping a stick he used to cook with to the ground and raising his hands toward Riley in a show of peace. "If you're a highwayman, all I have is this cooked rabbit . . . and I fixed it for you anyway."

"Where's my gun? My horse?" Ted Riley asked, looking around bleary-eyed before seeing the paint horse standing less than twenty yards away. Riley still had his hand on his gun belt.

The old man's voice took on a wise tone as he patted the big Remington pistol he'd shoved down his waist. He nodded at the horse. "If you mean Sheriff Fitch's big paint, well, he's doing fine as ever."

Riley starred at the old man, not liking the idea that he had the Remington. But he wasn't going to mention it right now. Instead he said, "How do you know about the horse, mister?"

The old man chuckled. "It's a big world, but not that big." He grunted, stooping down and picking up his stick. Riley saw two large carpetbags and an even larger leather-bound trunk lying on the ground near the fire. "I knew Sheriff Fitch when Sheldon was still being talked about as becoming, as the *Harper Weekly* news article called it, 'The Mecca of civility in an untamed wilderness.'" He grinned. "Strange how things can turn around so quick in this world, ain't it?"

"I suppose," said Riley. He rubbed his face, sitting

upright, feeling pain running all the way from his lower back down his left leg. "I didn't mean to steal his horse. It just turned out that way."

"Oh! And isn't that always the case?" the old man chuckled, busily turning the roasting rabbit above the flames.

"What I mean is, he'll get the horse back as soon as I'm finished—" He stopped himself, realizing how foolish it sounded. Then he said, "I'm not going to explain myself to you, stranger."

"I never asked you to," said the old man. "You started talking to me, I was just responding out of politeness." With his duster sleeve pulled low protecting his hand, he lifted the end of the thin iron bar that ran through the rabbit. He blew on the sizzling meat and inspected it closely. "Soon as this cools I'll pull some off and bring it to you on a plate." He grinned, saying, "Jackrabbit on a platter! Who do you know of that's eating any better on this fine desert night?"

Riley struggled up to his feet, saying, "I'll come over there for it."

"Well, then," said the old man, "you are *indeed* on the road to recovery. Careful though, you'll bust those stitches I put in you." Only then did he realize his shirt was unbuttoned; only then did he notice that he'd been sleeping on a blanket instead of the hard ground where he had fallen when he'd first arrived here.

"What?" Riley reached a wary hand behind him and felt the bandage covering his lower back. "How long have I been asleep? What have you done?"

"I don't know how long you were out before I got here," the old man said. "But I knocked you out early yesterday with some potent medication I've been de-

veloping for blocking pain." He grinned, using the
rabbit on the spit as a pointer. "I'm glad to see it
worked so well."

"What are you, mister, a doctor?" Riley asked, the
aroma of the roasted rabbit reminding his stomach of
how long it had been since he'd eaten.

"A doctor!" The old man chuckled. "No, indeed,
not I, although I am flattered beyond design that you
might think me so." He swept the battered silk hat
from his head. "I am Franklin Floyd Bright, sir, at
your service."

"You're developing medicine, are you an apothecary?" Riley asked, coming closer to the fire and the
rabbit on weak legs.

"Oh, heavens no, sir," said Franklin Floyd Bright,
holding the rabbit out to him. "I daresay if any re-
spectable apothecary heard you say that, you'd have
more than one bullet hole in your back!" He beamed
at his own humor. "Although if you'll permit my van-
ity to speak, I will say that most cures those noble
healers possess come from medical pioneers like myself. You see I am a—"

"You're a medicine drummer?" Riley asked bluntly,
finishing his words for him.

"Well, yes, that is one name for my profession. I
have traveled, supporting myself and my important life
work by selling liniments and health potions of my
own creation." He raised a finger for emphasis. "Nev-
ertheless, it was I, sir, not some academic doctor or
apothecary, who removed that bullet fragment from
your back without you feeling it!"

"Much obliged, sir," said Riley, "but I thought the
bullet had gone all the way through and come out
clean."

"Clean? Hardly, sir," said Bright. "I took out a fragment the size of chickpea. It was lodged down into your hip bone, right at the joint. Didn't you seem to be unusually sore?"

"Every step the horse took I felt like I was going to break in half," said Riley, managing a slight smile. Bright held the rabbit out to Riley, who broke off one of the hind legs and laid it quickly onto a tin plate that Bright pointed to beside the fire. Steam bellowed.

"I see you're feeling much better now," said Bright, watching Riley blow on the meat, then eat it. "Your appetite is  certainly in excellent working order, Mister . . .?" He waited for Riley to tell him his name.

"I'm Ted Riley. I didn't mean to be rude, it's just that I can't remember when I last ate," said Riley. "No offense, sir."

"No offense taken, Mister Riley," said Bright.

"I've been pushing awfully hard," Riley continued, "trying to catch up to a scalp hunter who kidnapped a little girl. I don't suppose you've seen a man and a girl traveling together, have you?"

"No, but a man traveling as hard as you said you are, I figure he's either on somebody's trail, or else there's somebody on his. I'm glad to hear it's you dogging somebody, instead of the other way around, else I might find I'm in a tight spot with you?" He posed it as a question and watched Riley's eyes, waiting for an answer.

"Mister Bright, you are not in a tight spot with me. I'm grateful for what you've done for me." He took another bite of rabbit, chewed and swallowed it quickly, then took a canteen of water Bright picked up and held out to him. He washed down his food, then upon consideration, said, "Mister Bright, if you run into a ranger and a sheriff along the trail behind me, will you tell them I'm after the girl and can't stop just now. They won't need any more explanation than that."

"Of course I'll tell them, if I see them. And should I run into Sheriff Fitch I'll tell him you'll bring his horse back as soon as you're finished borrowing it." He chuckled under his breath and shook his head. "I'm sure hearing that will tighten his jaw."

"I would appreciate you telling him all the same," said Riley, "maybe he'll be understanding." He finished the rabbit and drank some more water.

"I must advise you that you need to stay here at least a couple more days," said Bright, "until the surgery heals a bit. Riding a horse is out of the question for at least a week."

"Sorry, Mister Bright," said Riley, "I've lost too much time as it is. Come morning I'm heading out."

"That's about what I expected you'd say." Bright smiled, lifted the big Remington from his waist and handed it to Riley butt first. "But I felt I should tell you anyway, on the outside chance that you might heed good advice."

"I wish I could, Mister Bright," said Riley, taking the gun, checking it and holding it loosely in his hand. "But I can't let this man's trail turn cold on me. The little girl's life depends on it."

Haddon Marr liked the way things were going here. He had the woman waiting on him even though now that he'd gotten up and been up and around most of the day, he thought she would see that he no longer needed anybody's help. But she continued to bring him coffee, food, water. He smiled to himself, realizing that in her loneliness Lenora Lambert couldn't stand not having someone to wait on. Marr liked that. He also liked wearing her dead husband's clothes while

she'd scrubbed his buckskins and stretched and dried
them. He especially liked sitting in her dead husband's
armchair, watching Hilda and the big yellow hound lie
on the floor in front of the night's fire. Hilda stroking
the dog's head, the dog licking her hand, this was the
way some folks lived all the time, he thought, sipping
his coffee, the soreness in his chest waning now, the
wound quickly healing.

The cut in his good eye had also healed fast. He no
longer kept it covered. The eye was almost completely
bloodred and his vision was still a little foggy. But
unlike Crossed-eyed Burton Stowl, whose eyes were
never going to see straight, Marr knew that his sight
would get better with each passing day. All he needed
was some proper time to heal. This place looked like
the perfect spot for just such healing. He looked Lenora up and down, secretly wondering how pliable she
would be if he wanted to get her to do his bidding.
Of course he could make her do most anything he
pleased. But he took no pleasure in that. She struck
him as a fine, intelligent woman. It would be interesting to see just how far he could lead her.

"Mister Haddon," said Lenora, interrupting his
thoughts. She sat across the table from him, repairing
the bullet hole in his cleaned and softened buckskin
shirt, "where will you and Hilda be going when you
leave here?"

"I expect we'll go to Missouri, ma'am," Marr lied.
"I have some family there, two brothers who own a
freight company. They've always wanted me to take
up with them. Maybe it's time I do it."

"Oh, that would be nice, I'm sure," said Lenora,
taking a genuine interest in his and his daughter's future. "Hilda could go to school."

"Yes, ma'am," Marr smiled. "And if you don't mind

me asking, what will you do now that your husband is dead—that is, *deceased*," he corrected himself. "You don't plan on staying here, do you?" As Marr spoke he stood up and started to walk over to the coffeepot sitting on the hearth near the fire. Lenora started to answer, but as Marr came close to Hilda, the big hound growled low in its chest and sprang up from the floor into a guarding crouch between him and the child.

"Steady there!" said Marr, taken aback by the dog's suddenness. "Ma'am, call him back!" he said to Lenora, seeing that the big hound would lunge any second. Marr had left his pistol lying on the table while he'd sat there drinking his coffee. But he couldn't get to it now.

"Oscar! Oscar, stop it!" said Lenora, coming up from her chair, Marr's buckskin shirt falling to the floor. "Bad dog! Oscar, get back!" Boldly, Lenora took a step and grabbed the dog by the loose skin on the back of his neck. But the dog would have none of it. He slung his big head back and forth and pulled free of her. Marr back-stepped quickly away from Hilda. The dog settled a little, but still continued showing his teeth and growling at Marr. Hilda sat staring calmly at the commotion going on around her.

"Ma'am, he's gone mad!" said Marr. "Take that pistol and shoot him!"

"I won't shoot him!" said Lenora, picking up Marr's pistol from the table, clutching it to her bosom. "Oscar, stop it . . . lay down!" She put her thumb over the hammer of Marr's gun, intending to fire a shot and scare the dog away if she had to.

But upon seeing Marr back away farther, Oscar settled more, standing close to Hilda, as if protecting her.

"That's a boy, Oscar, settle down," Lenora coaxed.

She said to Marr, "He's never acted this way; I don't know what could have caused this!"

"Ma'am, the dog is clearly mad," said Marr. "You just don't want to see it. I'm sorry to tell you, but it's the truth. We'll have to shoot him."

"No!" said Lenora, tightening her grip on the pistol. "I can't shoot Oscar!"

"I'll shoot him for you, ma'am," Marr said in a soft tone, not wanting to get the big dog upset. "It's got to be done. A big dog like that will kill somebody before it's over. This time he went for me. Next time it could be you, or even little Hilda there. Ma'am, I've seen this sort of thing before. Trust me."

Lenora relented slightly. "Are— Are you sure he's gone mad?" she asked, her voice trembling.

"Ma'am, your dog has gone mad," Marr said firmly, working at keeping his temper under control. "You can see that as well as I can. You just don't want to admit it to yourself."

"No, he just got excited," said Lenora, "from not being used to having people around us. He's a good dog." Her eyes began to well with tears.

"Ma'am," said Marr, keeping his voice quiet to keep the dog calmed down, "ease around here and hand me that pistol. It's got to be done."

Weeping, Lenora did as Marr told her. She took a step around the dog and Hilda, and started to reach out and hand Marr the pistol. But then she stopped herself and drew the pistol back. "No, I can't watch Oscar die this way!" She walked briskly to the door and opened it, saying to the dog, "Come on Oscar, *out*! Go *out*!"

The big dog hesitated, whining low, not wanting to leave the girl's side. But Lenora continued to coax and command the dog until finally Oscar lowered his head and walked out into the darkness. Lenora let out a breath and slumped against the closed door, saying, "There, he's out. . . ."

Marr stepped over and took the pistol from her hands. "You can't tolerate a big dog doing something like that, ma'am. When an animal goes mad, all you can do is kill it quick before it hurts somebody."

"Yes, I know, I know," said Lenora, "stop saying it! I know it's true!" She put her hands to her ears. "Tomorrow, it can wait until tomorrow."

Marr eased the pistol into his waist and said quietly, "Yes, ma'am, tomorrow. If you'll get a rope around his neck, we'll walk him off somewhere away from the house and I'll take care of him for you."

"I just don't understand it," said Lenora. "He acts as though he's protecting little Hilda from something."

"Who knows what goes on inside an animal's head, ma'am," said Marr. "We both see that there's nothing to protect Hilda from here." He gestured with his arm, taking in all of the house.

Lenora gave him a curious gaze. "And he only turned aggressive toward you, Mister Haddon. Is that the way dogs do when they go mad?"

"Yes, ma'am," said Marr, "that's exactly the way a mad dog will do. Lucky thing he didn't turn on you while you were alone here with him." Marr watched her eyes begin to well up again. "But I can see how upset this has made you." He reached up with his fingertips and brushed a strand of hair from her face. "You quit thinking about it tonight. I'll take care of everything."

"All right, Mister Haddon," she said, turning away from the door. "You know more about this than I do." Marr smiled to himself watching Lenora walk away crestfallen to her room. Growl at me, you son of a bitch . . . Marr thought, hearing the dog whine softly outside the door.

In the night Lenora awakened more than once to the same soft whining of the big hound. Once she got up quietly, walked to her window and eased it open to look out and check on the dog. "Oh, Oscar," she whispered to herself, seeing him sitting with his head bowed, less than a foot from the door, as if at any moment he knew someone would let him inside. He raised a paw and scraped lightly on the door, then raised his head expectantly, waiting for a response that wasn't going to come. Lenora eased the window shut and wiped a hand beneath her eye. Since her husband's death Oscar had spent most nights curled in front of the warm hearth. It broke Lenora's heart to see him like this. She walked back to her bed and wept. She couldn't allow the dog to be shot, not for just one incident in a lifetime of faithfulness. The dog deserved another chance, and she would willingly give him that chance. She'd have to tell Mister Haddon her decision first thing in the morning.

# Chapter 18

Haddon Marr was sitting at the table drinking a cup of coffee when Lenora Lambert came into the room. He had made a fresh pot using the last of the water in the pail. On the tabletop his pistol lay broken apart where he had just cleaned and inspected each part and had begun reassembling the weapon. Early-morning sunlight streaked in through the front windows and across the plank floor. "You're getting up late this morning," said Marr. "I expect you wanted to put this off as long as you could." He smiled sympathetically. "I can understand that." As he spoke his fingers worked deftly, snapping the pistol together.

"No, Mister Haddon," she replied, "but I was up late thinking this over, and I decided to give Oscar another chance. Perhaps you're mistaken. Perhaps nothing like this will ever happen again."

Marr nodded as he snapped the pistol shut and spun the cylinder, listening closely to the mechanism. Then he reopened the cylinder and began putting the bullets in it as he spoke. After thinking it over and deciding how best to respond, he said in a gentle tone, "Well, ma'am, if that's your decision, I'll go along with it of course. But if the dog does like that again, you have to understand, all I can do is shoot him." Easy enough, he thought to himself. The dog would make another move on him, he'd see to it. Then he'd put a bullet in its head. This was no problem. Him and the dog weren't through with one another . . . he knew it.

"Thank you for being so patient with me, Mister Haddon," said Lenora. "I'm hopeful that Oscar won't do anything like that again."

"Yes, ma'am, and I as well," Marr smiled. He raised the coffee cup to his lips and started to take a drink when a man's voice from out caused him to freeze for a second, then set the cup down quickly and rush to the front window.

"Hello, the house!" the voice called out again. Lenora started toward the door. But Marr caught her by her forearm, stopping her. He had peeped around the edge of the window enough to recognize Ted Riley sitting atop the paint horse with a rifle lying across his lap. "Ambush!" he hissed.

"What?" said Lenora.

Thinking quick, Marr said, "It's one of the scalp hunters I told you about! He's the worst of the bunch! He's after little Hilda, because of her yellow hair! He'll kill her! He's the one who did all this to me!"

"Oh, my God!" said Lenora.

"Go see what he wants!" said Marr.

"You're not going to kill him are you?" she asked. "Please don't kill him! There must be another way besides killing him!"

Marr rubbed his injured eye gently. He could see the woman about to get hysterical on him. "No, I won't kill him." But he certainly wasn't ready to fight Riley again. Not in a fair fight anyway. Riley had nearly killed him the last time. The man was fast and accurate. Marr needed to get the drop on him without Riley being able to fight back. This was too close for Marr. He would have to plan a surprise for Riley.

"Just get rid of him! He's looking for me and Hilda. Tell him we were here but we're gone."

"Why not just say I haven't seen you?" Lenora asked.

"Because he's followed our footprints here!" Marr said, having a hard time not shouting at her. "Tell him we were here for a day, then left day before yesterday. Can you do that for me? For little Hilda?" He shook her by her shoulders.

"Yes, I can tell him that!" said Lenora.

"Hello, the house," Riley called out again. "Is anybody there?" He started to step down from his saddle.

"Hurry!" said Marr. "Don't let him get out of that saddle."

"Yes, I'm here!" Lenora called out, hurrying to the door, then outside, closing the door behind her.

Seeing her, Riley settled back into his saddle. He tipped his hat. "Morning, ma'am. I'm Ted Riley."

Lenora nodded. "Mister Riley . . . I'm Lenora Lambert." She said nothing more, but looked him up and down, checking his torn, blood-stained shirt with one sleeve shredded where he had torn it to make bandages for himself.

Riley noted her tight tone of voice, her closed demeanor. No "good morning, what can I do for you," nothing . . . "Uh, ma'am," said Riley, feeling a bit awkward, "I saw your smoke from along the trail. I'm looking for a man traveling with a young girl. I think they might have come this way. I wonder if you've seen them?"

Inside the window, Marr listened closely. "Might have come this way . . . ?" Who did Ambush think he was fooling, Marr thought. Hilda's footprints and the horse's hooves had led right to the door. Now it was up to whether or not Lenora Lambert could lie well enough to make Riley believe the two had been here and gone.

"Uh, no—" Lenora caught herself and quickly corrected her words. "That is, yes, Mister Riley. . . . They were here and they left. They left yesterday—I mean, day before yesterday."

"Ma'am, are you all right?" Riley asked, looking at her curiously.

"Yes, of course, I'm fine, Mister Riley," said Lenora. But she didn't look it. Her voice sounded strained. "It's still early, and I didn't expect anyone to come riding by this morning."

"I see," said Riley. "Did the man happen to mention where he and the girl were headed?" Riley already knew what her answer would be, he was just marking time, checking her reaction.

"Uh, no, he didn't say anything about where they were headed," said Lenora, visoring her hand above her eyes, although the morning sun glare hadn't yet gotten harsh.

As Riley looked at her, his eyes were searching the place peripherally. Over her shoulder he thought he might have seen someone's reflection in the window. She was too nervous. Her face was flushed. Riley could tell she was lying and that lying was not something she was good at. He'd already seen the small footprints of the girl. They lay right on the ground beneath him. But he wouldn't mention them. And he wouldn't ask her anything else. He had a hunch Marr was still here. If he was, Riley needed to get out of here, not only for his own sake but for the sake of this woman and Hilda as well. There was plenty of cover in the area surrounding the house. He could easily keep an eye on the place and find out what was going on. If Marr was still here, he'd soon know it.

"Well, then, ma'am, I won't trouble you any longer." Riley touched his hat brim with his fingers and backed the paint horse a step. "I'll try to pick up their trail down on the flatlands."

Haddon Marr watched from the window with his thumb over the trigger of his Colt. As soon as Riley turned the horse and rode out of sight around the first turn in the trail, Marr lowered the Colt and turned to see Hilda standing in the middle of the room staring at him. "He wouldn't be here if you had done what I told you to do in the first place!" Marr snapped at her. He wanted to say more, but the door opened and Lenora Lambert stepped inside, out of breath and looking scared.

"He suspects something," she said.

"I'll say he does," said Marr. "He knew you were lying to him. He thinks we're still here. He's not leaving."

"I'm sorry, I'm afraid I'm not a very good liar, Mister Haddon," she said. "What will you do now?"

Marr thought about it. What he had to do was get above Riley in the shelter of some rocks with a rifle. He had to drop the man before he knew what hit him. "Ma'am, I'm like you, I hate killing. If you could stall him for awhile so Hilda and me can make a break for it, I'll manage to shake him off our trail soon enough." Marr gave her a wistful look. "There must be somewhere for Hilda and me to live in peace."

"I'll do it," said Lenora. "I'll divert him somehow."

"Do you have a long gun?" Marr asked bluntly. "What I need is for you to make him think we're still here when he comes back. Keep him busy while Hilda and I make a run for it."

"I have my husband's old rifle. I know how to fire

it. But I won't kill him, Mister Haddon, please understand."

"I do understand," said Marr, "and I respect you for it." He felt like rapping her in the teeth, but he kept his temper in check and played along with her.

"There's a hidden trail that runs up through the rocks and back down to the flatlands, but it is terribly rough. Do you suppose you can ride it, as difficult as it is?" Lenora asked.

Marr just looked at her, then said, "I'll do my best. Just point me to it, then get that rifle and keep him busy while Hilda and I gain some distance on him."

Oscar watched from a cover of cedars as Haddon Marr, with the girl in his arm, hurried secretively from the back door to the small barn without anyone being able to see him from out front of the house. Moments later the dog still sat watching as Marr led the girl and his horse out of the barn and disappeared into the brush and juniper that had long grown over the path the dog often used in his pursuit of jackrabbit and deer. No sooner than they were out of his sight, Oscar stood up in a crouch, sniffing the air toward them, and loped along through the cedars parallel to them twenty yards away. When the dog cut over to the trail, Marr had mounted the horse and put Hilda on his lap. He pushed the horse hard over rock, through sharp brush and brittle red deadfall cedar.

Instincts made the dog keep his distance, sensing there was something wrong with this man. But those same instincts drove him to stay on the girl's trail. She had fed him, she had patted his head. But more than that, she had laid down beside him on his spot in front of the hearth. No person had ever done that, and no dog had even done that, not since he'd been a pup in his litter. She carried his scent and he carried hers. The two had become kindred. For reasons indiscernible to his canine mind, yet no less real, he yearned to be near her. Oscar loped along through the brush a safe distance behind them with unwavering resolve.

Inside the house Lenora waited, her dead husband's rifle leaning against the wall beside the window, the window opened enough for her to get the barrel pointed out when the time came. She paced back and forth, expectantly watching the trail out front of her house for the next hour. She stopped long enough to walk to her bedroom and flop down on the side of her bed. She began crying softly and picked up the picture of her husband from the nightstand. "Oh, Ballard," she said to the picture, "when does it quit being so lonesome?" Then, after a moment, she wiped her eyes, sat the picture down and walked back to the front window.

In the slope of brush and loose rock on the left side of the house where there were no windows looking out on him, Ted Riley eased down from tree to tree, using the cedars partly for cover, partly for a handhold. At the bottom of the sloping hillside he dropped the last few feet to the flat spot of ground and crept along out of sight until he ducked into the barn. To his surprise and disappointment he saw only one horse, a strong-looking black Morgan cross standing in a stall. The horse raised its head and nickered quietly toward him. But Riley noted that the door to the next stall had been left open, and there were fresh droppings lying in the newly turned straw. Riley searched the floor and saw a fresh single hoofprint in a spot of soft earth.

He eased out of the barn, to the back door of the

house and inside, certain that Haddon Marr and the girl had only left here since his earlier visit. But Riley had drawn the Remington just in case he was wrong.

When Riley stepped out into the short hall leading to the front of the house, he saw Lenora Lambert from behind as she stood peeping around the edge of the window toward the trail. He saw the rifle leaning against the wall only inches from her hand. He eased the Remington down into his belt. Keeping close to the wall he eased forward one step at a time, and made it almost to the front room before he heard the telltale sound of a pine board squeaking loudly beneath his boot. Lenora turned quickly, gasped at the sight of him and made a grab for the rifle.

"Ma'am, no!" Riley shouted, lunging the last few feet toward her.

She brought the rifle up. Riley saw her hand go around the stock, saw her finger go into the trigger housing. "Stop or I'll shoot!" she screamed. Hearing her say that at the last second let Riley know that he had nothing to worry about. Still, he snatched the rifle to one side and out of her hands. She came at him swinging her fists, but Riley held her out at arm's length, letting her blows glance off his shoulder, missing his face. She kicked at him, but Riley hiked his leg sideways to her, taking the kicks.

"Ma'am, stop it!" he bellowed at her, not about to turn her loose, unable to control her with one hand. She looked at the rifle looming in his right hand and shied back from it as if afraid he might hit her with it.

"Let go of me!" Lenora said.

Sensing that if he turned her loose she would take off running out the front door, Riley said, "Not until you settle down, ma'am."

"They're gone!" Lenora said. "I told you they were

gone!" She struggled slightly against his grip on her shoulder.

"But they just left, didn't they?" said Riley. "They were here when I came by earlier, weren't they?"

Lenora didn't answer. She stared defiantly.

"Ma'am, I already know they were here! Why are you trying to protect that man? He's a scalp hunter! I've got to get the girl away from him!"

"Men can change!" Lenora said. "At least he's trying to do something different! What are you doing?" Even as she spoke, she settled down a little.

Riley eased his grip on her shoulder a little in response. "Ma'am, I don't know what he's told you, but him and his bunch of scalp hunters are on the run right now for killing a bunch of folks at a water settlement. They killed that girl's mother and scalped her because of the color of her hair!"

"You mean Hilda is not his daughter?" she asked, a bit swayed by the conviction and sincerity in Riley's voice.

Riley turned her loose, seeing her demeanor change. He sighed. "No, ma'am. Believe me, he is no kin to that little girl, he's holding her captive."

"She didn't act like anything was wrong," said Lenora.

"I can't tell you why that is," said Riley. "Maybe he has her too afraid of him to say anything. But I'm telling you the truth. He's a scalp hunter—and the only changing him and any of his pals have made has been to go from scalping to robbing and looting towns between here and the other side of the badlands." He checked the rifle and saw that there had been no cartridge levered into the chamber. "Ma'am, are you here all alone?"

"Well, yes, my dog and I," said Lenora. "My husband is deceased."

"I see," said Riley. "Maybe for my own sake I shouldn't tell you this, but you can't shoot a rifle until you lever a round into the chamber . . . like this." He levered a round, showing her.

"Sir, I know how to operate a rifle. I wasn't going to do so until I knew for certain that you were coming back."

"He asked you to shoot me for him?" Riley shook his head.

"He asked; I told him no," said Lenora. "The same thing I would tell you or anybody else who asked me to do such a thing."

"But you agreed to keep me pinned down as long as you could, give him some time to get away?" Riley asked.

"Yes," said Lenora, indignantly, "thinking him to be an honorable man and protecting his daughter from someone who would do her harm, I did agree to help him any way I could. He promised me he wouldn't kill you if he could just get away. Said all he wanted was to live in peace, him and his daughter."

"So much for his promise," said Riley, unloading the rifle and leaning it back against the wall. "I'll make *you* a promise. I promise that right now you can find him somewhere along the trail, waiting to put a bullet in me from hiding."

Lenora looked saddened. She shook her head, ashamed. "I'm afraid I've been a fool, Mister Riley. I don't know why I believed that man. Perhaps I just wanted to believe someone, anyone. It seems like forever since I've spoken to anyone out here like this."

"Ma'am, your intentions were honorable," said

Riley. "That's all that counts. Don't be hard on yourself." He looked around, then said, "I have to go get my horse and get right on his trail. I'm afraid he's going to head across the border."

"The child will need someone to take care of her once you catch up to him," said Lenora. "I'm going with you, Mister Riley."

"Ma'am, I don't have time to spare and these are hard trails he rides. I'm sorry, it's out of the question."

"Me and my husband's Morgan can withstand anything the trail has to offer, Mister Riley. Besides, I put him on a hidden trail that is a shortcut down to the flatlands. I can show you. Otherwise, one wrong turn and you could be lost for hours, perhaps days. I'm coming with you."

Riley saw desperation in her eyes. "Ma'am, I saw your Morgan, he looks fit. Get him saddled and ready by the time I get back. You can come, but if you slow me down, I've got to leave you, for the child's sake."

"It's a *she,* Mister Riley."

"Ma'am?" Riley said.

"The Morgan, Mister Riley," Lenora said. "It's a mare, and I can assure you she'll stay ahead of you on these hard trails unless I hold her back."

"Yes, ma'am," said Riley, already seeing a difference in the woman. He offered a thin smile, touching his fingers to his hat brim as he headed for the door.

# Chapter 19

Haddon Marr lay at the edge of a cliff looking down at the trail below. Behind him lay a straight flat trail most of the way to the border. He gently rubbed his healing eye and practiced sighting his rifle on a few targets along the trail. On the ground beside him Hilda played with a piece of string she'd taken from her clothing and hummed quietly under her breath. Haddon turned from setting up an ambush for Riley and lay on his side for a moment watching her. Hilda sat with her sheared head bowed, idly winding then unwinding the string around one finger after another. The melody she hummed was some archaic child's song that Marr recognized but could not name. After a while, he reached up and cupped his rough hand on her cheek, whispering, "You are a true little angel, you are."

Hilda raised her eyes for a second, but continued to hum.

Marr raised a finger to his lips and said, "Shhh . . . You be real quiet, now. We'll be having a visitor any minute, unless I miss my guess."

Moments later, when he heard the sound of the horses' hoofs climbing up the trail to the level clearing beneath him, Marr waved the girl back farther from the edge out of the sight. "You stay right there," he said, "unless I wave you back up here."

He looked back down and watched Riley follow the woman up into his waiting rifle sights. "I knew I shoulda took that Morgan," he whispered to himself. Then he nestled the rifle butt against his shoulder and settled in for the shot.

On the trail, Riley caught a glint of sunlight coming from the cliff line above him and reacted instantly. Lenora Lambert hadn't seen the warning sign and continued speaking about her dog, Oscar, concerned for how he would fair while she was gone. Riley, in a split second before the rifle shot resounded, flung himself from his saddle into Lenora, hooking an arm around her, taking her to the ground with him. Lenora let out a short scream, then the fall partly knocked her breath out of her. The two landed off the narrow trail and rolled a few feet before stopping beside an ancient piñon clinging to the rocky, sloping hillside.

Riley rolled her over into the shelter of the piñon as another shot rang out. "Are you all right, ma'am?" he asked, his Remington out and cocked.

"Yes, I'm all right!" said Lenora. She breathed heavily, looking up wide-eyed toward the trail. "The horses! He'll shoot the horses!" She scrambled away from Riley and ran up the slope before he could stop her.

"Ma'am, stay down!" he shouted. He ran behind her onto the trail, but the horses had already bolted forward and stood out in the open, hugging a rock wall on the inside of the trail. A rifle shot thumped into the ground at Lenora's feet. She ran to the inside of the trail herself, into the cover of rock. Riley stood in the open long enough to fire two shots upward, hoping to distract Marr from getting a bead on Lenora

Lambert. With Lenora safely out of Marr's sight, Riley hurried out of the middle of the trail behind her, hearing a shot thump into the ground at his feet.

On the cliff Marr waved the girl forward. "You sit right up here where they can see you, angel," he said. Then he called down, saying, "Ambush, you should have been dead where I left you laying! I hate having to do a job twice!" He chuckled to himself.

"I'm not going back without the girl, Marr," Riley shouted in reply.

"Then you're not going back at all," Marr responded. "She's mine and she'll stay mine!" He turned to Hilda and said in a softer, lowered tone of voice, "Ain't that right, my little angel?"

Hilda nodded.

Haddon Marr laughed and looked back down, knowing the two were out of danger against the inverted wall of rock below him, but knowing there was nothing he could do about it. "Look up here, Ambush!" he shouted. "Hilda's sitting here on the edge wanting to tell you both hello!"

Riley ventured out from against the wall long enough to look up and see the girl sitting on the edge of the cliff. "Marr, you son of a bitch," he whispered to himself.

"Is that child on the edge of the cliff?" Lenora asked, when Riley stepped back in beside her.

"Yes, ma'am, she is," said Riley. "It's just Marr's way of telling us he'll kill the girl if it comes down to it."

"Then what must we do?" Lenora asked. "You can't just back off and let him keep her."

"No, ma'am," said Riley. "We're not about to back off. But we've got to be careful how close we press him. We've got to stay close and look for just the right time to make a move. The main thing is we don't let him shake us off his trail."

"Lenora Lambert!" Marr shouted. "Woman, you let me and Hilda down! You said you would hold him back while we got away! Now look at her, up here, her in danger! This is your doing!"

Before Riley could stop her, she blurted out in reply, "You, sir, are a liar and a scoundrel! I trusted you, but you deceived me! Hilda, I didn't let you down, child. Mister Marr is using you!"

"No, don't say that!" Riley warned her, pulling her back as she leaned out to shout up at Marr.

She gave Riley a curious look. "I think she should know who is doing this to her, Mister Riley."

"No, ma'am, not right now," Riley said. "Whatever her connection is to Marr, it has kept her alive. Right now that's all that matters. If she turns on him, I have no doubt he'll kill her."

"You're right, Mister Riley," said Lenora, after considering it.

"Ma'am," said Riley, "since we're riding together, if it's all the same with you, feel free to call me by my first name."

Lenora blushed and averted her eyes. "Thank you all the same, Mister Riley. But I shouldn't want to appear bold or presumptious. I almost made that mistake with Mister Haddon."

"His name is Haddon Marr," said Riley. "I respect your decision, ma'am. But at any time you choose, feel free to call me Ted."

"Thank you, Mister Riley, I will remember your offer," Lenora said.

As Riley spoke he kept his attention focused on the ground sixty feet above them. "Le— Uh, ma'am," he said, catching and correcting himself. "I'm going to have to go get those horses before one of them happens to wander out into his rifle sight. If I give you this pistol will you be able to cover me while—"

"Mister Riley," Lenora said, cutting him off, "it would be too dangerous, me giving you cover. . . . I'm not a good shot with a pistol. I'll be the one to go get the horses. You can cover me."

"No, ma'am," said Riley shaking his head. "If something happened to you I would never be able—"

Lenora had already turned and began running in a crouch along the rock wall toward the horses. The horses stood against the same wall but at a turn in the trail visible to the ridge above. "Ma'am!" Riley hissed in a harsh whisper. "I can't allow you to do this!"

But Lenora Lambert didn't even look back. She stopped long enough beside a spilled boulder to look back and up, seeing that in a few more feet Marr would see her moving toward the horses. "Lord, help me," she whispered, "here I go."

Ted Riley saw her make a run along the last few yards to the horses. He bolted out into the middle of the trail and looked up, seeing only Marr's rifle barrel and a sliver of the top of Marr's hat. Close to the rifle barrel he saw the girl sitting with her legs dangling over the edge. He couldn't risk firing at Marr, but he fired two shots straight up to draw Marr's attention to him and away from Lenora Lambert. "Marr! Come down here you coward!" he shouted. "Face me like a man!"

Face him like a man? Uh-oh, Marr thought. He took a quick glance back and forth, seeing what Riley was up to, saying a foolish thing like that. "There she goes," Marr whispered, seeing Lenora hurry back along the rock wall, leading the horses. "Thanks for letting me know, Ambush," he chuckled to himself.

Seeing the rifle barrel swing toward Lenora, Riley shouted, "Run, ma'am! Let the horses go!" He pointed the Remington, but could not force himself to take the shot and risk hitting the child.

Marr's rifle shot missed Lenora but kicked up dirt against Morgan's hoofs, causing the horse to rear and try to turn. Lenora struggled with the horse. Another shot hit the ground near her feet. "Ma'am, take cover!" Riley shouted. He instinctively aimed the gun up at Marr, but stopped himself from firing, seeing the child's legs swing back and forth without a concern in the world.

But Lenora wasn't about to turn the horses loose. Instead, she jerked the frightened Morgan down onto four hoofs, then flung herself into the saddle and batted her heels to the mare's sides, racing back along the trail toward Riley, leading the paint horse by its reins.

Another rifle shot ricocheted off a rock as Lenora rode past Riley, cut a half circle and ducked both horses over against the wall.

Above them Marr rubbed his healing eye and cursed under his breath. "Damn this infirmity!" He looked at Hilda, who sat calmly staring down at the empty trail beneath them. "Well, little angel, it's good to see you've gotten over any gun-shyness you might have had. I'm glad of it, because we'll be seeing a whole lot more of it between here and the border." He scooted back and stood up, dusting himself with his hand. Then he reached down, took Hilda by the hand and lifted her to her feet. "It's time we get on out of here. Don't you worry none, I won't let them take you away from me. We're together; we're staying together, dead or alive."

Against the rock wall below, Riley had breathed a

sigh of relief, taking the reins to both horses and pulling them farther in out of sight. He shook his head, took off his hat and ran his fingers back through his hair. "Ma'am, you sure work awfully well under fire."

"Well, I should certainly hope so, Mister Riley," Lenora said, catching her breath and fanning herself with her hand. "After all, my father was a cavalryman when he was younger."

Riley had no idea what that might have to do with anything. But he smiled slightly and said, "Well, ma'am, you've made him proud I'm sure."

They stood in silence for a moment as Riley looked back and forth along the trail, deciding what move to make. Finally, looking toward the spot where Lenora had gone to gather the horses, he said, "It's not far from where this wall goes out in the open to the next bend in the trail." Staring hard at the turn in the trail, estimating the distance, he said, "I'm guessing maybe twenty yards, twenty-five at the most."

Lenora also looked, then replied, "If we hit that exposed stretch at a run, we would be out of his range in seconds."

"Seconds can get long, ma'am, when a gun's pointing at your back. Are you sure you're up to it?"

"The way he has been shooting, yes," said Lenora, "I'm *positive*. Lucky for us his eye is still healing."

Riley looked at her. "He hasn't been shooting the best I've ever seen, but it only takes one bullet to kill you."

"Mister Riley," Lenora said frankly, "I know about death and dying. I have seen much of it in my time. So much that I daresay I no longer fear it, not if it comes to giving my life for some greater good. You needn't worry about whether or not I understand the severity of our situation. I do. Were it not for that child, I wouldn't be here; I wouldn't be involved in something this dangerous. But I am here, sir—I am involved. Once involved in something, I only know how to give it everything I have. I am not a halfway person, Mister Riley."

"Well said, ma'am," Riley replied. "I just need to make sure you know."

"I *know*, Mister Riley. Believe me," Lenora said. "Now let's have no more of this wondering where I stand because I'm a woman."

"You are absolutely right, ma'am," said Riley, ". . . you have my apologies. We are in this together, no matter how hard the trail."

"Thank you, sir," said Lenora curtly. "Now let us get mounted and ride." She glanced upward and said, "It's ironic that he can only be twenty or so yards above us, but by the trail that means he is over two hours ahead of us."

"How far does that put him from the border?" Riley asked.

"From where he's at right now he has only a short run to the border. I can't say how many miles, but he's less than a full day's ride, I can tell you."

"Then we best get at it," said Riley, stepping up into his stirrup and swinging over into his saddle, his wounds throbbing with pain, but not enough to stop him. Lenora stepped up atop the Morgan and rode close behind Riley alongside the rock wall until they reached a spot where they would begin being visible from the cliff above them. Riley stopped and said, "All right, ma'am, I'm going to put you in front of me while we make our run."

She gave him a dubious look.

"No, ma'am, not because you're a woman," Riley said. "It's because like you said awhile ago, I can provide you with better cover. So let's not argue, let's just do it." He had dropped his horse a step behind her as he spoke. No sooner had he finished his words than he slapped the Morgan mare on its rump and sent the animal racing toward the turn in the trail. He booted the paint horse out right behind her, looking back and up at the cliff line, the Remington in hand on the outside chance that Marr had moved the girl out of the line of fire. They made the turn in the trail and slowed and circled their horses for a look back. Seeing no sign of Marr or the girl up there, Riley said, "He's already cleared out. He's headed straight for the border right now."

"Yes, I'm sure he is," said Lenora, already turning the Morgan mare to the trail. "Let's not waste time talking." She batted her heels to the mare and took off along the treacherous rock path.

"Yes, ma'am," said Riley, "I'm right behind you."

The ranger, Sheriff Tackett and their prisoner rode onto the trail leading into Hueso Seco and saw a bullet-riddled sign lying in the sand that read POPULA-TION 127. The town's name had been completely blasted off the sign by endless shotgun, rifle and pistol fire. "How long since you've been through here?" the ranger asked Tackett after having him drop back until they were both twenty feet behind Toller. He asked quietly, keeping Morton Toller from hearing him as Toller continued to ride along in the afternoon sun.

"It's been a while," said Tackett, "but even then they could have cut that number of people in half and still been exaggerating."

"He's got a trick up his sleeve," said the ranger.

"I've been thinking that myself," Tackett agreed. "But this is the quickest way to the border and to

Piedra Negra. There's no water between here and the Ajo mines this time of year."

"I know it," said Sam. "We've got to go this way, like it or not. But let's keep ten feet between us once we get inside Hueso Seco."

"Sure enough," said Tackett, reaching back as they spoke and pulling a sawed-off double-barreled shotgun from beneath his blanket roll. He tucked the short shotgun up under his coat, out of sight. The ranger slid his rifle from the saddle boot and carried it lying across his lap. Ahead of them they saw five men begin to assemble slowly out front of a boarded-up saloon. Balls of sagebrush lay strewn about the street, rocking back and forth in the hot breeze. The ranger sidled up to Morton Toller and dropped a loop of rope over his head and tightened it before Toller could duck.

"Hey, what the hell, Ranger?" said Toller, caught off-guard. "I gave you my word I'd lead you to Black Rock! Don't you trust me even a little bit?"

The ranger let the rope sway between the two of them and said, "I don't trust you enough to make it worth talking about, Toller. But I'll give you *my word* that if you turn rabbit on us all of a sudden, you'll break your neck at the end of a tight rope." He threw two quick hitches around his saddle horn with a slight smile.

"What the hell is this?" a man wearing a black riding duster asked, stepping out into the middle of the street in front of the saloon as if to stop the ranger and Tackett from passing him on their way to the well in the center of the deserted town.

Another man stepped out beside him, this one wearing buckskins and a broad Mexican sombrero with eagle feathers hanging from the brim. He wore a brace of pistols standing high on his stomach, the butts for-

ward for a cross draw. Three more men eased forward
for a better look, seeing the prisoner in handcuffs with
a rope around his neck. "Is that two law dogs?" one
man asked another.

Noticing the two badges as the ranger and Tackett
drew closer, the man in buckskins said loudly, "Hey,
you two are law dogs, huh?"

The ranger and Tackett kept riding slowly toward
the well without answering. Morton Toller grinned,
giving a sweeping glance at a couple of faces along
the boardwalk, then staring straight ahead.

"Hey, I asked you a question, law dogs!" the man
in buckskins shouted.

But neither the ranger nor Tackett gave him a
glance. They rode on, keeping ten feet between them,
listening for the metal against metal sound of a pistol
hammer cocking or of a rifle lever being pulled back
and forth. The ranger eased his finger over his rifle
trigger. They rode on to the well another thirty yards
away. But on their way, the ranger heard someone say
to the man in buckskins, "I believe they just ignored
you, Buckskin Dave! What the hell did you ever do
to deserve that?" The men laughed among themselves.

"You two step down and water your horses," the
ranger said, turning his Appaloosa sideways to the
well to keep his eyes on things out front of the saloon.
"When you're finished, mount up and I'll step down
and water mine."

"What's the matter, Ranger?" Toller grinned. "Are
these boys making you feel a little unwelcome?"

"Come on, Toller," said Tackett. "Step down and
keep your mouth shut." He gave Toller a nudge to
get him started.

"I was just thinking maybe I could put a word in
for you with these fellows." Toller stepped down, still

grinning, and let his horse stick its muzzle down into a water trough beside Tackett's horse. "Since I'll soon be going free, I'd like to get on the side of law and order as quick as I can."

"I told you to keep your mouth shut!" said Tackett, stepping close to him, his fists balled tightly at his sides.

"Easy there, Sheriff," said Toller, seeing that Tackett was on the verge of losing his temper. "Every time you start thinking unpleasant thoughts about me, you just think of that little girl you're out to save."

"Quiet, Toller," the ranger said, giving a sharp yank on the rope. "We've got company coming."

Three of the men from out front of the abandoned saloon walked toward them down the middle of the sagebrush-littered street. The one in the buckskins stayed behind along with another man, staring toward the well. "How many of these men do you know, Toller?" the ranger asked without taking his eyes off them.

"None of them, Ranger, and that's the by God truth of the matter," said Toller, still grinning, but losing some of his devil-may-care attitude standing between the ranger and Tackett with three men coming at them down the middle of the street.

"Stop right there, you're close enough," the ranger said when the men got within ten yards of them.

"Close enough?" The three stopped, but the one in the middle said, "This ain't close enough to carry on a civil conversation."

"It's *close enough* for our purposes," said the ranger. "We've got nothing to talk about anyway."

"Well, I'm afraid we do, Ranger," said the young gunman, tightening his jaw. "See, that's our well you and your horses are using."

"Turn around and go," said Burrack, not even offering a reply.

The men stood firm. "Maybe you don't understand about the well, Ranger," the young man said. "Now that the town has pulled up stakes, we've taken over. Hueso Seco is our town now. So the fact is, you're going to have to—"

"Tackett," said the ranger, cutting the man off.

Sheriff Tackett swung the sawed-off double-barrel up from under his coat, cocking both hammers with his thumb. The three men stiffened on the spot.

"See what I meant by 'close enough'?" said the ranger.

"Back off, Tommy," said one of the other men under his breath. "It ain't worth a face full of buckshot."

"Nail heads," Tackett called out, correcting him. "Enough nail heads to ruin the rest of your day."

"Yeah, Tommy," the other man said quietly. "If Dave wants to collect some money, let him do it himself."

But the young man stood firm, saying, "You two back off, if that's all you're good for. I don't back off." His right hand poised near his holster.

"Tell your friend adios and get out of here," said the ranger.

"Tommy, come on," one of the young men said as the two of them backed away with their hands held chest-high away from their guns.

"Get away from me," said Tommy, "before you both wet yourselves."

The two men quickly turned and left, getting out of the line of fire.

The ranger waited until they were out of hearing

distance, then he said to the one remaining, "Tommy? Is that what he called you?"

"Yeah, Tommy Rowlings," said the young gunman, his hand still poised, but looking as if he didn't know what else to do with it.

The ranger nodded, still in his saddle, his hand on his rifle. "All right, Tommy, forget that your pals are watching. Forget that you want to look tough to that man in buckskins. Ask yourself one question: Do you really want to die with your face blown all over the street? Because that's where you're headed right this minute."

A tense silence passed. "How do I end it?" the young man asked sheepishly.

"Just like your friends did, Tommy," said Sheriff Tackett. "Let your bark down, step back and walk away."

The young man bit his lower lip. "Buckskin Dave told me to collect a dollar from yas for the water. He won't let me live it down if I don't."

"Tell him I said to come collect it himself," said the ranger, "just like your two pals said."

The young man wanted to say something else, but Tackett saw it and cut him off before he got started. "Boy, get out of here! We're not the kind of men you want to fool with. We're out here on serious business. I'll burn you down."

Tommy Rowlings saw the look in Boyd Tackett's eyes. "Wait! I'm going!" He backed off a step, raising his gun hand away from his pistol butt.

Watching him turn and walk back to the others, Burrack and Tackett heard the men already begin to taunt him for backing down. Tackett turned back to the two horses, which had been drawing water steadily. "Damn fool kid," he said, easing the hammers down on the shotgun and letting it hang loosely in his hand. The ranger watched the men out front of the empty saloon until Tackett and Toller finished watering their horses. Once Tackett was back in the saddle, Burrack stepped down and watered the Appaloosa, still keeping an eye along the dusty street. The man in buckskins stood facing them from fifty yards away with his feet spread as if poised for a fight, but the ranger knew none was coming. They finished up and rode on.

On the boardwalk by an abandoned mercantile store, Cinco Diablos had watched the scene play itself out in the street. Now he watched the three continue on their way, leaving the far end of town. He was certain that Morton Toller had seen him as he and the lawmen rode past. Now that Cinco saw nothing was going to happen here, he turned to the man beside him and said, "We better get on across the border, Bruno. Earles will want to hear about Toller leading these lawmen to our hideout."

"How do you know he's leading them there?" said Bruno.

Cinco gave him a cold stare. "You weren't with us this last trip we made. You don't know the things we did. I think the law will not rest until they find us."

"Then let's just kill these two along the trail and be done with it," said Bruno Kratz.

"You let me do the thinking," said Cinco. "Let's get out of here." The two slipped around the corner of the old mercantile and hurried to where their horses stood in the shade on a narrow alley.

# Chapter 20

The two lawmen and their prisoner made a dark camp along a dry southerly branch of the Gila river. The next morning before dawn they had headed out again toward the border. Morton Toller rode a few feet in front of them, his hands still cuffed but the rope no longer around his neck. Daylight had just cleared the eastern horizon and the sun's heat and glare had not yet begun to cast its wavering veil across the desert floor, when Toller stopped atop a rise of sand and rock and motioned for the ranger and Tackett to join. The two lawmen heeled their horses forward quickly and sidled up to Toller, who stood in his stirrups staring out across a stretch of cactus and sage. When the two stopped, Toller managed to step his horse a few feet away from them.

"What is it, Toller?" the ranger asked, staring out with him.

"I swear it's the biggest damn wind-devil I ever seen," said Toller. "See it? Right over yonder?"

The ranger only made a sweeping search in the direction Toller pointed, but Sheriff Tackett stood in his stirrups searching back and forth, seeing nothing. "You must be seeing things, Toller," he said gruffly.

Seeing Toller step his horse farther away from Tackett, the ranger realized what Toller was up to. "Get down, Tackett!" the ranger shouted, giving Tackett a shove from his saddle just before a bullet sliced through the air, followed by a rifle shot exploding. Burrack jerked the Appaloosa around in a half circle and batted his boots to its sides, ducking out of the way just as the sound of another rifle shot exploded. Tackett rose to his knees, still holding his reins. Without mounting, he jerked his horse back down the low rise of rock dirt until he was out of the line of fire. Morton Toller raced forward across the sand, letting out a loud hoot of laughter. "Adios, *necios*!" he shouted over his shoulder.

"Dang it!" said Tackett. " 'Fools' is right!" He ducked as another shot exploded.

But the ranger didn't duck. This time he saw the bullet kick up sand on the other side of Morton Toller as Toller raced away.

"They're shooting at him!" said the ranger, ready to kick his boots to the Appaloosa's sides.

"What? I thought it was some of his scalp hunters come to set him free!" Tackett shouted.

"They're trying to kill him!" the ranger shouted, already racing away while Tackett drew his rifle from his saddle scabbard and scurried up the crest of the rise to give him cover.

The ranger raced along behind Toller, hearing the rifles firing from a long ways off, seeing dirt kick as the bullets missed Toller and struck the ground. Suddenly Toller realized the rifles were firing at him. He jerked his horse to a halt and shouted, "Hey, you stupid bastards! It's *me*!" As he turned his horse facing toward the gunshots, the ranger shouted, "Get down, Toller! They know it's you!"

"What?" Toller shouted in disbelief. But even as he shouted, a bullet snatched his hat from his head and spun it high in the air. Toller saw what the ranger meant and hammered his boot heels to his horse's sides back toward Tackett, who had the only cover available within two hundred yards.

"Hurry up!" the ranger shouted as Toller raced past him toward cover. Burrack had drawn his rifle and began firing, keeping the Appaloosa moving back and forth, not giving the rifles an easy target. As Toller raced toward safety, the ranger fell in behind him, firing shot after shot at the two rifle positions. Before he'd reached Tackett and Toller, the ranger noted that the rifle fire had stopped. When he spun the Appaloosa to a halt, he saw a rise of dust running away in the distance.

"You sonsabitch!" Tackett shouted at Toller, swinging his rifle butt and getting a glancing blow on Toller's shoulder as Toller ducked away.

"Jesus! Take it easy, Sheriff!" said Toller, seeing the rage in Tackett's eyes. "Ranger, do something! He's gone mad on me!"

"You tried to get me killed!" Tackett shouted, taking another swipe with the rifle butt. "I don't care if he kills you, Toller," the ranger said. "I think you might be too stupid to live anyway."

"Don't forget, without me you'll never find Earles and the others. You'll never find the girl!"

"If you get yourself killed by your own men, Toller, you're not going to be much help to us anyway." As he spoke he stepped in between Toller and Sheriff Tackett, and stuck the hot rifle barrel up against Toller's chin. "The next stunt you pull like that, if Tackett doesn't kill you, I'll kill you myself!"

"All right, all right!" said Toller. "I saw a chance

and took it. You can't blame a fellow for looking out for himself, can you?"

"Remember what I just told you, Toller," the ranger warned him, lowering the rifle and taking a step back. "If your *own kind* wants to kill you, I think you'd better look at us as the best chance you've got."

Tackett calmed down and backed off. Looking out toward the rising dust, he said, "It looks like they're cutting out now. They made their play and missed. Think that's all we'll see of them?"

The ranger looked at Toller as he replied to Tackett. "Now that they know Toller sees what they're up to, they know they're not going to catch us off-guard again." He asked Toller, "What do you say? Will that be the end of it?"

"I think so," said Toller. "One thing's for damn sure, I ain't sticking my head up in front of them again. If this is all they think of my friendship, I reckon I'm quits with them for good. I'm glad I'm taking you to the hideout." He raised his voice as if the two gunmen could hear him from two miles away. "Hear that? You gawdamned traitor sonsabitches! I hope these lawmen kill every gawdamned one of yas!" Toller grinned, dusted his cuffed hands together and said to Tackett and the ranger, "There now, how was that?"

Three miles away, Cinco Diablos and Bruno Kratz slowed their horses to a halt and looked back over their shoulders in the direction of Toller and the lawmen. "Damn it!" said Cinco, "we missed that *idiota bastardo*! All those shots and you never hit a damn thing!" He gave Bruno a look of contempt.

"Neither did you!" said Bruno, returning the look.

"How do we face Earles and tell him we missed a chance to kill Toller while he brings law dogs down our necks?"

"Just like that I reckon," Bruno shrugged. "To tell you the truth, Cinco, I always thought you and Toller were saddle pals from way back."

"*Si*, we are," said Cinco, "so what is your question?"

"Well, I mean you are wanting to kill him awfully bad, not knowing for sure that he is leading them to Black Rock," said Bruno.

"You are too stupid to talk to!" Cinco stared at him for a second. "Toller is leading them there . . . I know he is, because it's the only reason they could have for not killing him or throwing him in jail. They're after the girl Haddon Marr has with him. It was a curse, keeping her. We should never have kept her."

"Well, it's too late to change it now," said Bruno.

"Yes, it is too late now," said Cinco, giving Bruno another look of contempt. He jerked his horse around toward the trail leading across the border. "Do me a favor, Bruno," he said. "We'll be in Mexico by morning. Don't talk to me anymore on the way."

"Suits me all to hell," said Bruno.

Jessup Earles had kept wounded Uncle Andy Fill with him, and the two had been the first to arrive at the sun-bleached shack standing on stilts against the side of a steep sandstone hill. But upon their second day there, as Uncle Andy lay on a flat quilt pallet in a corner nursing his wounds and Earles sat at the window drinking whiskey, Earles saw the Beldon brothers, Duke and Brozy, come riding up a trail through loose rock, cactus and creosote. It had been awhile since the Beldon brothers had ridden with Earles. He welcomed them heartily. The four men drank together throughout a day and a night until Uncle Andy Fill could no longer rise up from his pallet.

"Can I get a hand here?" Andy called out in a weak, shaky voice.

But the three only laughed. Brozy Beldon finally rolled a half-full bottle of whiskey across the floor to Uncle Andy, saying, "There, that ought to keep you smiling for a while."

"Sonsabitches," Uncle Andy grumbled to himself. Still, he snatched the bottle up and held onto it.

The next to arrive was Crossed-eyed Burton Stowl, who had spent most of the past five days dodging an army patrol along the border. On his last three miles into the Piedra Negra hideout, he met an old outlaw named Bud Langston, who upon hearing from Stowl that Earles and his scalp hunters had gone into robbery and raiding towns along the border, became interested in joining them. When Earles met the two in the dusty yard out front of the shack he had recovered from a bad whiskey hangover and was ready to talk business. He'd even dragged Uncle Andy Fill out with him and propped him against the front porch while he spoke to the men.

"There's enough towns along the border from here to West Texas to keep us busy the rest of our lives," said Earles. He grinned. "Is there anybody here who can't see what a perfect setup this is?" Nobody responded. "If you can't, you best think about going somewhere and crawling under a rock. This border is made for people like us, bold enough to take what we want in this world!" He laughed, looking from one face to the next. Then he stopped at Bud Langston and stared. "Well, Bud, what do you say? Are you in or out?"

"Count me in," said Langston. "This is a sure thing. I've always wanted to ride with you and your bunch, but I always said that sooner or later the scalp-hunting business was going to hit bottom."

"Then you're in, Bud," said Earles. He gestured a hand toward the Beldon brothers, saying, "Duke and Brozy here have already said they want in. It's time I let in some new blood."

As he spoke, Earles saw Cinco Diablos and Bruno Kratz riding up the trail toward the shack. "Here comes two more good men right now," he said. "Alls we're waiting on now is Toller and Haddon Marr. We'll be riding out of here to line our pockets soon." But when Cinco and Bruno dismounted and gave a nod to the other men, Cinco said to Earles with a worried look on his face, "Earles, Morton Toller is on his way here with a sheriff and that Badlands ranger."

Earls looked stunned for a moment. "Toller has turned on us?" He let it sink in, then said, "How far back are they?"

"We left them not far from the border. If they pushed as hard as we did, they could ride in here within an hour," said Cinco.

As he'd spoken the men had drawn closer around him and Earles. "How do you know they'll cross the border," Stowl asked.

His question drew a hard stare from Cinco and Earles. "It ain't likely that ranger would get right to the border and just stop there, now is it?"

"That's what he's supposed to do," said Stowl.

"To hell with what he's supposed to do," said Earles. "If Cinco says he's coming, damn it, *he's coming*, border or no!"

"Wait a minute!" said Bud Langston. "What Badlands ranger are you talking about? The one who rides the big Appaloosa?"

"Yes, that one," said Cinco.

"How do you know it's the same one?" said Earles.

"I saw him and the sheriff ride into Hueso Seco with a rope around Toller's neck! The ranger is riding the big Appaloosa. These two are out for blood. They backed down Buckskin Dave Ryder's men like they were schoolboys . . . acted like they didn't even want to waste time on them."

"Damn it!" said Jessup Earles. "Damn Morton Toller for bringing those law dogs down on us and damn Haddon Marr for dragging that kid along! It always gets everybody upset, snatching a kid, especially a girl. That's why those two lawmen are willing to cross the border."

Cinco looked all around, then asked, "Where is Marr anyway? Has he not shown up yet?"

"Hell, no," said Earles. "But he will soon enough. And when he does, I'm going to tell him he's got to get rid of that kid, one way or the other! If he gives me any trouble over it, I'll shoot the little nit myself and be done with all this nonsense."

Having heard about the ranger headed their way, Bud Langston had grown quiet and stepped back away from the others.

"All right," said Earles, trying to keep in charge of things, "this is just a little bit of a setback. We'll handle the lawmen when they get here. Everybody get ready for a fight." He looked back at Cinco and Bruno and said, "You two get yourselves some water and grub and get back down along the ridge. Keep watch for them."

"We're on our way," said Cinco. "If you hear us fire two warning shots, just realize that one of them has just blown Toller's heart through the back of his shirt."

While Earles and the others talked, Bud Langston eased his way over to his horse, stepped up into his saddle and rode away quietly toward the trail before anyone noticed him being gone. "Who's that?" said Earles finally, craning his neck for a better look at Langston as the old outlaw's horse began to raise a stir of dust. "Yep, it's him all right," Earles answered himself.

"That dirty bastard!" said Cross-eyed Burton Stowl, looking over at the hitch rail, seeing Langston's horse missing. "I was going to vouch for him riding with us!" He snatched his pistol from his holster and fired wildly at the fleeing outlaw.

"Save your bullets, Stowl!" said Earles. "He's too far away for you to hit even if you had two good eyes."

Eighty yards away, Bud Langston had ducked slightly as the pistol shots exploded behind him. But he only chuckled to himself and rode on. "Damn fools," he said to himself, "think I'm going to stay and fight that ranger with them. I rob banks for a living. This kinda stuff ain't putting one thin dollar in my pocket." He heeled his horse onto the main trail that meandered back toward the border. But before he'd gone two miles through a stand of sparse woodland, he rounded a turn in the trail and had to jerk hard on his reins to keep from running headlong into Haddon Marr.

Both horses reared face to face. "Whoa!" shouted Langston, seeing it was Marr and throwing his right hand up away from his gun. "Don't shoot!"

But Marr's reaction had been as quick as the strike of a snake in spite of his blurred eye. His pistol came up and fired just as Langston's horse touched down. The shot hit Langston in his right shoulder, twisting him from his saddle. He landed flat on his back. Only then did Marr recognize him as he coaxed his horse closer, his pistol pointed down at him.

"Don't . . . don't shoot!" Langston pleaded, holding up his left hand toward Marr, seeing how strange the scalp hunter looked with the girl on his lap. Hilda stared down at the wounded outlaw wide-eyed, her close-cropped hair standing out in every direction.

"Bud Langston?" Marr asked, tipping his pistol barrel up.

"Lord, Marr, what's got into you?" Langston groaned, lying in the dirt, grasping his right shoulder. "You've shot the hell out of me!"

"What are you doing out here?" asked Marr, offering no apology for his act.

"I came here with Burton Stowl to ride with you boys," said Langston. "Damned if I think it's a good idea from what I've seen so far." He reached his bloody left hand up for help. "Can you give me a pull here?"

"Grab on," said Marr, sidling his horse over to him. Lifting his boot from a stirrup, Marr allowed the wounded outlaw to hold onto the stirrup and pull himself to his feet with his left hand. "I'd offer to stay and help you, old pard," said Marr, "but I've got a bullet wound myself, and somebody is dogging me hard." He shot a glance back along the trail, then added, "I ain't seen them, but they're back there. I can feel them watching me. Hope you understand."

"I do," said Langston, wincing in pain, blood flowing down his arm. "If you'll just give me a—"

Before he could finish his words, Marr had booted his horse and took off, the girl looking back at Langston with a blank expression. "Well, thank you all to hell," Langston said bitterly. "I guess it's just my tough luck!"

But Marr didn't even hear him as he rode away, booting the tired horse into a run. Bud Langston stood in a wake of dust for a moment beside his horse as he rummaged through his saddlebags, took out a faded bandanna, shook it and pressed it to his shoulder. "A wound like this ain't something to play around with," he grumbled to himself, "get infected and die seeing things that ain't there."

After a moment he struggled up into his saddle using his left hand, turned his horse in the opposite direction Marr had taken and batted his heels to its sides. "Scalp hunters," he said, "the craziest sonsabitches in the world . . . what the hell was wrong with me, coming here in the first place?" He rode on, pressing the bandanna to his wounded shoulder while Haddon Marr raced on toward Piedra Negra.

Marr stopped only once, inside the stand of woods, long enough to look all around while he rested his horse and stepped down to stretch his back and give the girl a drink of tepid water from his canteen. As Hilda lifted the canteen and sipped from it, Marr stooped down enough to face her, his hands on his knees, and say, "You know there might soon be people who will come wanting to take you away from me, but I won't let them." He studied her eyes. "Do you understand me? Do you know what this means I'll have to do?"

She nodded her head without answering.

Marr gave her a curious look, then testing her asked, "What will I have to do? You tell me, Hilda."

She started to raise the canteen again, ignoring him. But Marr stopped her. He took the canteen and said, "Tell me, what is it I'll have to do?"

She shrugged. She didn't know.

Marr looked at her for a moment as if closely considering his next words. Finally he just said, "Well, it won't be very pretty, I can tell you that." As he spoke he ran his hand back across her close-cropped hair, judging it, wondering if it had grown any at all since she'd been with him. After a moment he thought he'd heard something in the woods. He gave a suspicious search as he capped the canteen and hung its strap around his saddle horn. "Let's go," he whispered.

He mounted the horse, swinging Hilda up onto his lap, and looked around once again, thinking he'd heard something in the brush. "I'm getting too edgy for my own good," he murmured to Hilda and himself, booting the tired horse along the trail.

A few minutes later, as Marr and Hilda approached the hideout at Piedra Negra, Cinco Diablos and Bruno Kratz stood up and watched from atop a large boulder embedded in the breast of the hillside. "Here comes Marr," said Cinco, "I think he has gone completely loco, just between you and me." They waved Marr on in among the boulders on the path leading up to the shack.

Out front of the shack the Beldon brothers were the first to see Marr approaching. They called out through the open door to Jessup Earles, who stepped out and stood with them until Marr stopped ten feet away and looked back over his shoulder. "It's about damn time you showed up, Marr," said Earles. "What the hell happened to you back in that town?"

"I decided it was time to go . . . so I went," said Marr, offering no explanation, no apology. "Is there any more to say on it?" He gave Earles a cool stare. "I'm back now and that's all that counts."

"You're back," said Earles, "but that kid has to go. She's had your mind twisted sideways ever since I gave her to you."

Marr's face lost all color; his jaw tightened. "She's not going anywhere. I'll kill any sonsabitch who comes near her." His hand snatched his pistol up from his holster. He fanned it back and forth, causing the men to take a step back.

"Whoa now, settle down," said Jessup Earles. "You're getting too far out-of-hand about this little child. We're your friends here, Haddon. You need to take a good look at yourself."

"Nobody comes near her," said Marr, still moving the gun back and forth slowly from man to man. "If any of you do, I'll kill you." He backed his horse and rode it at a walk across the dusty yard toward a smaller shack with half its tin roof peeled back and hanging loose in the hot breeze.

"Where you going, Haddon?" asked Earles. "Come on back here. You don't have to stay in that old hull. Stay in the house, with the rest of us." But Haddon Marr didn't answer.

Standing beside Earles, the Beldon brothers watched until Haddon Marr stopped his horse twenty yards away. Brozy said quietly, "I don't take kindly to having a man put his gun sights on me."

When neither his brother nor Earles answered,

Brozy said, "Reckon he even knows how much trouble he's caused everybody, keeping the kid with him?"

"Oh, he knows all right," said Earles. "And he knows he's got to get rid of her. He's just fighting himself over it. But he'll come around. I saw the new bullet hole in his shirt. He knows she's got to go."

# Chapter 21

Ted Riley and Lenora Lambert had pressed their horses hard until at length they had narrowed the distance between them and Haddon Marr to where they could see his trail dust no more than two miles ahead of them. But when they reached a small muddy watering hole at the base of a short cliff runoff, Riley knew they had to stop and water their horses or risk losing the animals. They stepped down, noting that Marr's tracks led straight past the watering hole. "He knows he's going somewhere nearby, somewhere where he knows there's water," said Riley. He looked along the trail, then at the soft ground around the edge of the watering hole. He saw paw prints of large and small creatures alike, as well as spindly bird prints. "We can't afford to pass up this water, but it looks like Marr can."

Lenora had already walked her tired Morgan over and let the animal drink. Riley walked the paint horse over and did the same. While both animals drew their fill of water, Lenora and Riley sank their canteens until they were both full. As Riley reached for his canteen, the thrashing sound of a horse coming through the brush on the other side of the water hole caused him to stand up, drawing the big Remington and cocking it. "Get back, ma'am," he whispered to Lenora.

On the other side of the water hole a steep slope covered with tall brush reached up the side of the cliff. As Riley stood watching and listening, an unwitting Bud Langston slid his horse down the last few feet toward the water hole. "Hello, over there," said Riley.

But the sound of a voice caught Langston by surprise and, seeing the gun on Riley's hand, he immediately grabbed his pistol with his good arm and swung it up, taking a bead on Ted Riley at a distance of no more than fifteen feet. Riley responded quickly. His shot hit Langston's gun hand, clipped his trigger finger off at the second knuckle and sent the gun flying into the air, its trigger gone. Langston hit the ground and let out a sharp yelp, grasping the bloody stub of his finger. Riley limped into the shallow water, walking toward him holding his gun out, ready to fire again.

"Damn, mister, why'd you shoot me?" asked Bud Langston, almost sobbing, holding up his severed finger for Riley to see. "My shooting finger, for God sakes! *Why?*"

With his free hand Riley helped Langston to his feet. "I saw you were about to shoot me," said Riley, "I couldn't risk it."

"But my shooting finger!" Langston wailed.

"Mister, I wasn't aiming for your finger," said Riley, "I was aiming for your chest. Be grateful for what you got." He watched Langston pull a bloody bandanna from inside his shirt where he'd placed it against his shoulder wound, and wrap it around his finger stub.

Seeing Riley look at the bloody bandanna, Bud Langston said, "That's right, I'm wounded already. So, I hope you're satisfied!"

"I didn't make you draw your pistol, mister," said Riley. "Who shot you?"

"That crazy sonsabitch Haddon Marr," said Langston. "Shot me not more than an hour ago, then took off, wouldn't even help me onto my horse."

"Did he have a little girl with him?" Riley blurted out quickly.

"Yeah, a real onion head," said Langston, attending to his finger as he spoke. "I'm gonna need to worry about infection," he said. "I don't suppose you've got any whiskey to spare, after shooting my damn finger off?"

"Sorry," said Riley, "no whiskey . . . If I did have, you'd be welcome to it."

"That's real comforting," said Langston with a trace of sarcasm, clutching his bandanna-wrapped finger. "You're after Haddon Marr, ain't ya?" He looked at Lenora Lambert as she walked the horses around the watering hole to where they stood.

"Yes, we're after him," said Riley. "Where's he headed?"

"I don't know if I ought to tell you or not," said Bud Langston, "at least not for free anyway. Not after you shooting me."

"I've got no money to pay you, mister," said Riley. "But don't forget Marr shot you too."

"That *is* true," said Langston, as if considering it. But then he held his wrapped hand up for Lenora to see. "Look here, ma'am, your husband has shot my finger off." He unwrapped it enough for her to see, then wrapped it again quickly. "It hurts like hell, I'll tell yas."

Lenora blushed at what Langston had said.

"I'm not her husband," said Ted Riley.

"Oh?" Langston looked surprised. He looked at Lenora. "You're not the child's mother then?"

"No," said Lenora, still blushing from what he'd said about her being Ted Riley's wife. "I'm concerned for the child's safety, that's all."

"Well, I can say you've got good cause to be concerned, ma'am. That's the craziest bunch of sonsa—" He stopped himself. "Begging your pardon, ma'am. They are not good wholesome family types, if you understand what I mean."

"Are you going to tell me where he's headed?" asked Riley.

"Yeah, all right, I suppose," said Langston grudgingly. "Stay on this trail till you come to a fork leading up into those blue hills over there." He started to point, then seemed to remember he had no finger to point with. He looked at his hand and shook his head. "Anyway, this trail will fork right and up. Just stay onto it till it narrows down to nothing. Then duck . . . 'cause there's eight or nine crazy scalp hunters there. They'll start shooting soon as they see you coming."

"Much obliged, mister," said Riley. "Is there anything I can do for you?"

"Ha," said Langston, flatly. "You've done plenty. Now you can get on out of here. I'd like to find my finger and be alone with it awhile." He looked down and searched back and forth in the dirt along the edge of the water hole.

Walking back around the watering hole leading their horses, Lenora Lambert looked over her shoulder, saying to Riley, "Oh, the poor man. I only wish there was something we could do for him."

"You heard him, ma'am," said Riley, "he just wants to be left alone. Besides, he's not much different than the men we're searching for. He was there with them. He knows how many there are, where their hideout is. We just caught him by surprise. I'm sure if it had gone the other way, he wouldn't lose any sleep worrying about leaving us both lying in the dirt."

"I understand that, Mister Riley," said Lenora, "but it seems such a cynical way to look at our fellow man."

"Yes, ma'am," said Riley, giving her a slight lift up into her saddle. He stepped up atop the paint horse and the two rode off along the trail in the hoofprints of Haddon Marr's horse.

Less than an hour later they paused at the same spot where Marr and the girl had stopped earlier. Looking at where Marr's horse had stood resting, Riley and Lenora saw Hilda's small footprints intermingled with Marr's big boot prints from when the two had stepped down for a moment. Riley looked all around within the sparse woods, seeing piles of brush that had blown in and tangled itself in scrub juniper and low-standing cedar. "This is a good place for an ambush," Riley said, almost in a whisper. "We need to be especially careful from here on—"

His words were cut short as he heard a sound coming from a bed of brush no more than fifteen feet away. The Remington came up cocked and pointed. "Come out where I can see you! Raise your hands!" Riley demanded.

He and Lenora heard the sound again, but no one came forward from the brush. A tense second passed as a hot, slow breeze swept by them and across the brush. Riley started to say something else, but before he could, a soft whimpering sound came from the brush, then a thrashing as Oscar came limping out toward them, his head hanging low in exhaustion. "Don't shoot!" cried Lenora. "It's my dog!" She ran to the big hound and caught him just as his legs gave out beneath him. "Oh, Oscar, what on earth are you doing out here?" Lenora said, sinking to the ground and resting the dog's sweaty head on her lap.

Riley walked over to her, leading both horses behind him. "He's just about run himself to death," he whispered softly.

"Yes, he has," said Lenora, stroking the big hound's head. "Following that little girl until he just couldn't keep up any longer. Didn't you, Oscar." She sniffed; a tear formed in her eye. "I guess we've both been terribly lonely." She smiled down at the dog, who lay panting, his big tongue dangling. "I was worried about how you would do while I was gone. All the while you were *ahead* of us . . . out to save that child. You saw the evil in that man and tried to protect little Hilda. You poor thing. When you tried to warn me I almost let him destroy you." Lenora cried softly until Riley stooped down beside her and put his arm around her shoulders, comforting her.

"Ma'am," Riley said as gently as he could, "there's nothing we can do for him. We need to get on the trail."

"Is he— Is he going to die, Ted?" Lenora asked.

Riley was stunned to hear her call him by his first name. "Ma'am," he said, "he's run himself out. He might make it if he lays here and rests some. You can stay here with him, ma'am, if you feel like you should."

"No," said Lenora, "when we get Hilda from these men, she'll be frightened. I think it would be good for a woman to be there for her."

"Yes, ma'am," said Riley, "that's what I think too. We can check on the dog on our way back through here." Riley reached out and lifted the big hound's head from her knee and laid it gently on the ground. Oscar only whined, looking up at Riley. Lenora noted how gently the dog had reacted toward Ted Riley, not at all the way he had acted with Haddon Marr. Riley stood up, lifting Lenora with him.

"Oscar, you rest now," said Lenora, tearfully, "I'll be right back for you." Riley winced and turned her away from the dog and helped her up into her saddle.

The ranger and Sheriff Tackett had heard the pistol shot in the distance a half mile ahead of them. They approached the water hole with caution, having seen the fresh tracks left by Marr's horse as well as the tracks left by Riley and Lenora Lambert. Knowing they were drawing closer to a confrontation, the ranger had once again dropped the loop of rope over Morton Toller's head and when they'd crossed the border. When the three arrived at the water hole, they saw Bud Langston sitting on a flat rock with his bloody bandanna-wrapped hand in his lap.

Looking at the three riders, seeing the badges on the ranger and Sheriff Tackett, both of them holding guns, Langston said, shaking his head, "There must be one hell of a fight brewing. . . . I've been shot *twice* just trying to ride *away* from it!"

"Bud Langston?" said Morton Toller.

"Yeah, it's me," said Langston. "Excuse me if I don't shake hands." He held up his wrapped bloody hand for Toller to see. "Got a finger clipped off; can't even find the damn thing for one last look." Seeing the rope around Toller's neck, he said, "Are they fixing to hang you?"

"No," said Toller, "not unless I take off too fast."

Langston nodded. Looking at the ranger and Tackett, he said, "I expect you've both heard of me?"

"Yes," Burrack said, for both of them, "we've heard of you. But if you're not siding with Earles, you can ride away."

"I appreciate that," said Langston. "I want you to know that I've broken no law lately. I was on the verge of it with Earles and his bunch, but they've got too many problems to suit me."

The ranger put his rifle back across his lap. Tackett lowered his pistol but kept it in his hand. "Who shot you?" Burrack asked.

"Some fellow riding a big paint horse," said Langston. "Told me he was aiming for my chest . . . guess he thought that my knowing that would make me feel better."

"A paint horse?" said Burrack. He and Tackett looked at each other. "That sounds like Riley, riding Fitch's horse."

"We've been following three sets of hoofprints," the ranger said. "Who's traveling with him?"

"There's a woman with him, riding a black Morgan." Langston shrugged. "I'm surprised she didn't shoot me too, but they seemed in a hurry. They were dogging Haddon Marr's trail pretty close."

"Did Marr have a young girl with him?" Tackett asked.

"Yep, he did," said Langston, as if he were growing bored with repeating the story. "He's headed for Piedra Negra. The man and woman followed him; I told them the way." He looked up at Toller and saw a look of disgust on his face. "Don't give me that look, Toller. What is it *you're* doing but showing them the way?"

"I've got no choice," said Toller. "Besides, Cinco Diablos tried to kill me! I don't owe nobody a damn thing."

"That's enough socializing," said Tackett. "Step down and let's water these horses and get on our way."

Bud Langston sat staring at the ground while they watered their horses, and he still sat staring as they mounted and started to ride away. The ranger circled his Appaloosa around to Langston and said, "Anything we can do for you?"

Bud Langston squinted up at him. "That's the same thing the man who shot me asked." He sighed, then said, "Obliged, Ranger, but no, I'm about as good as I ever will be. I'm just going to sit here awhile, if it's all the same to you."

"Suit yourself," said the ranger, turning the Appaloosa back toward Tackett, who held Toller's rope. The three rode on, hurrying along the trail as much as possible without allowing themselves to get careless in such perfect ambush country.

# Chapter 22

Ted Riley and Lenora Lambert stopped inside the cover of trees and saw Cinco Diablos standing atop the large boulder seventy-five yards above them where the trail turned steep up into the rocky hillside. Beyond Cinco a gray spiral of smoke curled upward from a campfire. Riley eased the paint horse back, motioning for Lenora to do the same. When they were completely hidden yet still able to see Cinco through the tree branches, Riley whispered, "Good, he didn't spot us."

"But how will we get any closer?" Lenora asked, the two of them stepping down from their saddles.

Riley searched the surrounding terrain looking for an answer to her question. Finally he said, "I've got to get around the guard on foot and work my way up there."

"Ma'am, I—" Riley started to speak but she cut him off.

"The matter is closed to discussion, Ted," Lenora said firmly, "I am going with you. I came here prepared for a fight, and that's what I'll give them."

"I understand, ma'am," said Riley, noting that once again she had called him by his first name. "I have to say that you are one courageous woman. It's been an honor riding with you."

"Shush now," said Lenora, looking embarrassed. "You sound as if we're neither one coming back."

"Well, ma'am, there is that possibility," Riley said softly.

"Nonsense," said Lenora, "let's not talk as if we're defeated." She offered a reassuring but unconvincing smile. "And after all we've been through and are about to go through, I think it proper that you should call me Lenora."

"Yes, ma'am, Lenora," said Riley, drawing the Remington and checking it, "I like the sound of that name." He finished checking the pistol and kept it in his hand, watching Lenora check her rifle. When she'd finished and looked up at him, Riley gestured toward the brush with the pistol, "Shall we, Lenora?"

She smiled and nodded curtly, "Yes, thank you, Ted."

They led their horses into the brush quietly and began working their way wide of the narrow trail and upwards through large rocks and woods until they stood out of sight around the side of the hill. When they reached a spot where their cover of brush and juniper ended, Riley motioned upwards with his pistol toward a point of rocks. Beyond that point smoke from the campfire drifted on a breeze. "I want you to keep the horses back here while I go up there and take a look around."

"You aren't going to try something without me, are you, Ted?" Lenora asked, giving him a wary look.

"No, Lenora," Riley said, handing her the reins to the paint horse. "We're both in this thing together. You have my word on that." Limping slightly from his healing wound, Riley moved upward in a crouch and lay flat upon a large boulder where he could look down on the house and the flat clearing tucked away deep inside a maze of rock. "So there you are," he whispered to himself, looking down at Haddon Marr, who stood out front of a small shack twenty yards from the house.

In the doorway of the shack Riley saw the child standing with a wooden bowl in her cupped hands. She raised the bowl to her lips and drank from it. Riley scanned the surrounding hillside, getting a look at any other ways out in case he needed one. He counted four men in the yard, all of them carrying rifles cradled in their arms as if prepared to do battle. One of the men was Andy Fill, who stood holding onto a weathered hitch rail for support. Riley didn't see Jessup Earles, but he knew that Earles must be inside the house. Nor did Riley recognize the Beldon brothers, but he realized that new faces could show up at any time. He had to make his move, get the girl and get out. Fifty yards from the front of the house Riley saw Cinco Diablos standing guard atop the large boulder, another man sitting nearby sipping from a canteen.

Scooting back from the edge, Ted Riley turned and ran in a crouch back down to Lenora inside the cover of juniper. "What did you see?" Lenora asked.

"Counting the two guarding the trail, it looks like there's eight in all. I didn't see Earles, but he's down there."

"The girl, Hilda?" Lenora asked.

"Yes, I saw her," said Riley. "She's eating. She looks all right in spite of everything she's been through."

"Then let's ride in there and get her out," said Lenora.

Riley just looked at her for a moment, then said, "Lenora, it'll be dark in a couple of hours. I'm thinking I should try to slip in there after dark without being seen, get her and get out."

Lenora thought about it and said, "And what shall I do?"

"I want you to cover me with the rifle. If something goes wrong and I have to shoot my way out, I need you somewhere up in the rocks in a good position to fight these men off."

"Very well," said Lenora, "show me where you'd like me to be. I will do my best to provide you with cover."

"You *are* a good shot, right?" Riley asked, needing to reassure himself.

"I am more than adequately proficient with a long gun," Lenora said, patting the rifle in her arm.

"I know you don't want to kill anybody, Lenora," said Riley, "but if I get in a tight spot down there . . ." He let his words trail.

"I've already resolved that issue in my mind," said Lenora. "If it comes down to your life and the child's depending on me, I will do what I must."

"That's good enough for me," said Riley. Taking the reins from her, he tied the horses to a thick juniper. "I want you up there where I was. It's the highest spot around here and it puts everything right there beneath you. I'm figuring it's about sixty yards from there down to the yard. Can you hit anything at that distance if you have to? Moving targets? In the dark?"

"Oh, heavens yes," said Lenora. "You have no worries in that regard."

Riley just looked at her for a moment. "All right then. Let's get you up there and get you all set."

They hurried along in a crouch to the top of the hill. Once flat on their bellies, Riley gave Lenora a second to study the house, the smaller shack with its disheveled tin roof and the men in the dusty front yard. Lenora licked the ball of her thumb and rubbed it on the front rifle sight. Riley said, "When it's dark, I'm counting on that campfire to give you some shooting light. You sit tight up here . . . don't do anything unless you hear shooting break out down there. If shooting starts, watch the muzzle flashes and aim about two feet behind them. That way you'll hit something or at least send them running for cover. If the shooting gets heavy, you move back and forth up here between shots, keep them from sighting in on you."

"All right," said Lenora, raising the rifle butt to her shoulder, practicing sighting it down into the yard.

Riley looked along the rough rocky terrain he would have to cross to get around on the other side of the clearing below and down to the small shack to the child. "I better get started now," he said. "It'll take me till dark to get around those rocks and climb down without being seen."

Suddenly it dawned on Lenora just how difficult it was going to be for him to get Hilda and make the trek back in the dark, especially if there were men shooting at him. Lenora saw the danger, but she realized they had no choice but to go forward with their plan. She turned to Riley with a concerned look and said, "You will be careful, won't you, Ted?"

"Believe me," Riley said, "I'll be as careful as I can." He backed away and out of her sight down the back side of the large boulder.

Darkness had already begun to close around the land by the time the ranger, Tackett and Morton Toller rode quietly along the last few yards of trail before it turned steeply up into the boulders. "Right around this next turn," said Toller, "we'll become an easy target for anybody standing guard up in the rocks." The three stopped. Toller looked back and forth between them and said, "Well, fellows, I guess that does it for me. If you'll take your rope from my neck I'll just turn this horse around and—"

"Shut up, Toller," said the ranger. "We'll let you go when we know we're at the hideout and that you're not going to turn around and tip off Earles that we're here. So sit tight. We'll remind you when it's time to go."

Toller cursed under his breath, but he settled himself and fell silent while the three of them stepped down from their saddles and walked their horses forward toward the end of the woods. In the failing evening light, Sam stooped down and saw that the two sets of prints they were following turned off along the bottom of the hillside. "Looks like Riley and whoever he's with went this way," he said, barely above a whisper.

"Do you think Riley and this woman are foolish enough to try to take this bunch on by themselves?" Tackett asked.

"I don't know," said the ranger. "But whatever move he *might* be planning to make, I don't want him and us out here shooting one another while Earles and his men get away. We're *this* close to getting that girl back; we can't afford anything going wrong." He stood up, nodded down at the spot where the two sets of tracks went off around the base of the hill and asked Toller, "Where did this take them?"

"It goes around the whole hillside," said Toller, "anywhere they climbed up will put them atop the hideout. The shack sits down in a clearing among some big boulders. You can see everything from atop this hill."

"Let's follow Riley," Burrack said to Tackett, "see what he's up to."

They eased the horses along through the juniper and brush in Riley and Lenora's footprints until they saw the paint horse and black mare standing quietly. "They've gone forward on foot," Tackett whispered, "so they've put some kind of plan into action."

"Yes," said Burrack, his eyes searching the hillside leading up to the large boulder. "Trouble is, they don't know we're back here. We can't do something to spook them, cause them to tip their hand to Earles."

"What's our move then?" Tackett asked.

The ranger looked all around. "It's going to be good and dark in another few minutes. You stay here with Toller and the horses. Let me slip up there and see if I can find Riley and the woman without them shooting at me." He looked at the top of the hill, estimating, then said, "Watch for me. If I want you to come up and join me, I'll give you a wave."

"Then you better hurry it up," said Tackett, "it'll soon be too dark to see you wave."

The ranger went forward in a crouch, not stopping until he stood at the base of the larger boulder where Ted Riley had left Lenora with her rifle. He climbed the boulder as silent as a ghost until he saw the woman lying prone with the rifle in front of her, peeping down over the edge. Dropping down onto all fours, the ranger crawled forward silently until he stopped at Lenora's heels. Rising slightly to get his needed leverage, Burrack lunged atop her, one hand clamping down on her rifle to keep it from going off. His right arm swung around her, covered her mouth and pressed her to his chest. She struggled wildly. He held firm, whispering quickly into her ear, "Listen to me, I'm Arizona Ranger Sam Burrack. I'm here to free the child, just like you and Ted Riley are!"

Lenora was having none of it; she continued to kick

and struggle. Burrack tightened his hold on her. "Ma'am, please!" he said. "If I was one of them, you'd already be dead! I'm here to help you!"

She settled down. "I'm going to take my hand off your mouth now," he whispered. "Don't get loud or they'll hear you down there. All right?"

Lenora nodded.

"There," said the ranger, taking his hand away but keeping his other hand on her rifle. She looked at his badge in the grainy evening light. "Oh, thank God!" she whispered. "You *are* a ranger."

"Yes, ma'am," he replied. "Where is Ted Riley, and what is it you two are trying to do?"

"He went around the rocks there," Lenora said, pointing toward the steep hillside surrounding the clearing below. "He's going to sneak in, get the girl and get out. I'm here to cover him."

"I see," said the ranger, venturing a peep down at the glowing campfire, seeing three men sitting closer to it now that chilled air loomed in the coming Mexican night. "Since you two have already put your plan in action, we'll back you both up in it. I have a sheriff and a prisoner with me. I'll get back and send Sheriff Tackett up here. He'll help you give Riley cover."

"I'll stay right here and keep an eye on things until you send the sheriff." She caught herself and said, "Ranger Burrack, where will you be?"

"I thought I'd slip down there myself," said the ranger. "Riley might need somebody a little closer to him if things heat up for him."

"Oh, thank you, Ranger Burrack," Lenora said. "I'm worried about Ted being down there all by himself. I feel much better now."

Ted . . .? Burrack caught the way she had referred

to Riley by his first name. "Yes, ma'am," he said, backing away.

But as he turned to leave her, she grasped his forearm and asked, "We're going to do just fine here, aren't we? Don't you think?"

The ranger looked at her for a second, seeing both courage and consternation in her face. Then he allowed a trace of a smile for reassurance and said, "Yes, ma'am, I believe we'll all be just fine."

Instead of waving Tackett and Toller up to him, the ranger moved swiftly back down to where they stood waiting. As he explained what was going on to Tackett, he took a pair of handcuffs from his saddlebags and handcuffed Toller with the scalp hunter's arms around a thick cedar tree. Burrack untied Toller's bandanna from around his neck and put it around his mouth. "Here's the deal, Toller," he said. "If you work this loose and warn any of your friends, I promise you I'll crawl back here if I have to and unload my Colt in you. Keep your mouth shut, and once it's over we'll turn you loose. Are we clear on everything?"

Morton Toller grumbled in a muffled tone, but nodded his head vigorously.

Sam slid his rifle from his saddle boot and turned to Tackett. "The first thing I'm going to do is see if there's a guard up in the rocks. If there is I'll take care of him so if Riley and I have to make a run for it, we won't have a rifle breathing down our shirts."

Sheriff Tackett nodded. "I'll get on up there and help the woman." He hesitated, then asked, "Ranger, are you sure you don't want me going with you?"

"We'll need some good shooting from up there, Sheriff," said Burrack. "I don't how good the woman is with a rifle."

"I understand," said Tackett, turning and heading away into the grainy darkness. The ranger gave a quick look around, then backed away himself and headed quietly toward the large boulder overlooking the trail.

# Chapter 23

The ranger stood in the darkness between the large boulder and a smaller one beside it. He listened to the voices speaking a few feet above him. Atop the rock Cinco Diablos said to Bruno Kratz, "This does it for me. We've been up here long enough. I'm going down to see why someone hasn't relieved us."

"Bring me some coffee if we have to stay up here longer. I'm starting to wonder if those lawmen are coming after us tonight."

"They are coming, Bruno," said Cinco. "You saw them with your own eyes."

"Yeah, but nothing says they have to come tonight," Bruno replied. "Maybe they want to get a good night's sleep first."

Cinco cursed under his breath and walked away, moving across the surface of the boulder and going down it too far away for the ranger to get to him in time. But that was all right, Burrack thought. He would get the other one right now. With darkness set in, Riley could make his move any minute. As soon as Cinco walked out of sight down to the house, where a lamp glowed in the front window, he climbed quickly and quietly up the side of the boulder, keeping his head down as he approached the man sitting huddled inside his coat, both his hands in his pockets, his rifle

lying three feet away from him. "It's about time somebody come up here," said Bruno, barely looking up.
"Cinco just went down to—"

The ranger's rifle butt silenced him mid-sentence
and left him sprawling on his back, knocked out cold.
Burrack jerked Bruno's pistol from its holster and
shoved it down behind his belt. He picked up the rifle
and flung it as far as he could out over the steep side
of the boulder. Then he rolled the knocked-out scalp
hunter over the steep edge as well, not hearing a
sound as the big man landed thirty feet below in scrub
cedars and rock. Without hesitating a second longer,
the ranger hurried down the same side of the rock
Cinco had taken. Staying on the rough edge of the
clearing, he hurried along through low brush and cactus toward the smaller shack, where another lamp
glowed in a window. But before he'd gone another
ten feet, he saw the dark outline of Ted Riley stooped
down in the brush. The ranger froze at the sound of
a gun hammer cocking.

"It's me, the ranger!" he whispered hoarsely, knowing he was taking a big chance on being heard by the
men over near the campfire.

After a tense second, Ted Riley came toward him
in a low crouch and stopped four feet away. "Ranger
Burrack!" he said, as if in disbelief. "You can't know
how glad I am to see you."

"I spoke to the woman; Tackett is with her now,"
the ranger whispered. "Where's the girl?"

Riley pointed with his pistol in the darkness. "She
was standing in the doorway here the last I saw of
her."

"Go check it out," said the ranger, "this is your
show until we get her out of here. I'm backing you."

Riley nodded and slipped away along the brush line

until he arrived at the rear of the shack. He eased around the side, staying low until he reached a window and stood up. Inside, Riley saw the girl sleeping on a pallet of straw. Marr had tied the rope back around her neck and the other end around a support post standing in the middle of the shack, reaching up to the rafters. He looked around and didn't see Haddon Marr. Hilda lay sleeping, all alone in the shack. Riley wasn't about to let this opportunity pass him by. He looked around at the ranger and tried to signal what he was going to do, hoping the ranger could understand.

Without wasting another second, Riley eased around to the rear door, opened it carefully and quietly, and slipped inside. Unsure what the girl's reaction to him would be, he carefully kept from awakening her as he loosened the tightly drawn knot in the rope and slipped it over her head. He reasoned that the girl must be exhausted and sleeping too soundly to feel him slip his arm beneath her and lift her up. Still he did so carefully, ready to clasp his hand over her mouth if need be. With her hanging limply in his arms, Riley hurried from the shack, back to where the ranger awaited him. But no sooner had he stopped and hunkered down beside the ranger, than he saw Haddon Marr walking back to the shack from the house, where he had been talking to Jessup Earles.

"We better hurry," Riley whispered.

But as they crept quickly along the brush line, Cinco Diablos and the Beldon brothers walked away from the fire and toward the large rock, stopping right in their path. The ranger and Riley dropped low to the ground, the girl still sleeping soundly in Riley's arms. The ranger held his rifle poised, ready to start firing should the men look their way. Suddenly the door of the shack burst open and Haddon Marr ran into the firelight with a cocked pistol in each hand. "Where is she? Who the hell took her?" he raged, fanning the pistols around wildly.

Upon hearing Marr's voice, Hilda whimpered in her sleep, not loud, yet loud enough for Cinco and the Beldon brothers to hear her. Their heads turned toward the sound and fixed on Riley and the ranger. "Get her out of here, Riley," the ranger whispered, even giving Riley a shove in the direction of the trail leading out of the camp in case he wanted to argue the point. Riley took off running with the girl, knowing the danger she would be in at any second when the lead began to fly.

Cinco and the Beldon brothers went for their guns at once. Burrack's rifle shot exploded, lifting Brozy Beldon off his feet and hurling him backwards. Even as the other two raised their guns to fire, their eyes had cut to Brozy for a split second. That split second was all the ranger needed to lever a fresh round into his rifle chamber. He fired quickly, his shot hitting Duke Beldon high in his shoulder, spinning him around. Seeing Duke take a bullet, Cinco fired wildly and fled out of sight into the surrounding darkness. "You sonsabitch!" Marr bellowed, seeing the ranger unclearly, given the darkness and his still healing eye. He fired but missed.

The ranger had more to think about than Marr right then. Shots sliced past him from the darkness from the direction Cinco had taken. Two more shots whistled past Burrack's head from the direction of the house. The ranger made a dive for the ground. Finding no cover, he rolled as bullets hammered the dirt around him. Jessup Earles ran down off the porch before the ranger could get a shot at him. But Burton Stowl wasn't as lucky. The ranger stopped rolling, threw his rifle butt to his shoulder and fired. The shot slammed Stowl against the front of the house. He slid down to the porch and pitched forward on his face.

From the rocks above the clearing, Tackett and Lenora Lambert had seen and heard the shots. They both opened fire on the area surrounding the campfire. Haddon Marr did a wild dance as bullets kicked dirt up around his feet, but then he raced away into the darkness in the same direction as Riley and the girl. The ranger didn't see Marr make the move; he was too busy ducking bullets from Jessup Earles and Uncle Andy Fill in the darkness. Badly wounded, Duke Beldon had managed to get on his feet and stagger into the firelight. Clasping his bloody shoulder, he raised his gun stiffly and shouted at Burrack, "You killed my brother, you law dog sonsabitch!"

The ranger's rifle shot hit him in the chest. Two more rifle shots hit him from above. The impact threw him sidelong into the licking flames. But Duke was beyond feeling the fire. His clothes ignited as he lay there stone dead. Black smoke billowed. Jessup Earles called out to his men in the darkness, "Cinco, Bruno, Uncle Andy, Haddon?"

Uncle Andy responded, so did Cinco. "Bruno is still up on the rock, Earles!" Cinco called out to him.

"Haddon?" said Earles. A second passed, and when he'd gotten no response from Marr he said, "All right, everybody stay out of the firelight and let's rush this sonsabitch!"

Cinco called out, "Ready when you are, Earles!"

"Now!" shouted Earles. He rose up and stalked forward shooting. Cinco and Uncle Andy did the same. The ranger lay still, not returning the fire, but rather watching the blue-orange muzzle flashes in the darkness. Bullets zipped through the air only inches above him as he held his fire until the last minute. When he did shoot, the only target he had was the dark outline of Jessup Earles lit only by the quick flicker of pistol fire. The ranger's shot hit something. Earles let out a loud yelp of pain and crawled across the ground looking for cover. Burrack didn't stay there long enough to find out what damage he'd done. He rolled away quickly, bullets from Cinco and Andy Fill hitting the ground where he'd been lying. By the ranger's count there were only two left. He crawled backwards in the darkness and took cover against the side of the shack.

"Come out, law dog," said Cinco Diablos. "It is only me and one more . . . and he is wounded. We will have a face-to-face showdown. That is how I have heard you like to fight. What are you afraid of?"

While Cinco spoke, the ranger picked up a tin can that lay alongside the shack. He scraped it on the ground, getting some dirt into it for weight, then he hurled it away from him. He heard it hit the ground twenty feet to his left. The two scalp hunters fired repeatedly at it. The ranger lay still against the side of the shack, prepared for a long night.

Riley didn't like leaving the ranger there to face the scalp hunters alone. But for the sake of the child he had to do it. He ran, holding her against his chest. Even the gunfire had not awakened her, not completely at least. For a moment she had whimpered and struggled slightly in Riley's arms. But he had lowered his face to hers and said softly, "Ssssh, it's all right, go back to sleep." And so she had.

Stopping a hundred yards down the sloping path leading to the trail, Riley listened for a moment to the sound of fighting going on back at the hideout. Pain pounded like a hammer in his wounded hip, but he disregarded it. He had no time for it. He had faith in the ranger, but he knew that the main thing he need to do was to get the child to Lenora and Sheriff Tackett as soon as possible. If he lost the girl now, the whole rescue attempt would have been in vain. Listening, he also heard the sound of boots running toward him. *Haddon Marr!* he thought instantly. He hurried on at a painful pace, his left leg beginning to weaken, until he felt the land flatten beneath his feet. Now he needed to get around to where he and Lenora had left the horses. From there he would make his way up to the rock where she and Tackett lay firing down onto the clearing.

Riley listened again and heard the boots getting closer behind him. He hurried along the path through the brush and juniper toward the horses. But he stopped to listen and see if the boots had also turned into the brush behind him. Standing stone-still he heard the boots come to a halt, no doubt having just reached the bottom of the hill. He imagined Haddon Marr standing there having no idea which way to go. A moment passed, then Riley breathed a sigh of relief as he heard the boots hurry on along the trail. But then, in her sleep, Hilda cried out, "Noooo!" And Riley heard the boots come to an abrupt halt.

On the trail, Marr listened closely, not hearing the sound again, but not having to. He turned and bounded through the brush like a man possessed. "I'm coming, little angel," he bellowed long and loud. Then he bellowed even louder, "Hurt her and I'll kill you, you *son of a bitch*!"

Riley summoned up his waning strength and ran limping through the brush, unable to keep from being heard and knowing that at any moment Marr would be upon him. His wound had drained most of his strength; making the climb around to the hideout and the run through the darkness had depleted him even farther. But whatever fight he had left in him he had to turn around and offer it up. He lay the girl in the brush and ran limping back toward the sound of breaking brush and running boots. Judging Marr to be no more than ten yards away and crashing toward him, Riley raised the Remington and fired, one shot, two, three. He cocked the hammer for the fourth. But he didn't get to make the shot.

Marr's pistol exploded, picked Ted Riley up and hurled him backwards like a limp scarecrow. The night spun above Riley. Stars rolled and pitched in the sky like ships on a turbulent sea. The Remington was still in his hand, but it was a worthless piece of iron now. He couldn't lift it. He looked up and saw Marr looming above him in the darkness. "This time I'll see to it your brains get spilled in the dirt," Marr said in a harsh whisper. He cocked the big pistol and held it out and down at arm's length, only inches from Riley's face. "Where is she? Where's my angel?"

Riley gasped for enough air to answer. "Go to . . . hell!" he rasped. He sank back on the ground, actually hearing a metal on metal sound as Marr pulled the trigger and let the hammer fall. Riley felt death come to him and it didn't frighten him. In what he knew to be his last second, he saw a black shadow streak above him between himself and the night sky as he heard the gunshot and felt the blast of hot powder in his face. He closed his eyes into a greater darkness. . . .

On the rock, firing down at the clearing, Tackett and Lenora both heard the single pistol shot, followed by a shrill cry of terror in the night. They listened intently. They heard another shrill cry, followed by a deathlike silence. "Lord God, was that the child?" said Tackett. "Was that her?"

"I don't know," said Lenora. "I—I must believe so." His voice sounded shaky.

"Marr has taken off with her!" said Tackett. He looked quickly down at the clearing. The gunfire down there had lessened. "Ma'am, it's up to you here! I'm going after little Hilda!"

"Yes, go! Hurry!" said Lenora Lambert. As Tackett hurried down the rock and toward the horses, Lenora felt tears well in her eyes. She had a crushing feeling that something had just gone awfully wrong for Ted Riley. "Oh, Ted, God bless you . . . you good man," she whispered to the night surrounding her.

Tackett raced downward through the brush, stumbling, falling, tumbling downhill, then catching himself, righting himself without stopping and continuing on until he fell to his knees out of breath among the horses. "Dang it!" he cried aloud in his frustration, wiping blood from his eyes where he'd cut his forehead in the dirt, pulling scraps of sharp brush from his hair, having lost his hat on the way down. "I'm coming, Hilda . . . I'm coming," he gasped, pulling himself up his horse's side, unhitching it and heaving himself up into the saddle. He turned the horse toward the trail below and batted his boots to its sides.

In the thin moonlight, the sheriff saw a figure hunkered down in his path and it dawned on him how careless he'd just been. He slid the horse to a halt as he made out what he was certain must be a pistol raising toward him. Tackett reached for his own pistol but found his holster empty, having also lost his gun as he'd tumbled downhill. He realized again how careless he'd been. "Oh, no!" he shouted, his hand gripping the empty holster with all its might. He braced himself for the coming explosion, wondering in an instant what was going to become of the child.

"Sheriff Tackett?" said a weak, broken voice. A chill ran the length of Tackett's spine, hearing the voice that way. But no explosion followed. He saw the pistol lower.

"Ye—Yes?" Tackett said, his voice shaky.

"Give me a hand?" said the broken voice.

"Riley? Ted Riley?" said Tackett. But he'd already answered his own question. He nudged his horse forward and stopped a few feet back, staring at Ted Riley, who sat with the child on his lap. Hilda clung to him, weeping softly. "Lord God! What's happened here?" said Tackett, stepping down from his saddle. He came to Riley and stooped down beside him. He smelled burnt hair, burnt skin; and he saw a black streak along the side of Riley's head.

"Got a match on you?" Riley asked calmly.

"A match?" Tackett said, stunned, wondering if Riley meant that he wanted to roll a smoke right then, right there. "Well, yes . . ." Tackett searched himself quickly and came up with a long sulphur match.

"Strike it for me," Riley said in a pained tone.

Tackett struck the match and saw the glow of light spread in a small circle around them.

"Over there," said Riley, nodding just out of the match's glow. Tackett stood and eased forward a couple of steps, then stopped cold.

"Lord God almighty," Tackett whispered.

"Careful, Sheriff, his hackles are high," said Riley, his voice a bit stronger. "He's still got his bark on. Give him all the room he needs."

"Lord God!" Tackett repeated. He stared for a moment longer, seeing Oscar the hound stand over Haddon Marr's torn and faceless body as if protecting his fresh kill. Blood foamed and dripped from the big dog's flews. Oscar returned Tackett's stare, his eyes fiery-red in the match's glow. He growled low, crouched and trembling, a part of Marr's hair, skin and ear clamped beneath one bloody front paw. "Lord God!" Tackett said for the third time. "He killed Haddon Marr? I can't hardly tell if that's Haddon Marr or not!"

"Yep," said Riley, "it's Haddon Marr . . . and yep, the dog killed him."

Tackett stepped back, feeling the match flame get closer to his fingers. "A dog kills a man this way, like it or not, the animal has to be destroyed."

"Whoever does it has to kill me first," Riley said softly but with conviction.

An hour had passed without the ranger making a noise or firing a shot in spite of bullets having flown by over his head and slammed into the side of the shack. More than once Cinco had called out to him, trying to goad him into saying something or making some move to give his position away. But Burrack hadn't responded. Finally Uncle Andy said in the darkness, "I believe that law dog has bit the dust on us."

"Don't talk like a fool!" said Cinco, twenty feet away in the darkness, lying prone behind a thick pile of firewood.

"I'm telling you, he's dead, or else he's lit out on us!" said Andy Fill. "He came here for the girl! Hell, Marr is gone! So is the girl, I'll bet you on it! They're all gone, even the riflemen up there! It's just you and me, in the dark like two idiots laying on goose eggs, thinking something's gonna hatch for us!" He laughed aloud. "We ain't gonna *hatch* a damn thing!"

"Shut up, Uncle Andy!" shouted Cinco.

"Bull! Watch this!" said Andy Fill. He walked right out into the firelight, waving his arms above his head. "Hey, up there, fire at will! Do you hear me? Take your best shot!"

*Don't shoot just yet, please don't shoot.* . . . The ranger held his breath, hoping Lenora and Tackett wouldn't fire right then, not knowing that Tackett had gone to see about the single pistol shot coming from down near the horses. To Sam's relief no shot came from the darkness.

"See?" Andy said to Cinco Diablos. "Everybody's gone. Just you and me." He laughed. "Hell, I'm going to finish Duke Beldon's coffee, since he's busy cooking." He laughed, jerking his head toward Duke's charred, smoldering body lying across the fire. He stooped down and picked up the tin cup Duke had been sipping from.

"You are loco," Uncle Andy," said Cinco, stepping in warily, looking all around and up into the darkness above them. "Has anyone ever told you that before?"

"Oh, yes, many times," said Uncle Andy. "But I never believed them." He grinned, sipping the coffee. "Hell, this coffee is still hot!" He looked all around and said, "It's only right that I never died in all this shooting. Not after as much bad luck as I've had of late."

"*Si*," said Cinco, "maybe you are right." His gun hand relaxed and hung down his side, his thumb letting the hammer down easily. He walked over beside Uncle Andy and reached out a hand. "But that was not Brozy's coffee, you fool. I had just poured that and was letting it cool."

"Like hell," said Uncle Andy. "It's in my hand now, and that's where it's staying!"

"Oh?" said Cinco, clasping Andy's wrist, "we'll see about that!"

"Time to settle all accounts, boys," said the ranger, stepping slowly into the campfire's glow. He held his cocked repeater rifle in one gloved hand, his big Colt in his other. Dust covered his bib-front shirt. His gray sombrero hung behind his shoulder on its rawhide string. A thin, dry blade of grass stuck to his hair.

"Damn you, Andy!" said Cinco.

"Well, hell!" said Andy, dropping the tin cup as he and Cinco made their move at the same time.

Above the clearing Lenora stared slack-jawed, hearing the ranger's rifle and pistol fire as one. She watched the men by the campfire fly backwards, leaving a red mist hanging in the air for a second as they hit the ground dead. "My merciful Lord in heaven, please let it end," she whispered, as if suddenly realizing what an ugly, terrible thing she'd been involved in. "I pray I never go through anything like this again." She had shut her eyes as she whispered her words to the wide dark night. When she opened them she looked back down and saw the ranger step closer to the campfire and look up toward her, not seeing her, she thought, yet certain that she and Tackett were there watching over him. He raised both hands, waving his guns back and forth slowly for her to see. "Good, it *really is* over," she whispered, as if the prayer she'd made had just been answered.

Beside the campfire, the ranger holstered his Colt and cradled the rifle in his arm. He turned and started to walk away, not seeing Jessup Earles walk quietly into the firelight, blood running down his right forearm, his pistol out at arm's length, his finger tightening on the trigger. He had the ranger cold and he knew it.

Burrack stiffened when the single shot exploded. It had caught him completely by surprise. He turned his eyes upward in the darkness, puzzled, and heard the rifle come bouncing down over the rocks. The last bounce landed the rifle ten feet from him at the edge of the campfire's glow. He looked around and saw Jessup Earles on his knees, staring at him wild-eyed. Earles' hands clasped his gaping chest as if to hold his blood inside him. "I had . . . you killed dead, Ranger," he said, gasping, his eyes turning upward, searching the darkness. "You . . . just remember that."

"I will," Burrack said quietly. His hand had gone instinctively to his holstered Colt. But it relaxed as he watched Earles topple forward like a felled oak and land facedown in the dirt.

He stood for a moment looking at Earles, then around the clearing, then up into the darkness again, raising both hands toward faces he could not see but that he knew were there. With a last look around him, the ranger walked all the way down the path and around to the horses, where he found Sheriff Tackett inspecting Riley's fresh wounds in the light of a small fire he'd built. "Howdy, Riley," said the ranger, touching his hat brim.

"Howdy, Ranger," said Riley, "I bet you never thought you'd see me again!"

"I had faith in you," said the ranger, his expression flat in a way that made made it hard to tell if he meant what he'd said. As the ranger spoke, Lenora Lambert walked in from the other direction, Hilda hugged against her side. Oscar the dog followed, his muzzle stained red with blood. Seeing Riley alive, Lenora immediately took over attending his wounds, keeping Hilda right beside her. Tackett walked to his horse, took down a blanket and wrapped it around Hilda's shoulders. Watching, Burrack wondered if Tackett was going to tell the child who he was. But Tackett didn't. Instead he looked at Lenora, watching how the child had taken to her. Looking at Oscar, the ranger asked, "Is this your dog, Lenora?"

"Yes," she said, without turning to him.

He looked at the bloody dog then at Tackett. "I'll explain everything later," said Tackett, just between the two of them.

"What happened to Marr?" Burrack asked aloud.

A tense silence passed, then Sheriff Tackett said, "Wolves got him."

The ranger raised a brow. "Wolves?" He looked again at the dog, noting its bloody flews.

"Yep, wolves got him," said Tackett, "I dragged his body out of sight a few yards up so the woman and child wouldn't have to see it."

*"Wolves?"* the ranger persisted.

Tackett stepped over closer to him and whispered, "I'll explain it to you later, Sam."

"I hope you will," said the ranger with a bemused look. To Ted Riley he said, "Riley, I still have to take you in. But owing to what you've done here, you won't be in long."

"What on earth are you talking about?" Lenora asked. She looked stunned.

"I'm afraid I was on my way to prison, Lenora," said Riley.

"There must be a mistake!" said Lenora. "This man can't be a criminal! He simply can't be!"

Tackett and the ranger stood quietly, letting Riley

handle it. "I broke the law, Lenora," said Riley. "I have to go pay up. But you heard Ranger Burrack. I won't be gone long."

"Oh . . ." Lenora sat quietly, hoping he had more to say. Riley looked at Burrack and Tackett. Both of them gave him a coaxing nod.

"Lenora," Riley continued, "I have no right to ask you, but do you suppose—"

"Yes, of course I'll wait for you, Ted," she blurted out, not letting him finish. She clasped his hand and, holding Hilda in her other arm, she looked at Tackett and the ranger and asked, "Who is going to watch over this child? Does she have family? If not, I propose that she stay with me."

"Ma'am," said Tackett, "she can stay with you until there's been time for any kin to come claim her. But I think I can assure you that there are none. It was just her and her ma."

"Bless you both," said Lenora to Tackett and the ranger. Her eyes welled with tears. "Look, Oscar," she said to the big hound, "we have a family again . . . a new start in life. As if on cue, Oscar ambled over and plopped down at Hilda's feet.

"Take me out and show me Marr's body," said the ranger to Tackett. "Then we'll go turn Toller loose, like I told him we would." He considered the irony that a man like Toller would go free while a decent man like Riley would have to go back and account for himself.

"Don't you believe me about the wolves?" Tackett gave him a wary look.

Without answering him, Burrack glanced toward Lenora, Riley and the girl, indicating that they might want a few minutes alone together.

"Oh, I see," said Tackett, understanding. The two

walked a few feet away from the firelight and stopped and looked back. "You know what happened to Marr, I reckon," he said to the ranger.

"It's just like you said, Sheriff," Sam replied. "In the midst of everything else happening, a pack of wolves wandered in and killed him."

Tackett thought about it and chuckled. "Yep, that sums it up."

The two lawmen looked back into the glow of the campfire. "It's good to see folks get what they want in life," said the ranger.

Tackett stood looking back at the man, the woman and the child for a silent, wistful moment. "Yep, it is," he sighed. Another silent moment passed. "Everything has a way of working together, doesn't it?" he said softly.

"I'm certain it does," Sam replied, watching red sparks from the campfire race upward, curling and dancing until they disappeared into an endless black velvet sky.

# Ralph Cotton

## JUSTICE                                   19496-9

A powerful land baron uses his political influence to persuade local
lawmen to release his son from a simple assault charge. The young man,
however, is actually the leader of the notorious Half Moon Gang—a
mad pack of killers with nothing to lose!

## BORDER DOGS                               19815-8

The legendary Arizona Ranger San Burrack is forced to make the most
difficult decision of his life when his partner is captured by ex-
Confederate renegades—The Border Dogs. His only ally is a wanted
outlaw with blood on his hands...and a deadly debt to repay the Dogs.

## BLOOD MONEY                               20676-2

Bounty hunters have millions of reasons to catch J.T. Priest—but Marshal
Hart needs only one. And he's sworn to bring the killer down...mano-a-
mano.

## DEVIL'S DUE                               20394-1

The second book in Cotton's "Dead or Alive" series. The *Pistoleros*
gang were the most vicious outlaws around—but Hart and Roth thought
they had them under control....Until the jailbreak.

Available wherever books are sold, or
to order call: 1-800-788-6262

SIGNET

# Charles G. West

### Hero's Stand                    0-451-20822-6
The town of Canyon Creek suffers under the
"protection" of Simon Fry's militia, supposedly sent
to keep the folks safe from Indians. But Jim Culver
knows Fry and his bunch for what they truly
are—and he's willing to stand against them.

### Savage Cry                    0-451-20691-6
Clay Culver thought the Civil War was the last battle
he'd ever fight, until he got word of his sister's
abduction—and suddenly had his own war to wage.

### Mountain Hawk                    0-451-20215-5
Mountain man Trace McCall must rescue his
beloved from a kidnapper without getting caught
in a growing conflict between white homesteaders
and Indians.

### Son of the Hawk                    0-451-20457-3
When a war party of renegade Sioux slaughters his
Shoshoni tribe, the young brave White Eagle has no
choice but to venture into the world of the white
man to find mountain man Trace McCall—the father
he never knew.

Available wherever books are sold, or
to order call: 1-800-788-6262

S309